SST

THE PUMPKIN SHELL

This is a story about marriage from a woman's point of view, in the Western world in the 1930s and through the Second World War and the years immediately following . . . Stevie enters into two marriages, primarily for the security they offer. However, she gradually realises that a safe and secure marriage is restricting. It is only when she commits to a relationship that does not offer security that she finds real self-fulfilment and happiness.

LOUISE PAKEMAN

◆

THE PUMPKIN SHELL

Complete and Unabridged

ULVERSCROFT
Leicester

First published in Australia in 2001

First Large Print Edition
published 2003

The moral right of the author has been asserted

British Library CIP Data

Pakeman, Louise
    The pumpkin shell.—Large print ed.—
Ulverscroft large print series: romance
1. Love stories
2. Large type books
I. Title
823.9′2 [F]

ISBN 0–7089–4937–1

Published by
F. A. Thorpe (Publishing)
Anstey, Leicestershire

Set by Words & Graphics Ltd.
Anstey, Leicestershire
Printed and bound in Great Britain by
T. J. International Ltd., Padstow, Cornwall

This book is printed on acid-free paper

Peter, Peter, Pumpkin eater,
Had a wife and couldn't keep her.
He put her in a Pumpkin Shell
And there he kept her very well.

— Old Nursery Rhyme.

1

Stevie cupped a handful of sand, and then let it run slowly through her fingers. She watched it as if it were an hourglass, and as the last grains slipped through she spoke to her husband.

'I'm going down for a swim, Martin.'

The only answer she got was a slight snore. Turning round, she saw that he was asleep. He had pulled his straw hat down over his eyes and only the bottom half of his face was visible. The sun glinted on the stubble on his chin. The fact that he had not yet shaved, and the straw hat, showed he was in holiday mode. And that, Stevie thought, was about as far as it went. In all her dreams she had never considered a honeymoon like this one.

For starters, she had always imagined some exotic foreign location, a beach, maybe, yes, but not in this select and quiet resort on the South coast of England. Nor, if she was honest, had she imagined that her bride-groom would be anything but young, good-looking and of course quite madly in love with her, as she would be with him.

Her musings were interrupted by another

bubbling snore. Martin's lips trembled slightly and a small froth of saliva appeared at the corner of his mouth. She turned away from him and, picking up a small smooth pebble that lay half-buried in the sand at her side, shied it angrily across the beach towards the in-coming sea.

There was another snore, this time not quite so soft, behind her. Irritated beyond endurance, Stevie scrambled to her feet and ran down towards the encroaching wavelets.

The edge of the sea was warm as it rippled in over the hot sand, but she ran on until the ice-cold sharpness of it made her catch her breath. She plunged in against the oncoming waves until the water was up to her waist before throwing her whole body in and striking out away from shore. The coldness of the water was cleansing and curiously relaxing. She swam for a few minutes before turning on her back and floating with the tide to the beach — and Martin.

He pushed the hat off his face and looked up at her, squinting in the sun, as she stood over him dripping raindrops of seawater as she peeled off her rubber bathing cap and shook out her short natural blonde hair.

'It's great out there,' she smiled down at him, her irritation melting now he was awake.

'better than sleeping.' She held out her hand. 'Coming?'

With a mock groan he allowed her to pull him to his feet and, not for the first time, Stevie thought what a splendid body he still had, trim and muscular with no hint of flab. He carried his age well.

Martin was a strong swimmer and within minutes all she could see of him was his head and two rhythmic arms. Not so bold herself, she remained in the security of the shallows.

As the warmer water here lapped around her and caressed her limbs she thought of her husband, the man to whom she owed so much, and wondered how she could broach the subject of something to fill her endless days without seeming ungrateful.

Even as she pondered it crossed her mind that she should be feeling something more than gratitude for Martin. They had known one another all their lives. At least, all her life.

★　★　★

Back in their hotel Stevie dressed thoughtfully for dinner while Martin was occupied in the bathroom. It still seemed strange to be sharing a room and they were both careful not to intrude on the other's privacy.

She chose a pure silk dress in a soft blue

3

that enhanced the blue of her eyes, making them appear more cornflower than their usual forget-me-not. Cut to perfection, the dress emphasised her young, voluptuous figure, leaving no doubt that she was now a woman and not the young girl, child almost, that her husband still seemed to consider her. Her hair brushed to a shining cap and her face made up with care, she was concentrating on threading the diamond pendant earrings that had been his wedding gift to her when he came out of the bathroom. For a moment their eyes held in the mirror then he turned away abruptly and shrugged himself into his shirt.

She examined herself critically; squirted herself with a light floral perfume, ran the comb once more, quite unnecessarily, through her sleek hair, then, remembering her purse, turned back to the dressing table to pick it up. In doing so she missed the look in her husband's eyes as he paused for a moment, his hands still on the knot of his tie.

When she turned towards him he had collected himself. 'I see you're ready. You look — nice.' As he spoke, the total inadequacy and banality of the word struck him.

★ ★ ★

Watching Martin as he sipped the sample of wine from the bottle that had taken him so long to select, Stevie wondered if he was really as knowledgeable as he liked to appear, or was it all part of the carefully built façade that he presented to the world? After the obligatory moment's hesitation, Martin put the glass down and with a slight smile and a nod of approbation, let the waiter know that it would do.

Stevie wondered if anyone ever said, 'No — it won't do.' At that moment, almost as if he had read her thoughts, the young waiter's eye caught hers, the shadow of a smile touching his lips as if they shared some secret joke as he turned to fill her glass.

'Thank you,' her voice was demure but she tipped her glass towards him the merest fraction, as if in salutation, as she drew it towards herself.

With a faint feeling of irritation that he couldn't account for, Martin raised his own glass to his lips as the waiter moved away.

'Hmm — a little sweeter than I really care for.'

Stevie raised her own glass and took a long, appreciative sip. To her it tasted just perfect. But then she was no wine buff.

'Martin . . . ' she began, then bit the words back and turned her glass slowly in her hand as she realised she had been about to say, 'I'm bored.'

'I hope you aren't finding it dull here?' he asked, almost as if she had spoken out loud. He glanced round the well-appointed and elegant dining room, which, like its patrons, exuded an air of well-bred, well-heeled good taste. 'Or me?'

His eyes met hers and, just for the briefest of moments, a shadow crossed his face. Stevie was awash with guilt, shame, and affection for this man to whom she owed so much.

She laughed, forcing a lightness she didn't feel.

'No, of course not, Martin. Not here — or with you. But at home . . . ' she added quickly, seeing his mouth tightening slightly. 'I shall be lonely when you are not there, there will be so little for me to do. I wish . . . ' She tailed off miserably as his mouth set in the stubborn line she knew meant he didn't intend to discuss the subject any further.

Of course he wouldn't. Why should she imagine he would? Wives of prosperous country town lawyers did not consider working in the early 1930s.

At that moment their main course arrived. Stevie concentrated on her duck à l'orange.

Martin smiled across the table at her kindly, almost paternally, as he passed her the vegetables. 'Maybe we should try and find some pastime for you?'

The tone of his voice did nothing to mollify her.

'Don't humour me, Martin, and please do stop treating me like a child!'

'I'm sorry, Stephanie,' The deliberate use of her full name made her smile. 'it's just that . . . 'now it was his turn to tail off helplessly.

'I don't mind you calling me Stevie,' she retorted. 'after all, you always have. It's just your attitude,' she finished lamely.

She dropped her eyes and concentrated on food, temporarily overwhelmed by the strength of her feeling. as they clashed verbal swords, she had been intensely aware of Martin as something other than the kind, avuncular figure she had known since childhood. She saw him as a man, and a very attractive one. It wasn't her name she was worrying about when she asked him to stop treating her like a child. No, he could call her whatever he liked if only he would see her as woman to his man; both desirable and desiring. The grim humour of the situation struck her for while women were slowly gaining the freedom to love, and even bed, whom they wished, here was she, the untouched bride of a man who saw her only as the child he had known for so long.

They lapsed into silence, each concentrating on the meal in front of them. A three-piece band was playing and Stevie found her eyes following the few couples who were dancing.

'Would you like to dance?' Regretting his brusqueness and suddenly anxious to please her, Martin spoke impulsively.

'Oh, yes please!' She dropped her crumpled napkin on the table and half pushed her chair away. 'But do you?'

'Of course,' he held out his hand towards her.'

As she moved into the circle of his arms and they paused for a moment to catch the beat of the music, she smiled into his eyes. 'I haven't danced with you since the days when I called you 'Uncle Martin'.'

He stiffened slightly, at this reminder of the difference in their ages. 'A lifetime away,' he murmured against her hair.

Stevie loved dancing, and she liked dancing with Martin. There was no need to make polite conversation and certainly no need to smile when he stubbed her toe — he was far too good a performer to do that.

Holding her in his arms, Martin was very much aware that this was indeed a different person from the gangly schoolgirl who used

8

to call him 'uncle'. He held her a little closer and bent his head until he was breathing in her perfume and could feel her hair against his face. He felt a swift surge of desire pulse through him, and his arm tightened round her.

'Perhaps . . . ' he thought, and still held her hand when the dance ended and they went back to finish their meal.

They had slipped into the habit of walking along the front before going to bed. But when they left the dining room they could see that dark clouds were in the sky and, away from the dance-band, the ominous sound of wind could be clearly heard.

'I'm afraid it looks like a storm.'

'We can get our walk in first,' Stevie loved the sea at night beneath a darkening sky. 'if we hurry,' she added and, suiting her actions to her words, began to run up the short flight of stairs to their first floor rooms. 'I'll just get a coat,' she called back over her shoulder. Martin followed her more sedately.

In her room he took the light summer coat from her and draped it round her shoulders. As he did so he smelt again that soft enticing perfume. His hands tightened on her shoulders and as he did Stevie swivelled in his arms so that she was facing him. Her eyes sought his and her lips, slightly parted, reached for his.

'Martin,' she murmured, tossing her coat on one side he pulled her to him and his mouth met hers. Then he carried her across the room and dropped her on the bed saying 'Forget the walk!'

As if to reinforce his words the sky darkened, there was a resounding crash of thunder and the heavens opened.

Stevie laughed softly in her throat, a sound that was a curious mixture of provocation, invitation and triumph, as Martin began to undress her.

They surprised each other in their lovemaking. Knowing Martin as she had from a tiny child, he had been an older, almost parental figure and as such asexual. To find him a passionate and highly skilled lover was both a surprise and a delight. Making love with Martin had the reassurance of being with a well-loved person and the excitement of being taken by a stranger.

Martin on his part was agreeably surprised to find that the child he had married out of a combination of true affection, compassion, and a sort of muddled sense of duty to his lifelong friend, had turned, overnight it seemed, into a sensuous woman who responded to him in a way he had never dreamed possible.

Aeons later Stevie propped herself on one

10

elbow and looked down on the man asleep at her side. She switched on the soft pink-shaded bedside lamp so that its roseate glow fell on his face. As she did so he opened one eye and looked at her.

'Hello wife,' he smiled as he said the word.

'Hello — husband,' Stevie responded hesitantly. It still seemed strange to her; she needed to make an adjustment somewhere. If this man with whom she had just shared such exquisite passion was her husband, then where was the 'uncle' Martin she had known all these years? Looking down at him she giggled softly.

'Can you share the joke?' He had both eyes open now and was looking up into her face.

'Oh, it was nothing, just a silly little verse someone put in my autograph book at school.'

'Tell me.'

'It's nothing,' she repeated, suddenly embarrassed, 'just a bit of nonsense.' But he was insistent.

'When I was young I married for fun — ' she rattled off,

'And never thought any danger,

'But oh, what a sin to get stripped to the skin

'And get into bed with a stranger!'

Martin laughed, pulled her down close to

11

him and kissed her in a manner that was neither that of an uncle nor of a stranger. Pushing her gently away, he held her at arm's length.

'I hope you don't feel that, Stevie?'

'That it is a sin, or that you are a stranger?' she teased.

'Both, but what I really meant was, I hope I'm not a stranger to you?'

'You, a stranger!' Twisting round she lay back in the crook of his arm. 'Far from it.' She paused for a moment before adding in a more serious vein. 'No — if anything, Martin, I felt I knew you too well, that was what made it seem like a sin.'

He laughed softly. 'I know what you mean, the thought of making love to you seemed almost incestuous,' he confessed. 'which is one of the reasons I held back; also I was waiting till I knew you were better — more yourself — I didn't want to take advantage of you.'

'Oh, Martin!' A wave of tenderness swept over her, fanning afresh the newly lighted flames of desire. She turned and kissed him and as their naked bodies touched they were catapulted into a new wave of discovery, each of the other.

★　★　★

Their new ability to make love finally turned the holiday into the honeymoon it was meant to be. But if Stevie hoped it would also mark a significant change in their relationship she was doomed to disappointment.

Though at night Martin became the tender, passionate lover, by day he was still much the same. Good, kind, 'Uncle' Martin deftly turning aside all her pleas that she be allowed to DO something.

All too soon they were on the way home. Silence had lain between them for some miles. Martin seemed preoccupied with the road ahead, or his thoughts, or both, but suddenly he turned to her with the smile that could in an instant take ten years from his handsome, but sometimes rather sombre, features.

'How about a horse?'

'A horse?' she repeated, wondering if he had said something else and she had missed it along the way.

'Yes, a horse. You always used to ride as a child, you could hunt this winter. Come to think about it, I might even hunt again myself. We'll buy two horses. That will give you something to do!'

Stevie opened her mouth to protest that what she really wanted to do was some work. Then closed it again without saying anything.

She had always ridden as a child, had her own pony; it might not be such a bad idea. In fact the more she thought about it, the better the idea seemed. A horse would give her some measure of companionship, a degree of mobility; as well as something to do.

'That would be wonderful, Martin. But please may I look after them myself, no 'hired help', no grooms?' She dropped her hand lightly on his thigh as she spoke. It was a spontaneous gesture of appeal with an undertone of feminine sexuality.

Martin had been about to say that of course he would employ someone else to look after the horses. He didn't want his wife smelling of horse. But the gesture fired his desire for this newly discovered woman at his side; a desire that since he had made her truly his wife was never far from the surface. She would soon get tired of the work; it would do no harm to humour her for a while.

'I don't see why not,' he turned to her for a second and smiled into her eyes then let his hand drop briefly onto hers.

Stevie, smiling back, had enough feminine wisdom not to push her point any further at the moment.

2

Stevie threw herself into the task of horse hunting with enthusiasm. It was, after all, about the only thing left for her to do. With the running of the household in the capable hands of Mrs Evans, a housemaid and a gardener, all of whom had been in Martin's employment for many years, and had known her as 'Little Miss Stevie' before their marriage, she was left with no more arduous household duties than arranging the flowers.

A few days after they returned from their honeymoon, Martin came home from the office to find Stevie had several hopefuls ticked off in the local paper, and had been on the phone and found out something about them.

'You have been busy,' he commented, absently pouring himself a glass of sherry.

'One for me too, please, Martin?'

'Oh, yes — of course. I'm so sorry my dear. I was preoccupied.'

He smiled at her as he handed her the sherry he had belatedly poured for her. 'Tell me about the horses.'

'Well — I haven't been so successful

finding one for you but this mare here,' she passed him the paper pointing with her pencil to the one she was talking about, 'sounds rather nice. I talked to the owner and she is only selling her because she is going to University and won't be able to hunt her this coming season.'

'Grey mare, eight years, fifteen hands, sound and reliable,' he read aloud. 'Hmm — sounds all right. I wonder if she is used to a side-saddle?' He passed the paper back to Stevie.

'Martin, I'm not going to ride side saddle, this is 1933!' Stevie protested.

'You might want to show her,' Martin pointed out, 'and ladies hacks have to be ridden in a side-saddle.'

'Well, if I do I'll just have to learn, and so will she,' she retorted.

'Hold on! You're talking as if you had already bought the horse, and you haven't even seen it yet!'

'Yes, but somehow . . . ' Stevie tailed off, knowing full well that to say that somehow she felt that this was her horse was the sort of argument Martin's clear legal brain would instantly reject. In his book you 'knew' or you did not know, and if you knew then your knowing had to be supported by facts, not feelings. Stevie gave a little sigh.

'Well, do you think, perhaps, we could go and see her?' Her voice sounded little-girl wistful.

Martin responded predictably. He smiled; his kind, paternal smile. 'I'm not too busy tomorrow,' he told her. 'I could leave the office about four o'clock and we could go then.'

'Oh, thank you!' How easy it was to be the little girl to his parent. Stevie jumped up and put her arms round his neck in a quick hug. 'I'll phone up and make sure that is all right,' and, she thought to herself, make sure she doesn't sell my horse to anyone else.

The following afternoon Stevie was dressed in jodhpurs and a neat workman-like shirt by three thirty. When Martin got home at four fifteen she was in a fever of impatience. She managed to conceal this as well as she could and bit back the accusing 'You're late!' that was on the tip of her tongue. If only she had her own car, her own money — but that line of reasoning never got her anywhere. It inevitably led to 'her own life', and brought her back to facing squarely just how much she owed Martin. Not only her way of life but almost her life.

As she climbed into the passenger seat next to him she fought back the memories that still sometimes overwhelmed her; triggered off by something she saw, something she did or something someone said. Or just flooded back, like now.

Just six months ago she had had the world at her feet and her life before her. She was twenty-one years old. In fact it was the day of her twenty-first birthday party when her life crashed into a million tiny pieces; until Martin had picked them up and put them together again.

Her father had insisted on a dinner-dance for her birthday, a sumptuous affair at a local hotel. He had been late getting home that evening and Stevie was already dressed in the exquisite white tulle dress inlaid with shimmering beads that he had helped her choose. When he came in through the front door and she looked down on him from the head of the stairs she thought he looked tired, old, somehow — beaten. Looking up and seeing her, he smiled and held out his arms in an extravagant gesture and the impression faded.

'Stevie, my little girl — you look just beautiful!'

'Not such a little girl now, Dad, I'm twenty-one today,' she quipped as she came down the stairs and kissed him. 'and if you don't hurry I shall be late at my own birthday party.'

'Which would never do,' he bounded up the stairs to change. Watching him, Stevie pushed her earlier impression to the back of her mind. Her father could never be old; he was the epitome of zest, zing and youthful enthusiasm, whatever his actual age.

He was down in the hall again in a surprisingly short time, looking incredibly young and handsome in white tie and tails. He held out his arm to her.

'Let's go,' he said as he offered her his arm smiling down at her, 'I wonder who will be offering you his arm — and his heart — by the end of the evening?'

Those were about the last words he spoke. Perhaps he really was tired, or just conscious of running late. If he had been alone in the car it would almost have seemed as if he had wanted to be killed when he drove out of the drive gates without looking. That was what the lorry driver kept saying afterwards.

All Stevie could remember was the scream of brakes and rubber on asphalt, the crash, the jolt, then a curious vacuum before she heard someone screaming — screaming — screaming — and realised it was herself. She tried to stop but she didn't seem to have control any more over her own voice. All she could hear were the terrible screams, and all she could see was her father's head in her lap and the huge red stain on the white dress.

The next thing she remembered was waking up in a hospital bed. Why was she in hospital? And why was Uncle Martin, her father's lawyer and lifelong friend, sitting by her?

Slowly, carefully and with infinite tenderness, he answered her questions, then and over the days that followed.

Her beloved father had been killed instantly in the accident. She, by some miracle, had merely suffered a few bumps and bruises and a great deal of shock. But more was to come. Not worse, for nothing could be worse than the sudden and violent loss of her father. She was absolutely destitute. Her father, it seemed, had been facing certain ruin and bankruptcy, a not uncommon fate among the farming community in the 1930s. The twenty-first birthday party for his daughter was to have been one final fling.

Guilt followed and mingled with her grief. If she hadn't wanted a big twenty-first party — if she hadn't worried about being late — if — if — if . . . Stevie tortured herself and sank deeper into a dark pit.

Martin watched her; the girl he had seen grow from a laughing baby to a sparkling young woman, and was filled with a deep compassion mingled with something else. The only thing he had ever envied his friend was his daughter, child of a brief and passionate marriage. It was a crazy idea; maybe he shouldn't even think of it — and yet, what was going to happen to her? Would she even agree?

Stevie agreed to marry him with the same dull acceptance she had given to all his other suggestions.

She must remind herself now how grateful she had been at the time for the haven that Martin had offered her when he proposed marriage, and not grumble at petty restrictions. She had what most girls her age would give their right arms for, a kind and loving husband who also happened to be wealthy, successful and good looking, a lovely home and everything she could want materially. She had a place in the world, position, and security; to look for the flaws was ungrateful both to Martin and the Fates that had brought her to this point, and miserably cheese-paring.

With a bright smile she pushed the memories back. She must live in the present. She laid her hand briefly over Martin's as he took the wheel.

'You're very good to me.'

'You're worth it.' He smiled back, squeezing her hand for a second before turning his attention to the road.

* * *

The mare, whose name was Fairy, was all Stevie had imagined, a rich rocking-horse dapple, with a silver white mane and tail that rippled in the sun. Stevie stroked her forehead gently as she nuzzled softly at her free hand, an instant rapport flowing between them.

'I like her.' Stevie turned to the owner, a girl a few years younger than herself, watching her with a curious strained anxiety. Stevie knew how she felt; she remembered standing by anxiously watching a prospective buyer looking at her last pony who had been sold when she went away to boarding school at fourteen. Would they like him; would they take him; and if they did, would they be good to him? She smiled at the younger girl, trying to convey her understanding and give her reassurance.

'I like the look of her,' she repeated. 'Can I ride her?'

Her owner smiled back. 'Of course. I'll saddle her up for you.'

While the girl was fetching the saddle

Stevie continued to stroke the mare gently. She knew that, no matter what, no matter how badly she behaved when she rode her, this was her horse. She could already feel the strong affinity that exists now and then between some people and some animals. It was more than liking, more even than love, as if the horse were a part of her.

She need have had no qualms; Fairy was as good to ride as she was to look at. When Stevie finally reined her up in front of Martin she felt as if they had been a team forever.

'Well, what do you think?' she asked him.

'I think you make a splendid pair. How do you feel about her?'

'Oh, Martin! Need you ask? I think she's just perfect!' Swinging her leg over the horse's rump she dropped to the ground and stroked the dappled neck.

'Then we'd better buy her,' he already had his cheque book out.

Finding a suitable horse for Martin did not prove such an easy task. He looked at one or two but liked none of them. Finally he asked a farmer/dealer friend of his to keep his eyes open for a good steady hunter before the next season; and so Huntsman, a huge, raking bay with a broad white blaze down his face and big kind eyes, finally arrived at Wingates. When she first saw him Stevie regretted her insistence on doing the horses herself; he was so very large and intimidating, but when she found that at heart he was just one big sook, she lost her fear of him.

The two horses kept her busy. So busy, in fact, that Martin insisted that they employ a part-time groom when the hunting season started.

'Once they are clipped and stabled,' he pointed out to her, 'they are going to need an hour or two's exercise every day. You will be flat-out exercising Fairy; you certainly won't have time to ride Huntsman as well, even if you dare!' he teased.

'The ground looks so far away from up there,' Stevie retorted, but she agreed to have some extra help.

When she rode into the stable yard a few days later she found Martin already home and talking to a young man. They were at the half-door of Huntsman's stable, the two men facing one another, each with an elbow on the top of the door. The big bay horse's head was between them and his ears flipped from side to side as if he were taking an active part in the conversation. As Stevie dismounted he raised his head; his ears pricked and whickered a greeting to Fairy. Both men turned towards her.

'Hello, my dear, had a good ride?' Martin

moved toward her with a welcoming smile, then turned back to the other man. 'This is Mr Jefferies — Tom Jefferies. Do you remember him?'

'Hello, Stevie.' The stranger, who it seemed wasn't a stranger at all, though for the moment Stevie could not place him, stepped forward with a warm grin. 'The last time I saw you, you had pigtails and braces on your teeth.'

'And you used to pull them — the pigtails I mean, not the braces,' Stevie retorted as memory, crystal clear, flashed back. 'but I thought you were in Australia?'

It was ten years since Stevie had last seen Tom Jefferies, 'the boy next door,' although next door had been the next farm and not quite as close as a suburban next door. They had attended the same kindergarten, met at the same Christmas and birthday parties, and been members of the same Pony Club. As a very small girl Stevie had always told her father, and everyone else, that when she grew up she was going to marry Tom Jefferies. Remembering this she felt a warm flush stain her cheek and quickly hid it by turning to unsaddle her mare. Anyway, all that was long ago. Before Tom's father had suddenly decided to sell up and pack up and had taken his family to try their luck at farming 'down under.'

'So I was, and so I have been for the last twelve years,' Tom told her. 'But Dad gave me a trip back to the old country as a twenty-first birthday present — and here I am!' Mention of his father and his twenty-first birthday brought a quick shadow flitting across Stevie's features. It was not lost on Tom, who cursed himself for a tactless fool. He had called first at her old home Willow Farm, but on finding strangers there had made his way to the Hare & Hounds, the village pub, to get himself put in the picture with all the local news before he tried any more visiting.

When they told him about the tragic death of Charlie Benson on the very night of his daughter's twenty-first birthday, he was stunned. He should have been glad when they told him about her subsequent marriage to Martin Colville; glad for her that after so much trouble she had found safe harbour. Yet somehow all he could feel was annoyance with the man. No, annoyance was probably too strong a word. It was more as if he felt that somehow his own personal feathers had been ruffled. He might have left the village without making any further move to meet up with Stevie again if it hadn't been for old Will, mine host at the Hare & Hounds.

'Reckon Miss Stevie will be glad to see you

again, Mr Tom,' shaking his head, 'from what I hear she still doesn't go out much or see many people. You and she were always pretty good friends when you were chillun. I remember seeing the two of you on your ponies. A good pair you made.' He had been about to add that he had always thought it might be a permanent sort of pairing up, then remembered that the lass was no longer 'Miss Stevie' but Mrs Martin Colville of Wingates and snapped his mouth shut quickly on a sigh.

'Can I use your phone, Will?' Tom asked.

His first instinct was to telephone Stevie. Then, hearing Muriel Shard's voice on the local exchange and remembering her reputation for gossip, he decided it would probably be better if he spoke to Martin first rather than Stevie. With a quick change of mind he asked for Martin Colville's office number instead of his home one.

Waiting for the phone to be answered he wondered what he was going to say; but a slight misunderstanding helped him out. Martin thought he had been given his number by a friend who had promised to look out for someone to help part-time with the horses. Tom started to explain, then thought better of it. Some inner demon of mischief let him go on with the mistake and apply for the job. Why not? It would be amusing — and he could use a little extra money.

'Tom,' Martin explained now to Stevie, 'is applying for the job of helping out with the horses.'

'Oh.' Stevie didn't know whether to be pleased or not. She was suddenly very conscious that both men were watching her reaction.

'Is it too late for afternoon tea?' she asked, stalling for time. It would be lovely having an old friend like Tom helping out with the horses; far better than a stranger. Yet somewhere, deep inside, some small inner voice was whispering a warning.

Martin glanced at his watch. 'Yes,' he answered her question, 'it's cocktail time now.'

In the gracious hall of the old manor house that was now her home, Stevie excused herself and ran lightly up the wide staircase to wash the dust and what Martin called her 'horsey pong' off before joining the two men for cocktails. When she walked through the drawing-room door a short while later, both turned to look at her with ill-concealed admiration. She was wearing a simple linen dress in a delicate lime-green shade and her blonde hair was like a sleek gold cap on her head. Tom envied Martin his good fortune while he, handing a glass to each of them as they stood side by side, thought involuntarily what a handsome young couple they made. With the thought came a stab of something like fear.

'Tell us about Australia?' Stevie broke the tension by putting the question to Tom as she took a seat near Martin. It was a question she was to hear herself ask many times in the days to come.

'Tell about Australia, Tom,' she would say to him, he would talk, and she would dream.

But today she only listened as Tom told them about their farm, or property as he called it, back home in Australia. Of the cattle, and the sheep, the horses and the dogs. The heat, the dust and the flies.

'Most of our riding is done for work, not pleasure,' he finished with a smile.

'It is a bit different here,' Martin replied. 'I don't think it will be long before the horse is superseded as a work animal and only kept for pleasure.'

'Not on the farms, not the heavy horses, surely?' Stevie protested, remembering her father's magnificent working Shires.

'Even, or especially, on the farms,' Martin replied. He turned towards Tom. 'You're not in a hurry, are you, you can stay to dinner?'

Then he wondered briefly what masochistic demon was driving him on.

So cocktails lengthened into dinner, and dinner into after-dinner brandy, and by the time Tom left Wingates the grandfather clock in the hall was very near the witching hour of midnight. He left with a promise to return in the morning to ride Huntsman. He had, it seemed, got himself a job.

3

'When were you thinking of stabling the horses?' Tom asked Stevie as they clattered out of the yard side by side.

'Any time, I suppose. It's September now and cubbing will start soon. The Opening Meet is the first week in November. They both have to be clipped out and really fit by then.'

Tom smiled slightly to himself. He had been in Australia long enough to have almost forgotten how an English country gentleman's life could be ruled by the foxhunting calendar.

'What are you smiling about?' Stevie asked; she had not missed the look of sardonic amusement that had flitted across his tanned features.

'Nothing really, I was just thinking how strange it seemed — so much work getting horses fit — just for pleasure.'

'All work and no play makes Jack a dull boy,' Stevie quoted, adding with some asperity, as she kicked her mare into a trot, 'and it seems it has the same effect on Tom.'

Tom grinned as he urged Huntsman to

catch up. He found Stevie stimulating when she was angry. She reminded him of the child Stevie whom he had liked so much. As tough as any boy, in spite of the rather ethereal quality her light blonde hair and forget-me-not blue eyes gave her, and so often angry, passionately defending some cause or other. He was already beginning to find her company as much fun as he had when they were children. He wondered fleetingly why he hadn't bothered to write to her over the years. He had wondered if the Stevie he had known was lost in Mrs Martin Colville; but her retort and the glint in her eye reassured him.

★   ★   ★

Tom came every day after that to help Stevie with the chores about the stables and to exercise Huntsman. In fact, as Stevie pointed out to Martin, Tom was riding the big horse far more than he was.

'He's doing a good job,' Martin replied, 'keeping him fit and exercised and my saddle warm for me. Don't worry, I'll be riding him when hunting starts.' He patted her hand in the way that still managed to irritate her. It was a gesture that somehow took them both back to the time when he had been 'Uncle Martin' and she a very small girl.

When the day of the Opening Meet came round it was not, after all, Martin but Tom who rode the big horse. Martin, who had come home from the office the night before sneezing and complaining of a headache, woke that morning with a bright spot of colour burning in each cheek, and almost hoarse. It was obvious he had 'flu.

'Of course I won't go and leave you here like this!' Stevie told him. 'I'll stay home and look after you.'

'Of course you will go,' Martin croaked. 'For one thing I don't need looking after, for another I'd much rather be left alone. Tom can take Huntsman and look after you.'

When she saw he really would prefer her to go Stevie gave in.

'You'll be the most handsome woman out today,' Martin told her as he watched her tie her stock. Indeed she looked a picture in her black hunting coat and boots and black bowler, with the white silk of the stock setting off her clear complexion and wonderful eyes.

'And you, my darling, would be the best looking man if you were going to be there. In fact we would make a very handsome couple.'

'Go on with you, and have a good day,' he smiled at her with an infinite tenderness, taking care to hide the longing and strange

33

nagging fear as he despatched her with a man half his age.

* * *

They set off early so that they need go no faster than a slow 'hunter's jog' on the five mile ride to the Meet and would arrive with fresh horses for the hunting ahead. It was a perfect day; early frost and fog soon gave way to a thin November sun that sparkled on the crystal beads of moisture hanging from the cobwebs caught between the leafless branches. It glowed too on the well-groomed coats of the two horses, now clipped and sleek. With plaited manes and polished bridle-wear they stepped out briskly, snorting occasionally with evident pleasure, knowing full well that it was a hunting morning.

Tom and Stevie rode in a companionable silence for a good deal of the way; their only conversation being desultory speculation on who would be hunting today; what horses would be out and how the scent would lie.

Scent was good and it was not too long before hounds found a fox who broke cover and gave them a good run, coming round in a semicircle until he went to earth almost where he had started a couple of hours and several miles before.

When Stevie saw the Huntsman calling for the terriers she turned to Tom. 'Let's go home. I hate it when they bring in the terriers and dig the fox out. I never think it's fair. When he has made it back to safety he's won as far as I'm concerned.'

She turned Fairy round and without waiting for his answer set off for home.

'Still the same old Stevie,' Tom teased as he reined in beside her. 'The soft heart in the cool exterior. But you're right,' he added. 'I don't like it myself. It doesn't seem quite British Sportsmanship,' he finished in an exaggerated and mocking accent.

Stevie laughed. 'They'd throw us off the field if they could hear us. Such talk is treason in hunting fraternities. What about Australia, do they kill the fox there?'

'They don't even have foxes where I come from.'

'Aren't there any foxes in Tasmania?' Stevie asked, genuinely surprised. Foxes were to her as much a fact of life as rain or sun. 'Tell me about Tasmania. What else don't they have?'

They rode the seven or eight miles home at a quiet but steady pace, with Tom regaling her with tales of his adopted country.

'We may not have foxes, but we do have Tigers.' he told her.

'Now I know you're having me on. There

are no tigers in Australia!' Stevie was indignant.

'There are Tasmanian Tigers.' And Tom whiled away the miles with what Stevie suspected were rather tall tales of sightings of the elusive marsupial special to the Island State.

Stevie could never have enough stories of Australia. Like a small child begging for a fairy story she was always saying, 'Tell me about Tasmania.' Even though she guessed that many of his stories should be taken with a pretty big pinch of salt, nevertheless there was growing within her a longing to see this strange wonderland 'Down Under' for herself.

They were back at Wingates by mid-afternoon. Stevie was glad they had come home when they did and especially glad of Tom's help as they rubbed down the horses and rugged them up for the night, then fed and watered them. She hadn't ridden so far in a day for a long time.

'I shall be stiff tomorrow,' she complained to Tom as she climbed the vertical ladder leading up into the hayloft through a hole in the floor. Dropping hay into their racks was the last job to do for the horses. The piles of sweet-smelling hay in the loft looked tempting, and impulsively Stevie flung herself down. 'Oh, this is good!' She patted the hay at her side invitingly.

'Are you asking me to join you in a roll in the hay?' Tom's tone was flippant but there was no banter in his eyes as he dropped down beside her and propped himself on one elbow to lean over her. 'Jesus, Stevie! How could you do this to a man?'

Her breath caught in her throat as their eyes met and held. She hadn't thought — hadn't meant anything — or had she? With a low moan she reached up and pulled him down on top of her.

'Stevie, Stevie, why didn't you wait for me?' There was a world of heartbreak in Tom's voice as he drew away from her a moment later.

'I didn't know. I didn't know you were coming back — and — and — I didn't *know!*' Her voice broke on a sob. With unsteady hands she undid the pin in her stock and none too carefully removed the silk tie. Tom was quick to interpret the invitation implicit in the gesture and his fingers trembled on the buttons of her shirt. He cupped his hands round one of her breasts and his lips eagerly sought hers.

Stevie responded to him with all the fervour and ardour of her ripe young body, but when she felt his hands moving towards

37

the buttons of her riding breeches she pushed him away.

'No, no, Tom! You mustn't, I can't, I'm married!' The last word was almost a wail. For one moment in the joy of their mutual loving, she had forgotten.

Tom sat up, suddenly angry and ashamed. He lashed out, directing his fury away from himself and at her.

'You wanted it as much as me.'

Stevie nodded bleakly as she buttoned up her shirt. 'Yes.' She looked up at him with tears glistening in her eyes, and he felt his anger ebbing away.

'Oh Stevie, Stevie darling. Why did you do it? You always said when we were children that you would marry me one day.'

'Yes, I know I did. But we were only children; and you went away, you never wrote or anything. I didn't know you would ever come back. Martin was there when — when — oh, Tom. He's been so good to me. I don't know how I could even think . . . ' She tailed off miserably as she stood up and brushed the hay from her clothes.

'Will you come in for a cup of tea?' she asked him, issuing the invitation hesitantly.

'No, not today.' His lips were set in a tight line as he threw hay down to the horses waiting below.

'I hope Martin will be better soon,' he threw at her as he climbed into his battered little sports car. With a roar he was gone and Stevie was left standing in the empty stableyard, one hand rose half-heartedly, the other limply trailed her silk stock.

4

'Hello, I didn't expect to see you up.' Stevie was surprised to find Martin reading a book in front of a roaring log fire in the drawing room. 'Are you feeling better? And have you had tea?' She was uncomfortably aware that she was gabbling. She hadn't expected to be confronted by her husband so soon.

He looked up and smiled. 'Hello to you, and the answer is 'yes' to the first and 'no' to the second question. I was hoping you would be back to have it with me. I'll ring the bell.' He leaned over from his chair and pulled down the handle of the ceramic bell knob by the mantelpiece. In the small silence that followed Stevie could hear it clanging on the kitchen wall.

'I'll just wash my hands and take my riding boots off. I'll bath and change after tea.'

'Don't be long; I want to hear about your day.'

Well, that you won't — not all of it, Stevie thought to herself. But she only smiled a quick, warm smile to her husband as she turned her back and ran down the hall to the downstairs cloakroom. Fitting the heel of her foot in the bootjack she jerked her leg savagely back and threw first one boot and then the other down on the floor. Washing her hands quickly, she rejoined Martin in the drawing room just as Elsie put the heavy tray with its silver tea set down on a small table in front of the fire.

'Oh, good. Mrs Evans has made some of her cherry cake. It's quite my favourite,' Stevie said as she dropped down into a chair opposite Martin.

He smiled at her. He loved what he thought of as her youthful enthusiasms, whether for cherry cake or horses. 'I expect you're a bit tired. Sit back and I'll be 'Mother',' he pulled the tray closer to pour out tea for them both. 'Was it a good day?'

'Mmm, very,' Stevie helped herself to a piece of cherry cake. 'but I didn't stay out too late. We had a really good run; several miles, then the fox went to earth; they were bringing out the terriers so I came home.'

'How did the horses go?'

'They were really good. They both seem to be experienced and reliable hunters.'

'And Tom? Did he have a good day? Why didn't he come in for tea with you?'

'I asked him but he said he had to get back.' The last thing Stevie wanted to do was

41

discuss Tom with Martin. But she was not let off so lightly.

'I've been thinking, darling. It seems absurd Tom living in lodgings in the village when we have so much room here. And during the hunting season it would be so much more convenient if he was on hand, what do you think?'

Stevie's first reaction was to cry 'No!' but she knew that would make Martin ask questions. So when she answered it was carefully and thoughtfully, as if she had given the matter a great deal of thought.

'I don't think that is really a good idea, Martin.'

'Don't you think Tom would like to come here?'

'I think he would rather be independent,' Stevie said, clutching at straws.

'Well, I think I'll ask him anyway.' Martin decided after a few moments' thought.

Stevie's feelings were in turmoil. One half of her said how wonderful it would be to have Tom so close, the other that it would be quite impossible.

Martin was not the sort of person to deviate lightly from a planned course of action. The only thing that could deflect him from having Tom live-in would be an adamant refusal from Tom himself. This he did not get when he broached the subject a week or so later.

'Thank you. But really I'm quite comfortable where I am,' Tom assured him.

'I'm sure you are, Tom. I just thought you would be more comfortable here. We have plenty of room and Stevie would enjoy your company; we both would.'

Tom glanced quickly at the older man. Was he a masochist, a sadist, or a blind fool? Probably none of them, he decided. Just a good friend with a kindly thought.

'I'll think about it,' Tom promised. Meaning to talk it over with Stevie.

'Yes, do that, and let me know. But remember you are more than welcome here.'

As it happened Tom neither thought about it for very long nor discussed it with Stevie because when he returned to his lodgings in the village later on that day, Mrs Burgess was waiting for him.

'I'm ever so sorry, Mr Jefferies,' she told him, drying her hands on her apron, 'but I'm going to 'ave to ask you to leave. It's like this, you see; my Bill 'as got another job, and we're leaving in a week. I'm ever so sorry,' she repeated, still drying her hands so that she appeared to be wringing them.

'That's all right, Mrs Burgess. It won't put me out at all. You've been very good to me while I've been staying here and I've been most comfortable.'

Fate, it seemed, was pointing the way with a clear finger.

A week later Tom moved into Wingates.

Martin seemed oblivious to the atmosphere between the two young people, and as the days passed without a repetition of the incident in the hayloft Stevie relaxed. Since Tom had moved in she had taken great pains not to be alone with him in what, in the best Victorian novels, would be called a compromising situation. In the evenings she was always careful to draw Martin into every conversation and had taken to being the first each night to make a move towards bed to avoid being left alone with Tom, even for a few short moments.

They still worked with the horses together and rode out with each other for exercise. But Stevie felt reasonably safe astride Fairy's strong back and Tom seemed as loath as her to take another toss in the hay.

It was almost as if they had both succeeded in deliberately sponging the incident and the emotions it had engendered from the slate of their respective memories. The relationship between them, however, surely but steadily deepened, building on the foundation of their childhood memories and their mutual love of horses until a deep friendship grew between them.

Martin made a rapid recovery from his 'flu and was able to hunt with Stevie on Saturdays when the hounds met within reasonable riding distance of Wingates. When the Tuesday Meet was close, Tom rode to hounds with her.

As Christmas drew near Stevie was more and more her old self. Much less often now Martin saw the dark shadow slide over her features that told him she was remembering. The lovely old manor house that had seemed so sombre with its bachelor master, and even in the early days of their marriage, came to life and he found himself really looking forward to the festive season. Their Christmas cards were already strung on lines of ribbon over the mantelpiece as well as standing on it, and Stevie and Tom had brought in huge armfuls of polished green holly bright with berries. Only one thing was missing, the mistletoe, and Martin had bought some this afternoon when he went to pick up their Christmas tree. It lay by him now on the car seat.

He daydreamed about holding it aloft over Stevie's head and kissing her, but when he got home she and Tom were down on the drawing-room floor making brightly coloured paper chains like two happy children. Standing for a bleak moment in the open doorway and watching them Martin felt old and *de trop*. But not for long. Stevie looked up and saw him and with a wide smile of welcome scrambled to her feet to draw him into the room and the warmth of the fire.

'It's really beginning to look like Christmas now, don't you think? What is that you've got? Ooh — mistletoe!' She laughed provocatively, adding, 'And what about the tree, have you got that?'

'I've got it,' he assured her, adding almost humbly, 'Will you let me help you with it?'

'Of course I will! We'll do it tonight, after dinner. We can all do it.'

'Not me, I'm afraid. I have to go out.' Tom knew that a cosy evening *à trois* was just what he didn't want. He was beginning to bitterly regret ever having accepted Martin's invitation to live with them. Watching Stevie play the devoted wife to Martin's doting husband was becoming just too much to bear. In that moment he made up his mind to leave as soon as he decently could.

With dinner over and Tom gone, Martin and Stevie settled down to the task of decorating the Christmas tree. Stevie had a bag of baubles she had bought in the village shop, but Martin had a surprise for her. He

46

disappeared into the lumber-room and came back with a battered, almost antique, biscuit tin. Stevie gasped in delight when she opened it. It was a treasure trove of Christmas tree decorations that would delight anyone.

'The family jewels.' Martin joked as Stevie drew out one twinkling treasure after another. 'They haven't been used since my mother died.'

'Oh, Martin, they're gorgeous!' Impulsively she reached up and, wrapping her arms round his neck, kissed him full on the lips, pressing her young body to him.

Martin held her close returning her passion. This was the first time since their marriage that she had spontaneously made the first move; he felt it was something of a milestone in their relationship. It also seemed to him a propitious moment to broach something that had been on his mind for some time. As they drew apart he took her by the hand and led her to a seat by the fire.

'There is something we have never talked about,' he said gently.

It crossed Stevie's mind, briefly, that there were many things she and Martin had never spoken of. But she merely smiled with unspoken encouragement.

He did not continue for a few moments, almost as if he found it difficult to broach the subject; as indeed he did.

'Children,' he finally said. 'How do you feel about children, Stevie?'

Stevie smiled and squeezed his hand. 'I haven't had a lot to do with them, really,' she told him, 'but I like them and I want them. If that is what you mean?'

'Then — how about — well suppose we try?' Martin found himself stammering and floundering like a schoolboy. It was as if their ages were suddenly reversed as Stevie, putting a hand on either side of his face looked into his eyes.

'Suppose we do?' she whispered before pulling his head gently towards her and kissing him once more on the lips. This time the passion was overlaid by a tenderness that was almost maternal. And in fact that was how she felt; warm, tender and maternal towards this kind and gentle man. If he wanted a child, then she would give him one; it was little enough for all he had given her.

★　★　★

Tom spent Christmas Day with relatives and Stevie and Martin did all the right and conventional things. In the morning they went to Matins at the village Church then came home to a quiet lunch before going to visit an old aunt of Martin's for Christmas Tea. This was something he did every year, he explained apologetically to Stevie.

'She would miss it if I didn't come,' he told her. 'She lives alone — well, with a housekeeper, but I'm her only family.'

They planned Christmas dinner for the evening when Tom would be back. Impulsively Stevie suggested, 'Why don't we bring Aunt Emma back with us for dinner?'

'That's a wonderful idea — if she'll come,' Martin agreed.

After some demur the old lady did agree to come back with them. Stevie suggested she stay the night but she was quite adamant that she could only come if she went home that night.

'I can't possibly leave Tinker Bell,' she said firmly. Tinker Bell was her beloved little Pekinese bitch.

'Bring her with you,' Martin suggested.

'Oh, no I couldn't do that. She wouldn't like it. She is like me; getting old and set in her ways.'

So Martin promised faithfully to have her back home, like Cinderella, before midnight.

They were a small but happy party at Christmas dinner. Stevie found Aunt Emma to be one of those old people who have a very young spirit. Far from being a drag on the party, she was the life and soul of it. Tom flirted shamelessly with her and she, equally shameless, enjoyed every moment of it and responded to his bantering with sharp and witty retorts. Every now and then he caught Stevie's eye across the table; and when he did she would feel her breath catch in her throat. Dear God — if only she didn't like him so much, find him so physically attractive. She dare not even think the word 'love'.

She half hoped that Tom would offer to take the old lady home and that Martin would accept his offer. But it was Martin who finally wrapped Aunt Emma's coat round her, settled her in the passenger seat of his car with a rug around her knees and drove off in the clear crispness of a frosty Christmas night. Stevie and Tom were left alone.

'Goodnight, Tom.' Stevie tried to make her voice firm as she turned towards the stairs.

But Tom caught her arm. 'Don't go yet — please, Stevie, have a nightcap with me for Christmas,' he pleaded.

Stevie felt her arm tingle where his fingers touched her. They seemed to be drawn together in a magic circle, as if entranced their eyes met and held. Or maybe she had just had a little too much wine? With a supreme effort she pulled her gaze away and, freeing her arm, walked with as much dignity as she could muster back into the drawing room.

'Just one drink.' She sounded a good deal firmer than she felt, 'better make it a soft one.'

'Just as Madam wishes!' Tom swept her a mock bow. 'But tell me, What are you afraid of?'

'Nothing, should I be? I just feel I've had enough alcohol for one evening,' Stevie retorted rather primly, refusing to look at him but she knew that she wasn't being strictly truthful. She was afraid. Not of Tom, no, but of herself and of the feelings she was keeping so carefully below the surface.

He handed her a glass of orange juice, his face suddenly serious. No mock bows now; all levity gone. Stevie's thanks died on her lips as she met the look in his eyes. She put the glass he had just passed her down carefully on the small table at her side.

'Oh, *Tom!*' She breathed his name, half whisper, half sigh through parted lips, and her eyes glistened with unshed tears, like someone in a trance or a dream, she stepped forward into his arms.

'Stevie — Stevie — ' he moaned against her hair as he cradled her to him.

He led her gently to the sofa by the fire and drew her down into the circle of his arms;

kissing her eyes, her hair, her lips; at first gently but with an ever increasing urgency. 'Oh, God!' he moaned at last. Then she thought of Martin who she was married to. Was it only yesterday that she had sat with him on this very sofa here in this room and promised to give him children? She pushed Tom away.

'Please don't, Tom. You and I, we can't — not ever. Please see that!'

He looked at her for a long moment. Then: 'I'm sorry,' he said simply and so humbly that Stevie felt her heart turn over. She wanted above all things to take him in her arms, comfort him like a small child and give him what he wanted. But she knew she couldn't.

'Don't be sorry,' she told him gently. She dropped her head and whispered, 'There's nothing to be sorry about; just — sad — because — because — I feel the same as you. Only we mustn't — we can't!' She raised her head on the last word and her eyes were swimming with the tears she could no longer keep in check. 'It's no good, Tom. I didn't wait for you, I had no idea you might want me to; after all there was no communication between us after you left, and now it's too late. I can't hurt Martin, I love him too!'

With a great gulping sob Stevie snatched her hand free from his and ran sobbing from the room and upstairs. She flung herself onto the large double bed she shared with Martin and the tears rained down her cheeks as her body shook in great racking sobs. It was true — she loved them both. Only her love for Tom was so much more intense; so much more a part of her whole being than her gentle affection for Martin. But above and beyond all that there were the hard cold facts. She was Martin's wife. It was Martin who had been there when she needed someone so desperately. Martin she had promised to cleave to until death parted them.

With a supreme effort she stilled the shaking sobs, dried her tears, then went to the bathroom and splashed her face with cool water until the blotches were less evident; carefully she re-made it with a light delicate make-up that was subtle rather than obvious, dressed in her prettiest nightie; brushed her hair till it gleamed; and sprayed herself with the expensive perfume that had been part of Martin's Christmas present to her. Wrapping a frilly bed-jacket round her shoulders, she propped up her pillows and picked up a book to wait for her husband to return. As an after-thought, she slipped out of bed and opened the door to his dressing room.

She had not long to wait before she heard him come up. He paused for a moment outside her door, even put his hand tentatively on the knob, before going into his dressing room. Seeing the door invitingly ajar and the light in her room, he came in to say goodnight to her.

He paused in the doorway. She looked so desirable, yet with it so curiously vulnerable and so very young that he hesitated to go any further. But she put down the book, smiled at him and held out her arms in invitation.

'It's been a lovely Christmas, thank you!' she whispered as he sat down on the bed and took her hand. She knew that he had done his best to make this a truly happy time, this first Christmas together and her first without her beloved father. It was almost a year now since that fateful night. In a couple of weeks she would be twenty-two. A woman — time to start behaving like one and not a girl, she told herself with some asperity. But her face did not betray her thoughts; her lips were smiling and if there was bleakness for a moment in her eyes, Martin took it to be remembrance of other Christmases and nothing to do with this one.

'Martin,' she whispered, almost shyly, 'you know what we were talking about yesterday — well — do you think we could — '

She neither finished the sentence nor heard his answer before he took her in his arms.

Their lovemaking that night was special; Martin was tender, passionate, and considerate as always, yet with a heightened urgency. But for Stevie there was a bittersweet quality to it. As she felt the hard strength of him between her thighs and her body instinctively arched towards him, she closed her eyes and bit her lip, afraid that the name she would cry out would be the wrong one.

Stevie lay wakeful long after Martin slept. It was true; she loved both men and hated to hurt either of them. At last she dropped into a fitful sleep and dreamed of a child; Martin's child who yet bore a striking resemblance to the young Tom, the boy she had grown up with.

Stevie woke tired and unrefreshed; in marked contrast to Martin who felt, looked and sounded on top of the world. There was a dull ache in her head that was echoed somewhere in the region of her heart. She felt old and committed; as if she were already heavily pregnant with the child they had tried to create the previous night.

'It looks like being a glorious day for the Boxing Day Meet,' Martin told her as he drew back the curtains.

'Uh-huh,' Stevie grunted sleepily. Boxing Day — she had forgotten that today she would be hunting with Martin. She yawned and stretched. It almost seemed like just too much effort.

She made the effort and enjoyed herself. Having decided to stick by her marriage come what may, Stevie had enough innate common sense and youthful optimism to make the best of it. Nevertheless she was glad that Tom was spending the day with relatives so that she didn't have to put on a good face for both men.

The vigorous exercise, the fresh air, the excitement and company of a day's hunting all combined to blow the cobwebs away, and by the time she and Martin jogged home in the deepening shadows of late afternoon, Stevie was feeling tired but relaxed and happy, with her problems pushed somewhere to a cubby-hole in the recesses of her consciousness.

They might have stayed there if Martin hadn't had to spend two nights away from home a few weeks later.

5

When Martin told her that he had to go to Liverpool for a few days to attend a court case with one of his clients, Stevie begged to go with him.

'I'd much rather you stayed here,' he told her, his finger under her chin, tilting her face up so that he could look into her eyes. 'I shan't have much free time at all and I don't like the idea of you on your own in a strange city all day. Besides, you'd miss the hunting and we're getting to the end of the season. It won't be long before Tom goes back to Australia, too. You and I will go on a holiday together a bit later on, around Easter — how about that?'

Reluctantly she acquiesced. Martin was right; she wasn't really a city person, she had little interest in shopping and clothes. She would be lonely and bored in Liverpool. She quickly repressed the sudden lilt in her heart at the prospect of a few days alone with Tom, and pushed the nagging fear that it might just prove too pleasant firmly to the back of her mind. As Martin had pointed out, the hunting season would be over soon and Tom would be leaving; it would be silly to miss out — on both of them.

For the first twenty-four hours she managed to keep Tom at arms' length, both literally and metaphorically. When he suggested on the second day that they go into the nearby town that evening to see a film they had been discussing, she hesitated, before saying 'yes'.

'I don't want any coffee, do you?' Stevie said, rolling up her table napkin and threading it carefully into its silver ring, the one Martin had given her as a Christening present.

Tom looked at his watch. 'No, I think we had better be going or we shall miss the beginning of the film.'

That wasn't quite what Stevie had meant; though she quickly agreed with him that they should be moving. She had developed a sudden revulsion to coffee; odd, because she had always claimed that she could drink it till it ran out of her ears. Now the aroma that she had once thought so wonderful made her feel rather nauseous.

The film proved to be as good as Stevie hoped, and when she felt Tom's hand reach for hers in a particularly tense moment she was so caught up in the story that she not only left her hand in his but automatically returned the pressure in an answering squeeze. It was only when it ended and the lights went up that she withdrew it.

They drove home through country lanes dappled with moonlight, cosily intimate in the physical closeness of Tom's little car. Stevie prattled happily about the film they had just seen, not noticing his taciturnity. She felt young and carefree, almost as if she were recapturing the youth that had been so tragically cut short.

So much so that as Tom drew up in the driveway in front of the house she instinctively turned to him to ask him to come in for a drink.

'Oh,' she laughed, embarrassed, 'I'm forgetting — you live here.'

'Too right I do,' Tom assured, 'but I'm still going to accept that offer.' He laid his hand lightly on her thigh for a brief second, and, butterfly soft though his touch was, Stevie was as aware of it as if he had laid a red-hot brand there. 'How about that cup of coffee we didn't have at dinner?'

'Yes, I feel like a hot drink — but not coffee — cocoa?'

'That will be fine I'll follow you in when I've put the car away.'

Stevie dropped her coat on the hall chair as she made her way through to the kitchen.

Mrs Evans had thoughtfully left a small plate of sandwiches under a muslin cover, with everything ready for her to make cocoa or coffee, as she pleased.

Stevie enjoyed pottering round in the kitchen doing the simple, homely tasks that she so seldom had a chance to do in her daily life. She was humming softly to herself the theme tune from the film they had seen that evening, when Tom came in.

He watched her for a few moments, letting himself dream that this was forever, this was for real.

'Hmmm?' He realised with a start that Stevie was speaking, asking him to carry the tray into the drawing room.

He laid it down carefully on the small coffee table and poked the fire into a blaze as Stevie poured the cocoa.

It was cosy and companionable sharing the simple snack together in the warm glow of the firelight and a single lamp. Stevie leaned back in her chair and kicked off her shoes, smiling at him over her cocoa mug.

'I enjoyed myself this evening, Tom. Thank you for suggesting it and taking me.'

'Thank you for coming,' he smiled back. 'The pleasure, I can assure you, is mutual.'

They relapsed into a silence in which there was no strain, merely the enjoyment each felt in the other's company. Stevie ignored the small wee voice deep down in her subconscious suggesting that now was the time to get up firmly and go to bed. She put down her mug, leaned back and stretched; like a cat, and like a cat she almost seemed to purr as she smiled across at Tom in pure contentment.

Looking back afterwards she couldn't remember actually seeing Tom move. It seemed that one minute she was sitting there totally relaxed, smiling at him in the firelight, the next he was kneeling on the floor by her chair, his arms locked round her body, his eyes on her face.

'Oh, Stevie!' he moaned.

Unable to help herself she bent her head till her lips touched his. It was like a match to a powder keg. All the love, the desire, the latent passion they had both tried so hard and so long to suppress, burst to the surface and when at last they drew apart and he took her by the hand and led her gently upstairs to her own room she neither could, nor wished to, resist.

He undressed her methodically and deliberately as she lay on the bed, her eyes on his face, neither assisting nor hindering him. For a long moment he just stood there, looking down at the sensuous loveliness of her young body, then swiftly he threw off his own clothes. He was already hard with desire and he took her swiftly, almost angrily, without saying a word.

Stevie felt her body melt and merge with his, while simultaneously it seemed a thousand stars exploded inside her.

'Tom, Tom . . . ' She repeated his name over and over as her hands explored his body and her legs twined round him holding him close.

They woke almost simultaneously in the early hours. As Stevie stirred she heard the grandfather clock down in the hall strike one — two — three. Without words their naked bodies moved together and now their lovemaking was slow, tender, with all the unhurried gentleness that had been absent the first time. Afterwards they lay in the circle of each other's arms, talking softly and at peace with themselves, each other and the world.

'You'll love Tasmania, Stevie,' Tom murmured against her hair.

'Uh- huh,' she muttered drowsily. 'Tell me about it.'

Tom smiled; how often had she said that to him in the past? But now he was telling her about his adopted homeland in a different way. He wanted her to love it as he did. He told her about the old homestead on the large sheep property in the Midlands that was his home; he described the countryside, the climate and the beautiful little capital city, Hobart, of the island State.

'You sound like a travel agent,' Stevie told him. She turned in his arms and with one finger traced the outlines of his face, his eyes, his nose, his lips, in the darkness. It was a strange gesture, as if, like a blind person, she wanted to know just what he was like and imprint his features on her consciousness for all time.

'Have I managed to sell it to you?' he joked, but there was an urgency behind his words.

'Do you mean — ?'

'Yes, I *do* mean. I want you to come back to Tasmania with me, Stevie.'

'You mean — leave Martin?'

'Of course.' To Tom she was being incredibly obtuse. 'Of course I mean leave Martin. Leave Martin, leave England, come to Tasmania with me and start a new life on the other side of the world.'

'Marry you?'

'Of course marry me, in due course. Martin will have to divorce you first; unless you want to commit bigamy. You and I belong together. We always have, Stevie. You know that as well as I do.'

She moved closer in the circle of his arms. 'Yes,' she breathed softly against his naked shoulder. 'I know.'

'Then you will come? You will leave Martin and come with me?' His voice rose in jubilation so that she put a finger gently on his lips.

'Ssh! Someone might hear!' she cautioned. 'Yes, Tom, yes; I'll come with you.' Lying here in his arms, relaxed and at peace from their recent lovemaking, it seemed not only so right that she should be with Tom, but so easy.

'Stevie!' His voice rose in excitement and once again she had to caution him. 'Stevie — ' Now it was a hoarse whisper shaking with the strength of his emotion. 'Do you mean it? Do you *really* mean it?'

'Of course I do!' she began but the words died in her throat as a fresh wave of passion engulfed them both.

'Oh, Tom!' Stevie pulled away from him at last and reaching out she turned the luminous bedside clock towards her.

'Look at the time, you must go, Mrs Evans and Elsie will be up soon and I don't want Elsie to come in with my early tea and find you here.'

'Don't you?' he teased. 'It might not be a

bad thing, then everyone will know, we won't have to tell anyone.'

'Don't be silly, Tom. You *must* go.' She was already sitting up and reaching for the nightclothes she had never put on.

'Only if you say you are really mine and you'll come away with me.' He had pushed her back down on the pillows and was straddling her with an arm each side.

Stevie laughed up into his face. 'Tom Jefferies, you're impossible. Of course I'm coming with you,' There was no other option, they belonged, they always had.

'Promise?' he insisted.

'I promise! *Now* will you go?'

He bent and kissed her lightly on the lips before springing from the bed, gathering up his clothes and padding soft-footed to the door.

When he had gone Stevie pulled her nightgown over her head and with a soft sigh settled down beneath the blankets.

She dropped into a deep sleep, waking only when she heard Elsie putting her tray of early morning tea on the bedside table.

She poured the tea with thoughts of Tom filling and flowing round her to enclose her in a cocoon of remembered delight.

When she finally pushed the tray to one side, and slid her bare feet out of the bed the floor seemed to come up and hit her and she sat back abruptly on the bed and leaned back on the pillows. Gradually her surroundings steadied and, cautiously this time, she once more got out of bed. Tom would already be in the stables and would soon be in for breakfast. She didn't want to miss a moment of him.

He was eating porridge when she got downstairs. The smell of bacon wafted up from beneath the silver cover on the sideboard. It seemed anything but appetising.

Tom pulled out a chair at the dining table. 'Hello,' Somehow he managed to make the simple greeting sound like a caress, 'aren't you having porridge?' he asked as she sat down without helping herself.

Stevie shook her head. 'No thanks, I don't feel very hungry.' Even the thought of porridge suddenly seemed nauseating, She poured herself a glass of orange juice, 'how are you this morning?' Just as if they had parted company the night before and not just a few hours ago.

'On top of the world.' His eyes sought hers across the table, saying everything he felt while his lips mouthed words that anyone might overhear.

'I was up in good time,' he told her, by which she guessed correctly that he had not been to his own bed, at all. 'I've finished the stables so we can take the horses straight out for exercise whenever you're ready.'

Half an hour later she met him in the stables, neatly dressed in jodhpurs and hacking jacket. The odd queasy feeling seemed to have worn off and she was looking forward to riding with Tom.

They jogged side by side through the quiet country roads, making plans for their future and talking of the homestead in Tasmania where they would one day live. When they weren't talking and planning they dropped into a companionable silence. They were completely relaxed and happy, with at least another twenty-four hours together before Martin came home.

'Would you rather I told him?' Tom asked her.

'No. I must tell him myself.' Stevie knew that was the least she could do.

'Are you sure? You won't lose your nerve?' He watched her frowning slightly and biting her bottom lip in the way he remembered her doing, even as a child, when faced with a problem she feared might be too big for her to tackle alone. As he did so a swift cold hand touched his heart. 'You will come back to Tasmania with me?'

'I'll tell him, Tom. But it has to be in my

own time and in my own way.'

The phone was ringing as she walked into the house. She crossed the hall and picked it up. It was Martin.

'Hello, darling. I'm just phoning to let you know I'll be home tonight, not tomorrow. The case is over a day earlier than we expected.'

'That's wonderful!' She had hesitated a moment too long, she knew, and her words sounded too hearty. It was not in her nature to be deceitful and she disliked herself in that moment but what she had to say could not be said over the phone.

'Is everything OK?' He sounded anxious. 'You sound funny.'

'Yes, yes, everything is fine. It's just this line. It seems rather poor. We can talk tonight.'

Slowly she laid the receiver back in its rest, her heart racing. It had seemed easy enough to tell Martin that she had fallen in love with Tom when she lay in the latter's arms; much harder facing it as something she had to do.

6

'Martin is coming home tonight.' Stevie told Tom, her voice flat.

'Tonight! Then — then that means . . . ' He tailed off, unwilling to put into words the bleak realisation that they would not have another night together.

Stevie nodded, equally loathe to verbalise the thoughts that were in both their minds.

'Oh, well,' ever the optimist, Tom determined to see the bright side of things. 'At least you will be able to tell him sooner. You *will* tell him, won't you, Stevie?' he pressed her when she did not answer immediately.

'Of course I will!' Stevie tried to inject a confidence into her voice she was far from feeling. Martin had sounded so joyful on the phone. So happy to be coming home sooner than he expected and so confident that she would be equally happy, She couldn't bear the thought of shattering his pleasure in coming home. But she loved Tom so much and wanted so much to be with him; to go with him and start a completely new life on the other side of the world. If only she could hate Martin as much as she loved Tom it would make everything so much simpler.

She toyed idly with the idea of not telling Martin at all; just packing up and going one day while he was at the office. But that, she knew, was the coward's way and would be just too cruel and hurtful to the man who had always shown her nothing but kindness and consideration. She owed him more than that. She felt so full and choked with emotion that she could eat little at lunch time, pushing her food round on her plate in a desultory fashion while she tried to keep a flow of casual conversation going between her and Tom. It was hard to talk about everyday things when her mind was so preoccupied.

After lunch she made her way up to her room, suddenly anxious that some little detail she had overlooked could give her away. The room seemed in order. Elsie had tidied it as usual and the bed was freshly made with clean linen. Feeling suddenly tired and overwhelmed, Stevie dropped down on the bed, kicked her shoes off and lay back with a sigh.

The distant sounds of the house were a soothing backdrop. Her eyes closed and, forgetting her problems, she allowed herself to relax.

She didn't hear the car drive up, or voices

in the hall, or Martin's steps on the stairs. The first sound that filtered through to her consciousness was the click of her own bedroom door, the one that opened into Martin's dressing room. She opened her eyes slowly to see him standing over her, a look of infinite care and tenderness relaxing his rather stern features. When he saw she was awake he sat down gently on the bed, taking one of her hands in his.

'What's this?' he asked her. 'Sleeping in the daytime, that's not like you, Stevie, are you unwell?'

She shook her head. 'I didn't mean to go to sleep, I just dropped off.' Smiling up at him she struggled to a sitting position. 'I don't know why I was so tired.' She looked over at the bedside clock. The fingers pointed to five minutes to four. She had been asleep for more than two hours.

'Would you like tea now?' she asked him as she got off the bed and moved over to the dressing table to comb her hair.

'I think I would. It's a long drive but I was glad to get away so much earlier than I expected. We won the case, by the way.'

'Oh, good!' Stevie had been so preoccupied with her own problems that she had forgotten why Martin had been away from home.

He busied himself putting away his

personal things in his dressing room.

'I'll go down and tell Mrs Evans we would like tea now,' Stevie told him through the communicating door. She couldn't tell him now, when he was tired from travelling and so pleased to be home, she went downstairs to see about the tea. She lingered in the kitchen discussing the evening meal with Mrs Evans before she went into the drawing room where Martin was standing with his back to the fire that he had just poked into a warm blaze.

He held out his hand to her. 'Come and sit down and tell me what you've been doing while I've been away.'

Stevie ignored the hand but sat down dutifully. This was a cue, a God-given chance to tell him. But the words stuck in her throat. Maybe after tea, 'Nothing much. Well, Tom and I went to the cinema last night.' At least that was the truth and a start. 'Perhaps that's why I was so tired this afternoon,' she finished lamely.

Martin looked down on her anxiously. He felt there was something wrong but he could not put his finger on it. At that moment there was a tap on the door and Elsie came in with the tea trolley. For a moment Martin forgot his anxiety. He was hungry; he had only stopped for a sandwich and a glass of beer on the way home; some compelling urgency was driving him to get back as quickly as possible. The pile of scones, so fresh from the oven that their butter was melting, looked very inviting. He helped himself to one as he sat down opposite Stevie, stretching his legs out to the now blazing fire. He watched her pouring the tea and noticed that her hand shook slightly and her top teeth were biting into her lower lip. She looked pale and tired, in spite of her rest and there was a tenseness about her that had been there following the tragedy of her father's death, she was not the carefree girl he had left behind a couple of days ago. What had happened; what was the matter with her?

Stevie, concentrating on pouring the tea without spilling it and immersed in her own troubled thoughts, was unaware of his concern or even of his scrutiny. She smiled at him as she passed his cup but the smile only touched her lips and never reached her eyes. Never for one moment had she imagined it would be so hard to tell him about Tom. She had been prepared to deal with his love for her. What she hadn't reckoned on was her own love for Martin, different from the passionate feelings she had for Tom but there all the same — quieter, more the love of a daughter for her father, but it was there and could not be denied or ignored.

She left her tea half drunk and only toyed with a scone. On his own fourth scone, Martin remarked on it as he passed his cup across to her for a refill.

'You don't have much appetite, have you been ill while I've been away?' Maybe that could account for it.

Stevie picked up her cup and gulped her tea down then took another bite at her scone as if to prove to him that she was perfectly fit and well. The defiant, almost guilty way she did it was not lost on Martin and he felt his concern for her grow to a nagging worm of worry that dampened all his pleasure at being home again with her.

'No of course I haven't been ill! There is nothing wrong with me at all. I've told you — I was just tired after the film last night.'

'Thank you.' He took the teacup from her outstretched hand, inwardly deciding that he needed to find out what was causing her to be so on edge.

'Hello, Tom.' He turned to the door as Tom came into the drawing room. 'How are things?' he asked as Stevie said, 'Will you have a cup of tea?'

'Oh — er — fine, thanks. Er — yes — please — I'd like a cup of tea,' Tom answered them both, looking from one to the other and trying to assess the atmosphere between them. He could detect a certain tension but not what he would expect if Stevie had already broken the news to Martin. He accepted the cup Stevie was passing him and sat down opposite her; although he was looking directly at her it seemed to him that she was avoiding meeting his eye. Martin, watching them closely, wondered at the added tension that Tom seemed to have brought into the room with him.

Stevie tried hard to steady her hand as she put her cup down; she had managed, with difficulty, to pour Tom's tea without slopping most of it into the saucer. She was aware that both men were watching her carefully, and the knowledge made her jumpy and uncomfortable. The silence between them all was lengthening. She was racking her brains for some small talk to break it when Tom spoke to Martin.

'Have a good trip? Successful in every way?'

'Very,' Martin smiled. 'We won and wrapped up the case far more quickly than I dared hope. I expected to be away for at least another twenty-four hours.' He looked sharply from one to the other. 'But it's good to be home; there is, I've discovered, no place like it.'

Stevie felt as if she were stretched on the rack. Every word that Martin spoke seemed to her guilty mind to suggest that he knew just what had happened between Tom and her. She found herself rushing in with inconsequential chatter about everyday things, Martin's journey, the horses, anything to keep talking and stop Tom plunging in with some wild confession. She fully intended to tell Martin, it was just that she had to do it in her own time, her own way, and this wasn't it. Tom was restlessly drumming his fingers on the arm of the chair; she was afraid that this was an outer sign of the inward impatience that could make him suddenly rush in and say something in spite of her assurances that she herself would tell Martin; when the moment came. It was with enormous relief that she watched him get up and replace his cup on the trolley. He gave her a meaning look as he said, 'Oh, well, this won't get the horses bedded down for the night.' He turned on his heel and left the room.

'Is everything all right between you two?' Martin asked as the door closed.

'Yes of course.' Stevie fiddled with the things on the tray, stacking cups together. Martin was making openings for her all the time; why on earth couldn't she take them?

76

She glanced up at her husband, only to find him looking at her with a slight frown. Hastily she looked away. She could feel her heart bumping against her ribs. The plain truth was she didn't want to see those handsome features darken with an anger that would, justifiably, be directed at her.

'I'll take this out,' she said, and before he could demur she stood up and began to wheel the trolley towards the door.

At the kitchen end of the hall, near the downstairs cloakroom, where they kept the riding boots and outdoor things, she almost bumped into Tom. He caught her arm. 'Have you told him, Stevie?' he hissed.

She shook her head. 'Let go — you're hurting me! Give me time, Tom. The poor man has only just got home.'

He dropped her arm and gave her a wan smile. 'Sorry, I want to get this thing settled once and for all. I feel I'm here in his house under false pretences.'

'And what about me? How do you think I feel, Tom? He is my husband. I love him, in a way. Not like I love you, but I do love him.'

'Then you must tell him, it's only fair,' he retorted in an urgent whisper. He leaned towards her and gave her a quick kiss on the lips before disappearing through the side door to the stables.

Tom excused himself from dinner that night; in order, Stevie guessed, to allow her to confront Martin with the truth. But she had still not said a word by the time they went to bed. She fully intended to then but, commenting that he had had a tiring day and that she, Stevie, still looked pretty tired, Martin kissed her and went into his dressing room to sleep, firmly closing the communicating door. Alone in the big double bed, Stevie felt a curious mixture of emotions, rejection, relief and sheer emotional exhaustion.

She woke to find Martin standing by the bed with their tray of morning tea in his hands. He smiled down at her.

'I thought we'd have this together. How do you feel this morning?'

'I'm fine!' she assured him, sitting up suddenly in bed. Too suddenly, for Martin began to swim in a curious mist in front of her and she was overcome with a wave of nausea. She dropped back on the pillows again and smiled up at him wanly, adding a weak, 'really' to her words.

He was immediately all concern. 'No, you're not. I could see that as soon as I got home yesterday. Now, you just stay right there and I'll ask Jock to call in and see you this morning.'

'No, don't, I'm all right, truly I am. Once I've had a cup of tea I'll be fine!' But even as she said it she knew she wouldn't. A cup of tea was the last thing she could face right now.

'No arguments!' Martin spoke with half joking severity. 'You look absolutely washed out. All you probably need is one of old Jock's iron tonics and you'll be right as rain.' Jock Campbell was the village doctor and an old friend, they joked and pulled his leg about the tonics he was so fond of prescribing for his patients. Martin patted her hand. 'Now you stay here and I'll get on the phone to him right away.'

Stevie relaxed, momentarily thankful that Martin had taken charge. She hardly dare admit it to herself but it was a relief at the moment not to have to face Tom who would, she knew, expect her to have told Martin everything by now.

★ ★ ★

'Well, young lady, there's nothing the matter with you that time won't cure!' Jock Campbell beamed down on her as he put his stethoscope away in his bag. He had brought Stevie into the world, seen her through all her childhood ailments and through the trauma of her father's death. He hadn't known whether or not to be pleased or sorry when she had married his old school friend, Martin Colville. There was the difference in their ages, and he wasn't quite sure whether the fact that they knew one another so well was an advantage. But it seemed to be working out well enough, and this should just set the seal on things.

'What do you mean? What's wrong with me?' Stevie asked anxiously.

'Wrong with you? Nothing is wrong with you, unless you call being pregnant 'wrong'.'

Stevie gaped at him in undisguised horror for a brief second before she managed to pull herself together.

'Pregnant!' she gasped. 'But I can't be, I mean . . . ' She tailed off lamely, realising the implications both of her condition and how her reaction to it must seem to Jock.

'Well, I can assure you there's a baby there,' he told her. 'As I said, nothing wrong with you that time won't cure,' he smiled kindly, 'look after yourself from now on, that doesn't mean you have to be an invalid, but just take care. I think maybe you had better stop this hunting.'

Stevie nodded. She was ready to agree with anything he said. If only he would go and leave her alone with her thoughts.

With a supreme effort she tried to look pleased. 'When?'

'Let me see — where are we now. February — and you're about two months pregnant — that means you can expect your little stranger around September.'

Stevie did a quick mental sum. If she was two months pregnant then it meant that she had conceived just about as soon as she had agreed with Martin to have a child, at Christmas. Oh, God! If only she had thought — if only she had known how things were going to turn out. How could she leave Martin now?

'I'll leave you to tell Martin,' Jock said from the door. 'I'll be seeing you soon. You can get up now — there's no need to stay in bed imagining you're ill.'

Stevie managed to smile as she bade him goodbye, but she had no intention of leaving her room, or even her bed at the moment. Not because she imagined she was ill, as Jock had suggested, but because above all else she needed to be alone to think this thing through and get herself together before she had to face either Martin or Tom.

She toyed with the idea of carrying out her plan to leave Martin and go now, at once. If she did that, there was the possibility that she could pass off the child as Tom's. It was an idea, but one that hardly appealed to her innate sense of justice and fair play. She could tell Tom and see if he was prepared to take her still, carrying another man's child. But that, she knew, was asking a hell of a lot of him and of his love for her. Or she could do nothing. Stay where she was, let Tom go back to Australia without her, and give Martin the child he wanted.

She went through the alternatives, seeing the pros and cons of each, knowing there was really no choice. She had to stay with Martin, even though her heart longed to go with Tom.

She started as the bedside phone shrilled. It was Martin. He sounded agitated.

'Stevie? I've just phoned Jock — he won't tell me anything, only 'time will cure you' — and I don't like the sound of that!'

In spite of herself Stevie chuckled. 'There's nothing to worry about, honestly, Martin.'

'Well, I'm coming home for lunch. See you soon!'

'No, there's no need for you to do that — ' but the line had gone dead. She would have to face him sooner rather than later.

Slowly she got out of bed, taking care not to move suddenly. But the nausea she had felt early on had passed and she was beginning to feel hungry and quite fit.

She dressed carefully, but did not go downstairs immediately. She wanted to see Martin before Tom. She had to make this decision herself; she couldn't face any pressure from Tom at the moment, and she had to tell Martin first.

When she saw his car turn in at the drive gates she made her way down the stairs. She reached the bottom just as he came in the front door.

'Are you all right?' he asked anxiously. 'Should you be up?'

'I'm quite all right, and yes I should be up,' she assured him, then all her carefully rehearsed ways of telling him fled and she blurted out, 'I'm pregnant!'

He looked at her for a moment as if he couldn't take it in. 'You mean — you mean — you're going to have a child?'

'I think that's what 'pregnant' means,' Stevie retorted dryly, forcing her lips to smile.

If he noticed her lack of enthusiasm he didn't remark on it. Taking both her hands in his, he looked into her face. 'Oh, Stevie, I'm so happy!' Then, anxiously, 'I hope you are too?'

She dropped her eyes from his face and turned slightly away. 'Of course I am, Martin, its what we both wanted, isn't it? Now, come and have lunch.'

His obvious happiness and pleasure were like a knife turning in her heart. She knew that the decision had been made. Only there really had been no decision to make.

7

Stevie was prepared for an ugly scene with Tom when she told him she had changed her mind. She had decided not to mention the baby but found it so hard to justify her apparent change of mind that she let it slip.

She wasn't prepared for Tom's reaction. He recoiled from her as if she had announced she had developed leprosy.

'Do you mean,' he spluttered, 'that you and he were — when you let me — '

'Tom,' she protested. 'he's my husband!'

'But I thought — I didn't think it was like that between you. He's so old. And the way he treats you — as if you were his daughter, not his wife!'

'Tom!' Stevie was suddenly angry. 'You're being stupid — and naive. He's my husband — we're married — and I love him!' It was so true; she did love Martin. Only not in the way she did Tom. Not with an all-consuming passion as if he were flesh of her flesh, bone of her bone; the other half of her that made her whole. She wished she could convey all that to him. But it was too late now. The time had passed.

'I think you're a whore!' Tom spoke softly which somehow underlined all the anger and hurt in his bitter words. 'I feel sorry for Martin!' He turned on his heel and left her, standing there, the tears raining down her cheeks.

She ran upstairs to the sanctuary of her bedroom and flung herself, sobbing, on the bed. Dear God, what had she done? To lose Tom was bad enough; to see the contempt in his eyes was unbearable. She railed against the baby, this tiny, unseen monster who had so effectively wrecked her life. She lay on her bed wallowing in misery and self-pity till the sound of car wheels spinning on the gravel of the drive took her to the window to see Tom's car roaring out of the gate.

Turning from the window she saw an envelope had been pushed under her door. She knew, before she tore it open and read the terse note, what it would say. He had gone, and she would never, ever see him again.

The note itself was by way of being a formal written notice and obviously intended for Martin as much as for her. He was sorry to leave without warning, he wrote, but a sudden family emergency necessitated it. He was returning to Australia at once.

He gave no forwarding address. There was

no way she could contact him even if she wanted to.

Meanwhile, Stevie realised, there were practical things to see to — such as two horses out in the stables expecting to be fed and bedded down for the night.

Putting on her old stable clothes she went out to see to them. Her mare, Fairy, whickered to her in affection when she heard her step on the cobbled stable yard. Sliding the bolt on her box Stevie stroked the soft neck, then buried her face in it, relishing the strong, sweet smell of horse that assailed her nostrils.

'He's gone — for good,' she told the horse in a choking voice. Fairy nuzzled her gently as if to comfort her. 'and I won't be hunting you, or even riding you much,' she told the mare as she leaned against her and gently stroked the dappled neck. As the full extent of her loss overwhelmed her she felt another wave of resentment against the cause of it — her unborn child. How could someone who was not even a person yet have such a devastating influence on her whole life?

She realised as she fed and watered the two horses that in a practical sense they were really going to miss Tom. He had looked after the horses almost entirely; exercising not only

Huntsman but also Fairy, taking her out with him on a leading rein beside the big bay horse, when Stevie, was too busy to ride. Martin was going to be anything but pleased when he came home and she broke the news to him.

It seemed a better idea to phone him at the office; the sooner he knew about the situation the sooner he could do something to remedy it.

'Tom has left,' she told him. There seemed little point in preamble.

'Left! What do you mean?'

'I mean he has gone. Something to do with his family. He's going back to Australia. He left a note for you.'

'Just like that! And what about the horses? I don't want you messing about in the stables — not now.'

Stevie repressed a sigh. It had begun. 'Don't do this' — 'Take care.' 'I've done them for tonight,' she told him. 'I thought I had better tell you straight away, you may be able to find someone else.'

'I'll try!' Martin sounded exasperated, as indeed he was. Getting someone at a moment's notice would not be easy, and the last thing he wanted was Stevie doing it. Damn the fellow; surely he could have given them a bit more notice, whatever the emergency. 'I'll try,' he repeated. 'Don't you worry.'

The problem was solved more quickly and easily than either of them expected — that same day, in fact. Hearing there was a job going, Martin's office boy recommended his sister, Liz Fenton, who had had to give up her previous job to nurse their mother through her final illness. When Stevie learnt that Liz had worked in Sir Hugh Braithwaite's stables, she knew her horses would be in good hands. Even better — Liz turned out to be about her own age, and an old acquaintance from Pony Club days.

By the time Martin came home that night, Liz Fenton was in charge of the horses, and Stevie's mind was at rest.

'I'm sorry about Tom going,' Martin said with a shrug. 'I liked the fellow. We're lucky to have found someone else so quickly. I didn't like the idea of you doing the horses in your — '

'Don't say it!' Stevie cut in. 'If you keep saying 'your condition' to me I'll scream!'

Martin smiled at her vehemence. 'I'll try not,' he promised. 'how about the girl, what was her name — Liz? Did you like her? Do you think she'll be suitable — as a stop-gap anyway?'

'I like her very much. But what do you

89

mean, as a stop-gap?'

'Until we sell the horses. You won't be hunting now in — now — and I'm so busy that I don't know that I will bother without you.'

Stevie was aghast. 'Martin! I don't *want* to sell Fairy. I love her; I'll never, ever find another horse I like so much. I'm pregnant; that's a condition that isn't going to last forever. The horses can be turned out for the summer if we're not riding. We don't have to sell them. Once this — once the baby is born I'll be able to think about riding again. Please don't sell Fairy!' Suddenly keeping Fairy became of the utmost importance, she was more than a horse to her, she was a friend and a link, however tenuous, with Tom..

Martin smiled at her in the way she found so irritating. He was being 'kind Uncle Martin', humouring her.

'All right, we won't sell them. We'll turn them out for the summer, and see how you feel about it in the autumn.'

'Thank you.' She turned away to hide her irritation. She knew she would feel the same in the autumn.

For Stevie the next few weeks were almost as hard as the period just after her father's death. Emotionally she felt empty and drained, grieving for Tom as if he had died.

But she couldn't let anyone see how she felt. Physically she felt tired and sick. It was nearly lunch time each day before the appalling nausea left her, and she spent the mornings lying in bed, for there was no need for her to get up, wallowing in self-pity and a growing bitterness against the child she saw as the cause of all her trouble.

Martin found her morose and difficult to get along with these days but, making allowances for what he still termed, in his own mind, 'her condition', he did his best to be considerate and humour her. All of which was possibly the worst thing he could do. What Stevie needed more than anything was something to do, something to think about, something to make her snap out of it and get on with the business of living.

She found the middle three months of her pregnancy somewhat better. The sickness miraculously stopped and she felt fit and well; physically, that is. She still grieved for Tom and the 'might have been', scanning the post eagerly each day, for a letter with an Australian stamp. A forlorn hope, she knew.

As the days passed and she grew more cumbersome her resentment grew too instead of diminishing. If only Martin would not 'cherish' her but would let her *do* something. It was back to the early days of their marriage when she had wandered the house and garden aimlessly looking for some chore, anything, to fill her days, and had spent hours curled up on the big sofa in the drawing room with a book.

Martin was disappointed that she seemed to take so little interest in the baby, or what he was beginning to think of as 'his son', he was so sure it would be a boy.

It was a hot July afternoon, a Sunday, and Martin in an attempt to rouse Stevie from her lethargy had fetched Aunt Emma over to have tea with them. He had insisted that Stevie come with him to fetch her, feeling that both the run and the company of the bright old lady would be a tonic.

He was right. Stevie liked her and not only responded to her cheerfulness and warmth but also for the first time in months actually began to show some enthusiasm.

'Hello, my dear.' The old lady kissed her warmly on the cheek. 'My, but you do look pretty, your condition suits you.'

Stevie returned her smile; there was that hated phrase and she hadn't really minded. Pregnancy, she decided, must be mellowing her, at last.

As they sat in the shade of the large weeping willow on the lawn, chatting away, Martin looked from one woman to the other.

It had been a good idea to bring Emma over. Who would have thought that it would take an old lady like her to brighten up someone young like Stevie?

'Have you got the nursery ready yet? Do let me see it.' She turned now to Stevie with an eager smile.

'I haven't even decided which room to use.'

'Well let's go and choose one now.' She was already on her feet, one hand held out to Stevie to give her a helping pull

Martin smiled to himself and took her other hand. Stevie even managed a smile as she allowed herself to be hauled to her feet.

There were eight bedrooms in the old house and only three were in use, so they had plenty of choice. Emma suggested a room at the side of the house that looked out on the gardens and caught all the morning sun. There were three rooms in a row on this side of the landing, which, as she pointed out, made an ideal suite. A night nursery, a day nursery and a bedroom for the nanny.

'I suppose you'll be having a nanny?' she asked.

Stevie hadn't given it any thought. In fact she hadn't really thought far into the future, about actually having a baby in the house.

'Of course,' Martin said quickly, and Stevie, even though she told herself she hated this baby and didn't want it, felt a quick stab of disappointment. Of course they would have a nanny to look after the baby, just as they had a housekeeper to look after the house, a gardener to look after the garden and a groom to look after the horses, leaving nothing for her to look after or do.

'They all need re-decorating. Something bright,' Emma mused as she looked round the rooms, adding, almost as if she could read Stevie's thoughts, 'Well, here's something for you to do, Stevie, plan your nursery suite.'

Looking round the rooms that had been empty for so long Stevie suddenly felt a throb of excitement. Yes, this was something she could do.

The next six weeks passed quickly and much more happily for Stevie as she immersed herself in wallpaper patterns, paint charts, curtain materials and furnishings. Martin, only too glad to see her happy and enthusiastic, gave her a free hand and an open cheque book to do as she pleased with the room.

When everything was finished and the last of the decorators had finally left, Stevie took Martin and showed him. The night nursery had been done in a soft lemon and the day nursery had a bright Nursery Rhyme frieze running round the entire room. She had rummaged about in the attics and found an old rocking horse that she guessed had once been Martin's. Its saddle was torn and it had lost most of its hair, but she had got the saddle repaired by the local saddler and robbed Fairy of several inches of her shining silver tail to replenish the sparse mane and tail. Now the horse stood in the window, awaiting a new rider.

The nanny's room she had decorated in soft greens and furnished as a comfortable bed-sitting room.

Martin looked around in amazement. It was indeed a transformation. 'Is that old Prince?' he asked, pointing to the horse. 'My word, I went some wonderful rides on him when I was a child, I don't think I've ever had a better horse.'

Stevie turned to him, laughing; for the first time in months she was happy and felt as if she were achieving something. Poor Martin, she hadn't been much fun to live with lately. Impulsively she reached up and kissed him on the cheek. 'Thank you!'

'What for?' He smiled down at her, taking one hand in his own and squeezing it gently.

'For everything,' she told him. She wanted to say for being patient, for loving me, for not probing too deeply. She looked round the room waiting for its new occupant. 'I'm beginning to look forward to this baby,' she told him, and surprised herself by meaning it.

Martin felt a surge of happiness; he had known that for some reason she did not share his joy in looking forward to their child. It stood like a wall between them and he had not known how to tear it down. Now, it seemed she was doing it herself.

'I think I've only just got it done in time. I've only another two weeks to go and the monthly nurse will be here next week. Ugh!' She pulled a face. 'I don't really want her here before the baby is born!'

She hadn't really wanted to have the baby at home, preferring the idea of going into a nursing home, but Martin had wanted his son to be born in the family home. Jock Campbell had pronounced her fit and healthy and everything progressing normally, so there had seemed little point in making an issue of it. A nurse had been booked to stay for a month and then a nanny would take over. Everything was organised now; there was nothing left to do but wait.

As it happened she did not have long to do that either, for she went into labour a few nights later. The monthly nurse was summoned and fortunately was able to come early; Jock came and looked at her, said that there was no hurry — plenty of time yet

— and went back to take his early morning surgery. As the hours went by and the pains grew steadily more frequent and more compelling Stevie moaned and railed inwardly to herself. No one had told her it would be like this — so long — so slow — such damned hard work. It was nearly twenty-four hours later, in the early hours of the first day of September that her daughter was born.

'Oh, no, it can't be!' Stevie moaned when Jock told her it was a girl. Martin wanted a son, and she had only wanted a child for Martin; absurdly, it had never crossed her mind that it might not be a boy. She turned her face away and refused to look at the baby.

Then Martin was there, holding her hand and smiling into her eyes. 'We have a daughter,' he said softly. 'What shall we call her?'

'But you wanted a son!' Stevie protested wearily.

'And we have a daughter — what shall we call her?'

Stevie's mind flashed back to her childhood and her two favourite dolls. 'Susan Elizabeth,' she murmured as she closed her eyes.

8

Squeak, creak, clunk, and squeak, creak the familiar sound played to the rhythm of the steadily rocking horse was immeasurably soothing to the child in the saddle. She had a hand on either side of the strong wooden neck, its dapples darkened and stained by more than one generation of children's hands. It felt as reassuring as the rhythm was soothing. Something unchanging in a world that seemed to be shifting perilously around her.

She was alone in the nursery. Nanny was in her own room and baby Michael asleep in his pram in the garden. Nanny was probably asleep too, so to all intents and purposes she was alone in the house. Everyone else had gone to something called a funeral.

Her small serious face puckered and she rocked the horse more fiercely. Maybe if she rode hard enough things would be different; she would ride away from the darkness in the house back to the sunny days before God took Daddy.

'I hate God!' she said aloud, somewhat appalled at her own temerity; but when nothing disastrous happened, like the ceiling falling in on her or Prince bucking her off, or even Nanny rushing in to scold and spank, she said it again.

'I hate you, God!' Clunk — clunk . . . she was rocking so hard now that she couldn't hear the squeaks and creaks, only the clunk, clunk. 'What did you take my Daddy for? I want him!' As she wailed out the last words she stopped rocking and let the choking feeling inside her take over. She slid off Prince; much as she loved him she felt the need for something she could cuddle. She ran across the room and sat down cross-legged on the floor, hugging Teddy to her as tight as she could. She loved Teddy; he slept with her every night and had been the recipient of all her troubles ever since she could remember, but he couldn't explain to her why God had taken Daddy. Sitting there on the nursery floor, Teddy held tight to her heaving chest, the top of his plush golden head damp with tears, Sue felt totally alone and bereft of comfort. She also felt angry with God who had taken her Daddy, angry with everyone who had let Him, and angry because no one had explained the 'why' of it all to her. They treated her as if she was a baby in a pram, like Michael, not a person of four years old.

She could hear cars on the gravel drive.

She ran to the window, but the nursery was at the side of the house overlooking the garden and she couldn't see much. Still clutching Teddy she went out onto the landing; the end window faced to the front and by standing on tiptoe she could see the cars slowly coming up the drive.

It was here Nanny found her and took her firmly back to the nursery. 'Tch, tch!' she clucked as she sponged her face, washed her hands and combed her hair. 'How did you manage to get dirty and untidy again after I cleaned you up?' Sue didn't bother to answer because she knew it was a statement rather than a question, and if it were a question Nanny would answer it herself anyway. Which she did.

'I suppose you've been playing on the floor.'

'No, I haven't!' It was true she had been on the floor, but not true that she had been playing there. Sue's voice was truculent. She always argued with Nanny, on principle.

'Well, there now. You look respectable again,' Nanny told her as she combed her thick fringe into place. 'Mummy may want to see you, downstairs.'

Sue's lips set in a mutinous line. She didn't think Mummy would want to see her; and anyway she didn't want to see *her*, nor did she particularly want to go downstairs.

There must be a lot of people downstairs because even in the nursery Sue could hear the sound of their voices, all talking at once, it seemed. She climbed back on Prince and rode him slowly and thoughtfully; the steady rhythm and the squeak, creak, clunk familiar and reassuring.

'Oh, there you are — do you know where Nanny is?' Stevie stood in the doorway feeling, as always with her daughter, totally inadequate.

'With Michael. She just fetched him in,' Sue told her; before turning towards her mother. 'Why did you send Daddy to God?'

For a moment Stevie recoiled as if she had been slapped. The child looked positively furious.

'I didn't, Sue. I didn't, really,' she protested. 'I — I didn't want him to go — any more than you did.' She walked across the room and put her arms round the stiff, unrelenting little body, trying to lift her down from the horse, but she clung tightly to the mane. How on earth could the child think such a thing? Stevie felt the ready tears start to her own eyes and was fumbling for a hanky while Sue rocked, squeak, creak, clunk, even harder, then Nanny came in, carrying Michael in her arms.

'Oh, there you are, Nanny.' Stevie gulped back a sob. 'I just came to ask you if you wouldn't mind bringing the children downstairs for a few minutes . . . ' She looked at her son, Martin's son, as he lay in the other woman's arms. In the strange way that very young babies have of looking quite old, Michael's small, wizened face had an uncanny look of Martin just before he died. Stevie was overwhelmed with love for both him and her dead husband.

'Let me take him, Nanny,' she said. 'Will you bring Sue down?'

Sue snatched her hand away from Nanny's reaching one. 'No! I don't want to go down!' She scowled at her mother.

Stevie, her arms now full of the baby, looked down on Sue helplessly. She knew she should have left Michael in Nanny's care and taken the child's hand herself. Why was it that she always seemed to say and do the wrong thing with her daughter? God knew the relationship between them was hard enough already. With an effort she smiled down at her. 'Please, Sue, come down with me?' she begged. The child didn't answer verbally, but placed her hand in Nanny's and meekly followed her mother down the wide staircase to the waiting guests below.

Stevie looked round, almost as if she

expected Martin to materialise and take her precious burden from her. In her wake the child did much the same thing. To both, it was incomprehensible that there was no more Martin, no more Daddy for their lives to centre on.

Stevie almost wished she had left the children in the nursery. Michael was the focal point of so many cluckings and tearful platitudes that she felt she would scream; and in the attention he got, the son that Martin had hardly seen, Sue was sadly neglected. In an attempt to level things out Stevie handed the baby back to Nanny and held out her own hand to Sue.

'Perhaps you would take Michael back up to the nursery, would you, Nanny? I'll look after Sue for a while.'

She should have known it was not the right thing to say. The child snatched her hand away. 'I can look after myself!'

'Of course you can! What Mummy really meant was that she needed you to look after her.'

Stevie turned gratefully to smile at Jock Campbell who had moved to her side and was talking to Sue. He had taken a special interest in the little girl ever since her birth and, in fact, was her godfather. Sue looked at her mother critically for a moment then turned to the man. 'No, she didn't, Uncle Jock,' she said firmly as she held out one small, plump hand to him. As the child led him away Stevie heard her repeating her question, 'Why did Mummy send Daddy away?'

She couldn't hear Jock's reply but was pretty certain that, whatever it was, he would do his best to rid the child's mind of the idea that she was responsible for Martin's death. Why, if it were anyone responsible, it was Sue. Stevie checked herself hastily: she mustn't, even for a second, think along those lines, much less ever let the child get the barest hint of such a thought. It was no more Sue's fault than it was hers. It was just one of those terribly unfortunate things that Martin should have contracted measles from Sue. They had all been so worried that the baby might get it that no one had thought of Martin, or even realised that he hadn't had it as a child.

Alone in the crowd for a few brief seconds as Nanny took Michael away and Jock moved away with Sue, Stevie let the thoughts creep in like the spearhead of an invading army, opening her defences to fresh waves of unhappiness, loneliness and self-blame.

She moved among the guests like someone in a dream. Part of her wished them all away, a million miles from here. The other part was grateful to them for providing a buffer between her and the grief that would assail her once they had gone and she was left alone.

When that moment finally came and there was only Jock between her and absolute aloneness, she turned to him in real gratitude.

'Thank you,' she said simply. 'I don't think I could have got through that without you. Can you stay — or will you come back for dinner?'

'No, on both counts,' he told her, his warm smile cancelling out the curtness of his refusal. 'I really can't, but I would if I could. I want you to go and lie down and rest. Take a couple of those tablets I gave you; they'll make you go out like a light, and that's what you need at this moment.' When she looked as if she might demur he took her hands in his and held them for a moment. 'Please do as I say, Stevie. I'm being your doctor now, not just your friend. You need the rest.'

Suddenly her eyes brimmed with tears as memories flooded in; she nodded her head, unable to trust her voice. She felt a vague uneasiness about Sue, but Nanny would have to cope; she couldn't. She turned and walked slowly up the stairs.

★ ★ ★

If it was hard for Stevie to comprehend that Martin was really gone, it was almost impossible for Sue.

'Nanny,' she asked, as she stood by watching Michael taking his bottle. 'Nanny, why didn't Daddy come to his party?'

Nanny looked up, startled. Dear God, didn't the child understand yet?

'Because,' she began, with far more confidence than she felt, 'because he couldn't,' she ended lamely.

'Why not? Did Mummy send him away?'

'No, dear, of course Mummy didn't send him away. He — he had to go. God wanted him. He was ill, you see, and God thought it would be better for him to go to Heaven where He could look after him.'

Sue was silent for a while, digesting this piece of information. Only one thing was certain: whomever she asked about Daddy, they all said he was with God. She turned away and began playing with her dolls, muttering, 'I *hate* God!' Nanny deemed it wisest not to hear. But a few minutes later Sue had another question.

'Nanny, what's war?'

'War? War is when people fight — when two countries fight each other.' The political situation and the outside world in general had been pushed into the background lately in this troubled household, but at the child's question she felt cold fingers of apprehension touching her. Involuntarily she gave a little shiver.

'Are we going to have a war?'

Nanny wished she could say 'No' and be sure she was right. She shook her head. 'I don't know, Sue,' she answered truthfully, then, remembering that she was talking to a four-year-old child and not one of her own contemporaries she became brisk, bright Nanny again. 'But don't you worry about it, it won't be anything to do with you anyway.'

Sue didn't say anything, just looked at her solemnly for a moment then turned abruptly away and ran through the communicating door to the day nursery. She clambered up on Prince's back. Here she could ride away to imaginary worlds and forget about all the horrid things that seemed to be happening, like God taking Daddy away and everyone talking about war.

★　★　★

Stevie closed her bedroom door behind her with relief. It had seemed an intolerable effort just to drag herself upstairs. Jock was right; she needed the rest — the oblivion of sleep

107

— more than anything. Slowly she kicked off her shoes and peeled off the plain black dress she had worn for the funeral. She looked at it in distaste and threw it into a corner of the room. She never wanted to wear it again. Then with a sigh she turned back the covers and slid between the sheets. She closed her eyes, remembering as she did so that she had not taken the tablets Jock had given her. She was so tired it didn't seem necessary. She was soon in that betwixt-and-between state, neither awake nor asleep, and the thoughts and memories running through her mind, no longer seemed distressing, but friendly and almost comforting. It was as if Martin were actually with her in the room. Five years, almost six, she had been married to Martin, and by and large they had been good and happy years. What a child she had been, though, when she first came to this house as his bride.

Her mind ranged idly over the high and low spots of those years. The trauma and grief of her parting with Tom. Sue's birth and the disappointment that she was a girl when she had been so sure the baby would be a boy, and that a boy would somehow make up to Martin for her shortcomings as a wife.

It was Aunt Emma who had once more come to her rescue, briskly pointing out the superiority of girls, and generally jollying Stevie out of her black self-pity. She had stood as godmother to Sue and taken a real interest in her, far beyond the gifts of jewellery she had bestowed on her at her christening and first and second birthdays. She had also remembered the child generously in her will. That had been another black spot in the preceding years, Aunt Emma's sudden and unexpected death during her sleep one night. If only she were here now, Stevie thought, missing her more sharply than at any time since her death. She hadn't even got Tinker Bell, for the little dog that had been the old lady's constant companion had herself died only a few short months after Stevie took her in.

Martin had adored his baby daughter — more than she had. Perhaps if she hadn't had a Nanny and had looked after her herself, maybe they would have been closer now? She had to admit that she found the child difficult. But in spite of that her relationship with Martin had steadily improved after Sue's birth; they had become excellent friends with a deep sense of companionship between them even though they lived much their own lives, Martin absorbed in his work and she in her horses and hunting. She had been annoyed at the time to find she was pregnant again, but overjoyed when she had the son she was so sure Martin wanted. What an ironic twist of fate that he should barely have lived to see him and would not be here to watch him grow up.

With these thoughts came a wave of anger that shocked her with its intensity; anger against Martin for dying; anger against Sue who had caught measles in the first place and given it to Martin.

It sometimes seemed to Stevie that Sue was the source of all trouble. If it hadn't been for her . . . She checked her thoughts. Perhaps she should take Jock's wretched pills after all.

True to his promise they put her out like a light. In fact, when she next woke it was long past dinnertime. Without thinking she moved her hand over the bed; but there was no other body to touch; only a void as cold and empty as the place in her heart. Now she let the tears flow.

* * *

Exactly a week later England was at war. Stevie's first reaction was panic. She was finding being a widow difficult enough; to be a widow in wartime seemed altogether too much. Until he was no longer there to turn to, she had not realised just how much she had always relied on Martin to get her round corners, to smooth out the bumps of everyday life; just to be there, a bulwark against 'them' and 'things' when she needed him. Now she found herself thrust into this position with the other members of the household looking to her for guidance.

Jock was a tower of strength in these difficult days. His friendship with Martin had been a lifelong one, starting at family parties and going through prep school, public school and eventually university. He had also been Stevie's family doctor for as long as she could remember, so it was as natural as breathing that she should turn to him now, and equally natural that he should help her.

Jock had married young, while he was an intern, but his lovely young wife had died tragically while still in her twenties, leaving him with a two-year-old son, Matthew, now just through medical school and about to join his father in the practice.

★ ★ ★

At first the war did not seriously affect their lives at all. In fact, tucked away as they were in rural Shropshire, it seemed hard to believe

111

that they were a country at war. Elsie and Liz Fenton were both called up, Stevie sold Martin's horse and sent Bobbin, the pony she had bought for Sue, to the horsebreaker in the village to be trained for harness so that she could drive him to the old governess cart she had unearthed from the stables. She ploughed up one of her two fields to grow potatoes, and put a temporary fence down the other one. She cut off part of the vegetable garden for a poultry run and bought a dozen Rhode Island Reds to keep them in eggs, and a Jersey cow to keep them in milk, and settled down to 'Dig For Victory' as the hoardings exhorted and to generally become as self-sufficient as possible. She and Nanny, who, thank God, was too old to be called up, joined the local Red Cross and what spare time she had left she devoted to committees and 'good works'. She was almost grateful to the war for keeping her busy. She was surprised to wake up one morning with the thought in her head, 'I am almost happy!'

The daughter of a farmer, she knew what she was about with her animals and her crops, and enjoyed the work. Mrs Evans continued to run the house and Nanny took charge of the children, leaving her with ample time and energy for all her other activities.

Michael was a placid, easy baby who didn't

cry nearly as much as Sue had done. Maternal feeling, Stevie felt, was not really one of her strongest points, but she felt a warmth and closeness to Michael that she had never been able to feel for Sue. Not that she didn't love the child, it was just that, somehow or other, they always seemed to be at odds with one another. One thing Stevie was thankful for, though — Sue adored her baby brother and showed no signs of being jealous.

The even tenor of her days, and those of a great many people in the sleepy little Shropshire village, was soon disturbed by the arrival of the evacuees. They came by the trainload, lonely and frightened, their shock at the trauma of being uprooted from everything they had known expressing itself in timidity or aggressiveness according to their individual natures. Most of them were from the deep heart of Cockney London, and the country was as alien and as terrifying as another planet. To the inhabitants of the village, some of whom had never been as far afield as their own capital city; they were indeed creatures of another world. Stevie found herself with the daunting task of matching children with homes and villagers with children.

At the end of the day she arrived home

exhausted and dispirited and with five unplaceable children crammed sulkily in the restored governess cart behind Bobbin.

'Don't you 'ave no car?' a grubby ten-year-old with wild red hair and a mass of freckles demanded truculently as she picked up the reins.

'Well, yes, I do,' she told him.

'Then why are you using this old horse and cart?'

Stevie felt herself bridle at Bobbin and her beautiful little governess cart being referred to in such disparaging terms. 'I'm saving petrol,' she answered rather more shortly than she had intended. And that was the sole conversation they managed on the mile and a half trip back to the house. She attempted one or two pleasantries but they all met with a stony silence.

Stevie couldn't blame them. She would no doubt be feeling just the same in their place. Her heart had bled on their behalf as she had tried one after another of the cottages, only to be met with a blank refusal to take them in, or the thinnest of excuses. But to be fair, outweighing those people were the ones who had opened their doors and their hearts with a warmth and generosity that she knew she herself hadn't shown. She had been prepared to take two children home with her and

114

Nanny had been warned to have one of the spare bedrooms opened up and ready. They were going to have quite a run-round to get beds fitted up for five children.

She unharnessed Bobbin and put him in his stable, watched by five pairs of eyes, then shepherded her small flock indoors. She took them in the back way through the kitchen where they were met by warm baking smells. If Mrs Evans was surprised to see five children trouping in after her she didn't show it.

'Kettle's boiling,' she told Stevie with a smile. 'Would you like a cup of tea?'

'Would I!' Stevie flopped down in one of the rush seated ladder-backed chairs around the scrubbed kitchen table. 'And I'll have it here, please.' She looked at the children. 'Maybe I should go and tell Nanny.'

'I'll tell her, I'll take her a cup of tea.' Mrs Evans smiled at Stevie, thinking the poor lass looked washed out. 'You sit there and have your tea. And what about you, children, would you like a glass of milk each?'

With one accord they shook their heads with as much vehemence as if she had suggested poison.

'Tea, then?'

The shakes for the most part changed to nods. Mrs Evans poured the tea and put a plate of freshly baked biscuits on the table.

'Help yourselves,' Stevie told them. They looked at her for a moment with round blank eyes then fell on the biscuits.

That night Stevie was asleep almost as soon as her head hit the pillow. For the first time since Martin's death she didn't reach out to the empty space at her side, hoping for the impossible: the familiar comfort of his body next to her.

She eventually found billets for three of the children and two, a brother and sister, ten and eight years old respectively, remained at Wingates.

Stevie didn't know whether she had been lucky or whether it was due to Nanny's experienced handling of children, but once they had settled in, Brian and Gladys proved to be surprisingly easy. Brian had a best friend also billeted in the village and in the same form in the school, so he spent a lot of time with him and when he was at Wingates was either busy with his model planes or absorbed in what to him was a whole new world, the great outdoors as represented by Stevie's garden and fields. He had been the child, she realised, who had asked the question about Bobbin, and it hadn't been meant as an insult, as she had felt at the time, but was an expression of genuine interest.

Old Phil, the gardener, gave him a patch of ground all to himself and he dug and hoed and planted to his heart's content. When Stevie realised his interest in the animals, she offered to teach him to ride, harness and drive Bobbin and to milk Daisy, her Jersey cow. He proved not only an apt pupil but also a real help.

Gladys, on the other hand, was all 'little woman', to quote Nanny. She loved helping with baby Michael and took Sue under her wing; Sue in return liked them both and was far easier and more tractable with them than with either Nanny or Stevie. So all in all, wartime life at Wingates settled into a pattern of busy, well-filled days where everyone had both something to do and someone to do it with.

Stevie was almost happy as she settled into the new routine. She lived each day as it came, not worrying too much about the war, which seemed far removed from their daily life. She would have been content for this way of life to go on indefinitely.

9

Sue climbed up the drive gate and, leaning over as far as she could, peered up the road. The gate had to be kept closed in case Michael escaped from Nanny and toddled down the drive and into the road. She, of course, at five and a half, was much too sensible to do that. But it was annoying having the gate shut. She always seemed to tear her clothes or something when she climbed it, and how on earth was she going to be able to see Brian and Gladys coming home from school if she didn't climb it? Not that the torn and dirty clothes worried her too much; it was just that Nanny and Mummy did get so *scratchy* about little things like that.

She could see a figure in the distance; just turning the corner, but only one and it looked like a grown-up, too tall even for Brian who had shot up quite astonishingly in the year he had been at Wingates. Hanging onto the gate with one hand and balancing somewhat perilously, Sue shaded her eyes with the other hand as she peered down the road into the sun.

The stranger was drawing nearer now and she could see he was wearing a khaki uniform, which she knew meant he was a soldier. But she had never seen a soldier in a hat like that before, sort of lop-sided, up one side and down the other.

He was near the gate now, heading for it in fact. Was he coming to her house?

'Hello,' he said as he stopped and smiled at her.

'Hello,' she replied solemnly, remembering, fleetingly, Nanny's oft-repeated injunction not to go chattering to strangers, particularly men and especially soldiers.

'Are you coming to see someone at our house?'

'Well . . . '

'Why isn't your hat like other soldiers'?' He was so slow answering her first question that she couldn't wait to fire the next one at him.

'Because I'm an Australian soldier,' he told her. 'And yes, I was coming to see someone at your house — I think.'

'Are you coming to see me?'

'That depends on who you are!'

'I'm Susan Colville!' she told him with as much dignity as she could muster hanging onto the top of the gate. 'And these,' she added with an airy wave of her hand, 'are

Brian and Gladys who live with us because of the war.'

The soldier turned round and smiled at the two older children who had just reached the gate.

'Hello, Brian and Gladys,' he turned back to Sue. 'If you are Susan Colville then I think you are one of the people I have come to see,' he told her.

She clambered down from the gate and stood back as Brian pulled back the heavy latch and pushed the gate open for his sister and the soldier.

'Who else have you come to see?' she asked, adding as a magnanimous after-thought, 'You can call me Sue.'

'Stevie — your mother,' he told her. Then almost to himself, 'if she'll see me.'

Sue slipped her small hand ingenuously into his large brown one. 'I'll take you to her.'

The soldier looked down on her untidy fair head as he matched his step to hers. He reminded himself that this small person exuding personality had been the cause for his abrupt and angry departure from this house six years ago and that then, and for some time after, he had harboured a searing resentment against her. He was relieved to find that, confronted by the child herself, he felt none of the hate he had nurtured for the unborn nameless being that had, or so he thought then, brought his whole life crashing about him in ruins.

'I'll take you in the back way because I can't open the front door,' Sue told him, keeping a tight grip on his fingers as she led him round to the back of the house.

He had little choice but to go with her. She marched him firmly through the kitchen, as if he were some prize beast, explaining in passing to Mrs Evans, who was just pouring water into the teapot, 'He's come to see Mummy.'

With his free hand he pulled off his hat and as his eyes met those of the woman a flash of recognition passed between them. But he only had time to nod a greeting before Sue had dragged him through the kitchen into the familiar hallway.

'Mummy comes in for tea,' the child told him as she led him towards the drawing room door.

He barely had time to wonder where she came in from and what she did with herself before the door was flung open and his small captor led him towards the woman reading the paper deep in one of the big chintz covered armchairs.

He felt his breath catch in his throat at the sight of the smooth blonde hair, and when

121

she turned round it was as if time had stopped. He pulled his hand free from the child's grasp and with her name on his lips took a hesitant step toward her.

Hearing the door open behind her Stevie put down the newspaper and turned round, expecting to see Mrs Evans with the tea trolley.

The room seemed to spin round her as she jumped to her feet and she clutched the back of the chair for support.

'Tom!' Her eyes were riveted to his face. It was, in fact, almost all she was aware of. It was as if the two of them were standing together in some charmed circle quite apart from the rest of the world. Dimly she was aware that Sue was standing there looking at them; gradually the sense of being enclosed faded and she could hear Sue's voice.

'I found him at the gate, Mummy. He said he'd come to see me and someone else. I forgot to ask him his name — '

'Tom,' Stevie supplied like an automaton. The spell was breaking and with the arrival of the tea trolley it was dispersed completely.

Stevie glanced down at the trolley. It was only set for two people. Sue usually had afternoon tea with her these days; it was part of Stevie's deliberate attempt to get to know her young daughter better and, hopefully, to improve their relationship. She was about to ask the housekeeper to bring in another setting when Mrs Evans took the child firmly by the hand.

'Come along now, Miss Susan, you can have your tea in the kitchen with me and Brian and Gladys.' Ignoring the child's protests she led her firmly away.

Left alone Tom and Stevie faced each other across the tea trolley, the memory of their parting like a spectre between them.

'How?'

'Where?'

They both stopped speaking as abruptly as they had begun, and laughed nervously.

'Sit down and have a cup of tea.' Stevie sought refuge in the safe role of hostess.

They sat like prim strangers on either side of the tea trolley. Stevie could feel the rigid set of her shoulders as she poured the tea, giving him sugar and milk without the need to ask. As she passed the cup over to him she could see her hand shaking and even hear the faint rattle of the cup in the saucer.

As he took it from her Tom looked up and smiled his thanks. In the brief moment in which they looked into each other's eyes everything seemed to go 'Zing!' and Stevie knew that no matter what had happened to each of them in the years apart the chemistry between them was still there, and it had lost none of its power.

Stevie was the first to turn away.

'And how is Tasmania? And your farm?' she asked as she poured herself a cup of tea.

'Tasmania is — well — Tasmania. I've left Dad in charge of the farm, so it should be in safe hands.'

'While you help us poor old Poms to win the war?' Stevie supplied with a smile.

'Too right!' he smiled back. 'And what about you? They told me in the village about Martin. I'm really sorry, Stevie.' He was telling the truth, he had liked the man, and Stevie must find it hard to cope on her own.

'Thank you,' her face clouded. 'it hasn't been easy,' she answered his unspoken thought, 'but I have certainly learned a lot and I'm really enjoying my farming now.'

'Farming?' Tom raised his eyebrows.

'Oh, yes!' Stevie retorted, nettled by the tone in his voice. 'We have dug or ploughed all the land we could, and we grow what we can. I keep hens and a cow, so we are almost self-supporting. I'll show you round after tea. I have to milk the cow anyway.'

'You milk the cow yourself?'

'Of course. I am a farmer's daughter, remember?'

'I'd forgotten,' he admitted. 'I just never

picture you in that sort of role, that's all.'

'How do you picture me?' As soon as she had spoken she wanted to snap the question back, but it was too late.

But Tom answered her seriously, and if he saw the provocativeness of her query he didn't respond. 'As the 'lady of the Manor', with nothing more serious to do than ride to hounds.'

'Oh.' Illogically she was disappointed.

'And,' he added, in the same level tone without a trace of levity, 'the sexiest woman I've ever slept with.'

'Tom!' In spite of herself she laughed. With her laughter the tension between them was dispersed and they were soon chatting together with all the old camaraderie.

* * *

He volunteered to milk the cow for her, once he had seen she really could do it, and helped her feed the hens and collect the eggs. He admired her vast vegetable garden and conceded that her potato crop looked good. Though not, he assured her, as good as a Tasmanian paddock of potatoes.

The three children came round with them, Sue clinging in a proprietary manner to Tom's hand. Brian fired questions at him about everything from life in the Australian Army to Tasmanian farming practices. Gladys was awestruck. His exotic uniform, his accent, his good looks, all gave him a roseate glow in her eyes. She wasn't in the least surprised that Mrs Colville was in love with him. Beneath the exterior of rather plain, slightly scraggy eleven-year-old there lurked, as Nanny had remarked, a being that was 'all woman', and her female antennae had been quick to pick up on the magnetic energy flow between Tom and Stevie. But, being Gladys, she kept her findings strictly to herself.

'You'll stay for dinner, of course?' Stevie asked Tom as they retraced their steps to the house.

'Well, I had hoped I could persuade you to come out to dinner with me,' Tom replied.

It was on the tip of her tongue to refuse. Then 'Why not?' she thought. It was a long time since she had been out to dinner with anyone, let alone a man.

'Why not?' she spoke her thoughts aloud. 'Yes, I think I'd like that!'

'The only thing is, I haven't a car,' he told her with a rueful grin. 'Can you spare the petrol or do we have to go in the governess cart behind Bobbin?'

'I think I can spare the petrol, just this once,' she assured him.

He took her to a hotel familiar to them both
from prewar days. In spite of rationing, the
King's Head still managed to put on a good
menu. It had a large dining room with part of
the floor cleared for dancing. Some half a
dozen couples, most of the men in uniform,
were moving round the small area to the
seductive beat of a fox trot.

'Come on,' Tom said, holding out his hand
to her after they had been shown to their
table, 'let's dance.'

She moved into the circle of his arm and
even though she had not danced for some
time, and never with Tom, she was soon
fitting her steps perfectly to his and they were
moving together as one person. Imperceptibly
his arm tightened round her and his lips just
touched her hair as they circled the small area
oblivious of anyone else.

They danced every dance, in between
courses and after the meal, and she knew that
nothing had changed. She wanted him as
much, or more, than ever. The music, the
wine they had drunk, Tom's presence itself,
the long months without a man, all made her
quick to acquiesce when he suggested they
spend the night in town rather than go home.
Explanations could wait till morning.

The quality of their lovemaking had lost nothing. In fact it seemed to Tom that her years with Martin had given Stevie a poise and maturity, a confidence in her own ability to please, that truly made her, as he had jokingly said, the sexiest woman he had ever slept with.

Stevie sighed deeply and stretched out her hand to Tom, feeling with reassurance the naked body at her side. Oh, but it was good to have someone lying by her again. She hadn't realised just how lonely and bleak her nights had been since Martin died.

Feeling her touch him, he grunted and stirred in his sleep, turning over towards her.

'Tom.' Stevie whispered his name as her gently exploring hands caressed his body. Barely awake he turned into her arms, and as their naked bodies touched he awoke thoroughly to urgent life.

'Stevie!' There was a timbre to his voice that made her stiffen slightly in his arms; a distant warning bell rang somewhere disturbing the peace and relaxation that followed their lovemaking. 'There's something I haven't told you.'

She turned slightly in his arms and put one finger gently on his lips. 'Then don't bother.'

'I have to. I should have told you before. I'm married, Stevie.'

Her heart, even her breathing, seemed to stop, she became rigid in his arms. 'You can't be!' Maybe if she refused to believe him he would laugh and tell her it wasn't true.

But even as she spoke she knew, deep down, that he was speaking the truth; and slowly anger, blind, illogical unreasoning anger, seeped through her whole being taking charge of her until she was aware of nothing else. With an abrupt movement she sat up in bed, snapped on the bedside light, pushed back the bedclothes and leapt out of bed.

'You — you bastard!' she spat at him, eyes blazing, managing to look, in spite of her nakedness, amazingly like an avenging angel. 'You absolute bastard — how dare you *seduce* me when you're married!' She was grabbing her clothes at random and thrusting her head, feet and arms into what, rather astonishingly, seemed to be the correct holes.

'Stevie — look — ' Tom began but with a magnificent gesture she put her hand on his chest and pushed him back on the pillows.

'Stay there! Don't you dare try and follow me. I'm going back home and I never want to see you again, Tom Jefferies. Never!' The last word came out as a sibilant hiss as she realised that her voice was rising and getting dangerously loud in her anger. She gathered up her bag and made for the door, her exit somewhat marred when she realised she had left her keys on the dressing table and had to turn back into the room for them.

Stevie drove back through the still dark country lanes as if pursued by demons. Fortunately at this hour, somewhere nearer five than six, no one else was abroad or she might not have got there in one piece. As it was, the first sharp edge of her anger had worn off when she let herself in through the door of Wingates and crept, like a thief in the night, up the stairs of her own home to her bedroom. Once there she tore off her clothes almost as quickly as she had put them on, pulled her nightdress over her head and slid between the sheets in her own empty but familiar bed. She would have liked a bath but was afraid that the noise would waken the household.

Much to her surprise she must have dropped off to sleep, because the next thing she knew Mrs Evans was drawing the curtains back with some hideously cheerful comment about its being a nice day. A steaming cup of strong tea was on the bedside table and somewhere along the landing she could hear Sue's childish treble arguing about something with Nanny.

Everything was so normal, so much as usual, that she wondered if the previous night had been a dream.

She managed a smile for the housekeeper as she pulled herself up in bed and reached for her tea. 'Yes thank you' she answered demurely to the older woman's kind, 'I hope you had a pleasant evening?'

The sharpest edge of her anger had worn off by now; and she was left with nothing to sustain her or soothe the dull, hard ache left in its place.

Why had it never occurred to her that Tom might be married after all these years? He could not have known that Martin would die and that when he next came back to England she would be a widow, nor even that he would come back to England at all. It was totally unreasonable of her to expect him to wait for her forever. All the same, he could have told her when they were talking and comparing notes, not waited until, she might as well face it, she had thrown herself into his arms.

Sue burst into her room, almost cannoning into Mrs Evans. 'Mummy!' She was all indignation. 'Nanny says I've got to put a dress on. I don't have to, do I? I want to put my shorts on.'

'Do as Nanny tells you,' Stevie snapped. 'I've told you before, Nanny is the boss, not me.' She knew only too well that the quickest way to lose Nanny was to support the children against her, and then how would she cope with the four of them? So, even though she secretly couldn't see why the child shouldn't wear what she liked, within reason, she was not going to take her part against Nanny. 'Run along now, Sue, and get dressed. I'm going to have a bath.'

'But Mu-u-mmy!' Susan wailed, cutting off when she realised that she was only playing to Stevie's back and had no hope of being listened to. She stuck out her tongue at her mother as she retreated to the bathroom, a gesture of defiance she would never dare make to her face. It made her feel better.

★　★　★

Ping! Ping! The swift jets of milk hit the bottom of the metal bucket, the sound gradually changing to a splash, as the level of the milk rose. Stevie's head was against Daisy's warm golden flank; the rhythmic movement of her own hands as she milked, the sound of the milk itself falling into the pail, the steady chewing of the cow as she munched through her morning feed, even the occasional shuffle of her feet or the swish of her tail, were all so familiar that they had a soothing, hypnotic effect on Stevie. Gradually her anger subsided and her world shrank to the small comforting one of the byre and the sounds and smells that were a part of her everyday life.

When Daisy stopped munching and her flank tautened, Stevie knew someone was there, so Tom's voice didn't startle her.

'Have you had breakfast?' he asked. as if they had parted amicably at a reasonable hour.

'Have you?' she parried, without turning her head.

'No, and I'm starving; it's quite a walk from The King's Head on an empty stomach, first thing in the morning.'

'Too bad!' was the only comment that came to mind. She ran her hands over the soft, now flaccid, udder and got up from the stool.

'You'd better come in,' she told him, 'and have breakfast with me.'

She took the milk through to Mrs Evans in the scullery. 'We have an early visitor,' she said as she handed the bucket over to be strained through muslin into a large bowl and left to stand for the cream to rise. 'Mr Jefferies has come for breakfast.'

The wry humour of the situation struck her as she and Tom sat opposite each other at the breakfast table.

'I didn't expect to be breakfasting with you here,' she told him.

He grinned back at her; the teasing, lopsided grin that she knew so well. 'I thought we should talk, at least. You didn't give me much chance when you left in such a hurry.'

'Is there really anything to say?'

'I think so. At least you could hear my explanation.'

'Explanation! What is there to explain, for God's sake? The tables have turned, that's all. You're married now and I am not. Otherwise the situation is as it was before. It seems we do have one thing in common: a remarkable talent for being married to the wrong people at the wrong time, but you may feel you are not married to the wrong person at all.'

'That's just it, Stevie. I do. Which is why I'm here this morning to talk to you. But if you really feel there is no point in it then I'll go, I promise you.'

'Oh, Tom!' Everything she felt echoed in the two simple syllables; all the love, the passion, the tenderness, the aching loneliness of the years without him. She reached across the table and touched his hand in a brief gesture. He looked up and smiled across the breakfast dishes and for a brief moment understanding, pure and perfect, flowed between them.

Stevie drew her hand away, and leaned back in her chair, the spell was broken. 'All right, Tom Jefferies, talk! And make it good!' She smiled a quick, bright smile, hoping to cover up her moment of softness and vulnerability. She pushed her plate away, leaned her elbows on the table and cupped her teacup between her hands, using it as a shield between them.

Tom too pushed away his plate. 'I was livid with you when I left here,' he began with a rueful smile. 'hurt too, but angry mostly.' He held up his hand to stop her when she would have interrupted him. 'Yes — I know now that I didn't really have any right to be angry at all. By any standard I was in the wrong. In fact, anyone could say I behaved quite despicably, or, as you English would say, 'like a cad'. All the same I *was* angry, and very hurt. I got a passage on the next ship back home, and I suppose the rest was inevitable; I was caught on the rebound.'

'You mean you met someone on board ship?'

He nodded. 'You could say that. I think the way I put it says it better. I was 'caught'. On the rebound. Oh, I admit I laid myself just about as open as I could; I drank a bit too much, flirted a lot too much and before I knew where I was it was a fait accompli. Unfortunately, Beryl's father happened to know my father; in fact it turned out she lived quite near us. I should have picked someone from interstate,' his smile was wry. 'I knew it was a mistake before we left the ship; long before I walked up the aisle. I should have been a cad then and got out of it, but there didn't seem much point. I had lost you, so it didn't matter who I was married to.'

'And now?'

'Now? Oh — we've rubbed along all right. So long as we don't see too much of each other we manage to make it work; and then of course there is Simon — our little boy, he is about Michael's age,' his face softened when he mentioned his son. 'When this shindig blew up over here my itchy feet really gave me trouble and I saw it as a marvellous excuse to get back here, and, what's more, be seen as a hero for doing it, so — here I am!'

Despite herself Stevie smiled. He looked like a small boy who had got away with a successful raid on the larder. But she soon grew serious again.

'And what about me, Tom? Where do I fit into all this?'

'Stevie, you know where you 'fit', as you put it — with me. You and I belong together;

we always have. You know that as well as I do.'

'You mean Beryl will divorce you and we can get married?'

He nodded. 'Yup.'

'And if she won't? What then, Tom?'

'We'll cross that bridge when we come to it. Meanwhile, I'm here and you're free and Beryl is a whole world away. If we love one another a little and spend some time together, who is going to be hurt?'

Stevie sighed. 'You're very persuasive, Tom Jefferies, but then you always were.'

10

Tom spent all his leave at Wingates, settling in with them as one of the family. He helped with the chores as a matter of course, bringing what he called 'Aussie expertise' to most of them, showing Stevie short cuts she had not imagined, and smoothing out the wrinkles.

On one point Stevie was adamant. He occupied the spare bedroom and she insisted that he be back in it early in the morning, long before Mrs Evans woke her with her early morning tea. He laughed and called her prudish, but on this point she would not budge. Until they were married she would not bring their relationship out into the open.

The question of Tom's divorce was the only cloud on her immediate horizon. Beryl had flatly refused to consider divorcing Tom and he had no grounds on which he could divorce her.

Stevie felt as if she was living in limbo between Tom's leaves, just existing in some grey hinterland waiting for him to come back and change everything. When he arrived the whole house seemed to spring to life; the children were easier and less quarrelsome, Mrs Evans fell over herself making the rations stretch to exciting and appetising meals, Nanny was all smiles and even Michael, still too young to join in some of the more exciting activities with Tom, seldom grizzled. As for Stevie herself, as she lived through each golden day in his company she knew that ahead lay a night of loving. Counting the days off between his leaves she wondered how she had survived the years of her quiet celibate life between Martin's death and Tom's return.

* * *

'Tom? What's the matter?' The minute she picked the phone off its hook and heard his voice Stevie knew there was something wrong, this was not just one of those 'social' calls; she could hear it in his voice.

'I'll be coming tomorrow, not in a fortnight,' he told her. There was a pause then, 'this is it, Embarkation Leave.'

'Oh, Tom! — How long?'

'That's the rub; only forty-eight hours. Stevie, I was wondering, Do you think, maybe you could come and spend it in a hotel with me? We could have every minute together then.'

'Where?'

'Well, I thought if you came this way I wouldn't even have to waste time travelling.'

She thought rapidly. It was only two nights. Nanny and Mrs Evans could cope and she could get old Phil to milk Daisy.

'All right,' she told him. 'I'll come.'

*   *   *

Her petrol coupons wouldn't stretch to going by car and the trains were both over-crowded and late. However, she still managed to arrive first at the quiet little hotel, the only one in the tiny Welsh border village that Tom had chosen for their rendezvous. As she went to sign the register she remembered just in time that she was booked in as Mrs Jefferies.

'Tom!' She was in his arms almost before he was through the door of their room. 'Oh, Tom!'

He held her close for a long moment then, turning and quietly sliding the lock on the door, he picked her up bodily and put her down on the bed. Without a word they began to undress each other.

Afterwards, as they lay naked together, their passion temporarily sated, he turned towards her, propped himself up on one elbow and slowly let his eyes travel down her body. 'I intend to keep you like this, always, in my mind. No matter where I go, or what happens.'

She laid a finger tenderly on his lips. 'Shh! Don't tempt Providence, you'll be back, we'll do this again, and again.'

'Oh, Stevie, I hope so! I do hope so!' With a catch in his voice that he could not control he dropped down over her body, holding her close and burying his face in her shoulder.

Stevie held him tightly in her arms, part lover, and part comforter. 'Of course we will,' she whispered in his ear; resolutely ignoring the cold shiver of doubt that rippled down her spine.

They spent their few precious hours together living with an intensity neither had known before. They walked the hill paths hand in hand. They drank together in the little bar, just the two of them in a charmed circle all their own; even though the room was full of other people, and they made love with a depth and intensity that neither of them had known they were capable of; they clung together and finally they wept in each other's arms as the moment of parting drew irrevocably closer.

★ ★ ★

'Mummy, why doesn't Uncle Tom ever come to see us now?'

Stevie looked at her daughter in exasperation. How often had she asked that question in the last few months?

'Oh, Sue! Do stop asking me. I've told you he can't, he's in the war — he's fighting somewhere.'

'Where?'

'I don't know. He isn't allowed to tell me.'

Sue sighed. 'Don't you wish you knew, Mummy? Don't you wish he would come and see us again, like he used to?' She pursed her lips in deep concentration. She was colouring in a picture and she had to be very careful or she went over the lines and then it didn't look nice, or as nice as it should. 'I miss him, don't you, Mummy?'

'Yes, I do,' Stevie answered patiently. 'I miss him very much.' Dear God, how she missed him. The ache inside her was like a huge gaping hole that nothing, but Tom, could ever fill. News of him would help a little and she hadn't even had that for weeks.

Sue looked up then and saw the hurt and pain in her mother's face. 'I expect he'll come back,' she said cheerfully.

In spite of herself Stevie smiled. If liking a person could bring him back then what could love do?

Apart from the eternal ache that was Tom, or, rather, not Tom, and waiting, and hoping, and praying for something, anything that would tell her he was all right, Stevie was not greatly affected by the war. She worked hard and played little, watched for the postman to come, listened to the news, read the papers and waited.

The weeks slipped into months and the months grew into a year and more, and still there was no news of Tom.

*   *   *

The war suddenly seemed a great deal closer when she opened the front door one evening to see Jock standing there. One look at his face, and she knew something was wrong.

'Jock, what is it?' She reached out and almost pulled him into the hallway. 'What is it?' she repeated as he still stood there looking at her. 'Matthew?' She asked in the little sitting room she used instead of the drawing room these days, and without asking him poured a stiff whisky.

It had to be Matthew. Nothing else could make Jock look like that; his son was all he had.

He nodded, accepted the whisky gratefully and took a long sip. It seemed to have the desired effect. 'I just heard, he is missing.'

Stevie let out her breath on a long sigh. 'Then there's hope, you *must* hope, Jock!'

'I know that's how I felt when I first heard, then somehow this evening I could only think of the worst, I don't know why I came to see you, I had to talk to someone, I suppose I thought you might understand, I couldn't think of anyone else.'

Impulsively Stevie dropped to her knees at his side. She put her hand on his arm and looked up into his face. 'Whatever you do, you have to go on believing that he is alive. You must, Jock!' Afterwards she was to wonder just why she had spoken as she had, even to reproach herself. If Matthew was dead, wouldn't it be better if he began to accept it now rather than go on living with false hope?

He looked into her face then, and his ravaged features managed to form themselves into something almost like a smile. 'Thank you,' he said quietly, 'thank you, my dear.'

He wondered if she would ever guess how much he had to thank her for. His grief at what he had allowed himself to believe was the loss of his son had been so great that he had seriously thought of ending things; all too easy for a doctor to do that. Instead something had prompted him to come to

Stevie, whom he had known for so much of her life that he still tended to think of as a child. Maybe he had come *because* he knew her so well; she was almost family to him.

Now, as he looked into her face, he forgot his own trouble for a moment and remembered that she too had known grief. He was wrong to think of her as a child; this was a woman kneeling by him, begging him not to lose hope.

'You have to keep on hoping and believing as long as you possibly can,' she was saying to him now, 'otherwise you just can't keep going,' her voice dropped almost to a whisper and she turned her face away as she got slowly to her feet.

'Stevie,' he caught hold of her hand, keeping her by him. 'Thank you,' he repeated, but he did not let her go. 'I'm sorry — is it Tom?'

She turned and looked at him, and he knew that his intuitive guess had been right.

Her eyes brimmed with tears. 'I just haven't heard anything — not a whisper since . . . ' but that stolen weekend was a secret, 'since he had Embarkation Leave,' she finished. She turned away from him, pulling her hand free. 'I'm supposed to be cheering you up, not wallowing in my own self-pity!'

'You have cheered me up — and made me

feel rather ashamed for losing hope like that.'

Before he left that night they made a pact to each call on the other if they needed their faith bolstering or moral support in any way. Neither actually mentioned the dread 'if' that loomed large in their minds.

It was a pact they both kept; a few weeks later Jock heard that Matthew was relatively safe in a German Prisoner of War Camp, but the months crept by and still Stevie had no news of Tom.

★　★　★

The night he had come to her seeking comfort had subtly altered the relationship between Stevie and Jock. She no longer saw him as a kind, avuncular figure but as a man who could love and suffer, and he no longer saw her merely as a child, or as a patient, but as a friend and woman. Neither of them ever brought up Tom's name again.

11

'Now the war's over do you think Uncle Tom will come and see us again?'

Stevie was ironing the hem of one of her daughter's dresses which she had just let down in the hope that it would do another year. Rapidly growing children and clothes rationing were a bad combination. She stared at Sue blankly for a few seconds, while the iron continued to rest on the dress; the smell of scorching fabric brought her to her senses as quickly as a whiff of sal volatile.

'Damn!' To cover her confusion she carefully examined the scorch, which fortunately was only a brown mark and not a hole and was on the inside anyway.

What on earth had made Susan think about Tom after so long? Stevie often wondered if there was some kind of mental telepathy in operation between her and her ten-year-old daughter. Maybe it was Sue's habit of bringing up in conversation the very subject that was occupying Stevie's thoughts that made the relationship between them so difficult at times.

'I doubt it!' she answered the child tersely.

She had long since given up hope of ever again hearing news of Tom.

'No — I don't think he will. He's probably back in Australia by now. Pity,' Sue added, looking up at her mother to see what reaction she was getting, 'he was nice. I would have liked him for a stepfather. We might have all gone to Australia, that would have been fun.'

Stevie felt a wild desire to slap her daughter. But instead she merely snapped, 'Well, he's not your stepfather, and we're not going to Australia or anywhere else!' She held up the dress; the singe mark was quite invisible from the outside. 'That will do, hang it up, will you?' She handed the cotton dress over to Sue who grabbed it in such a way that it almost needed ironing again.

'I hate dresses!' she grumbled.

Stevie sighed. She was such a tomboy. Maybe Nanny had been right. She shouldn't have sent her to the village school. She sighed again and pulled the basket of ironing nearer. She missed Nanny, and not only to do the ironing; she had left when Michael started school a year ago; gone into retirement near Portmadoc on the Welsh coast with her recently widowed sister. They called it retirement but they took boarders during the summer; Stevie was taking the children to stay for a couple of weeks later in the year.

148

'I suppose,' Sue returned to her original subject, 'you could always marry Uncle Jock.'

'Sue! I don't have to marry anyone! Now will you please take that dress to your room before I have to iron it again.'

Sue obediently headed for the doorway but as she went she turned and threw back over her shoulder, 'Well, couldn't you?'

Stevie managed to resist the temptation to throw a blouse she was ironing after her daughter's retreating figure. Damn the child, she was getting too precocious for words. But perhaps she was right, she *should* think of marrying again, if only for the children's sake; in fact Jock had said as much himself and had let her know that, like Barkis, he would be willing. But she could never quite let go of the hope that one day Tom might come back.

The sudden shrilling of the telephone interrupted both her reverie and her ironing. She started towards it but heard Sue clattering back down the stairs and a few minutes later the child called, 'It's Uncle Jock, Mummy. He wants to know if we can go for Sunday lunch, shall I say yes?'

Stevie hesitated for the barest second before answering. 'Tell him we would love to, and thank him!' She heard the child relay the message and guessed from the way she did it that the invitation had already been accepted and asking her if it was all right was a mere formality.

* * *

Stevie smiled and sighed as she relaxed in the deep chintz covered armchair. They were drinking coffee after lunch and Jock was sitting opposite her in a similar chair. The children were out in the garden playing with a half-grown Labrador puppy that belonged to Matthew, who was standing at the window, watching them. He put his empty coffee cup down and left the room to join them, whether because he wanted to be with them or because he thought the puppy needed his protection Stevie was not sure.

'How is Matthew?' Stevie asked, 'has he decided what he is going to do?'

'He seems very well, none the worse for his time spent as a guest of Adolf Hitler; at least, nothing that Mrs Carter's good cooking won't put right.' Jock's treasure of a housekeeper had been with him ever since his wife died, and was locally renowned for her cooking. He smiled at Stevie over the rim of his coffee cup. 'I'm glad to say he's going to join me in the practice.'

'Oh, good, I'm so pleased.' Stevie knew that more than anything else in the world

Jock wanted his son working with him, though he would never press him to do so.

'And what about you, what are you going to do now? No evacuees to look after; no more need to dig for victory; what will you do with yourself?'

'I've been wondering that myself. I couldn't go back to the sort of life we lived before the war; even if that were possible. I couldn't get the help in the house, for one thing. I need to *do* something. When the children go away to school, which I suppose they will some day, I'll have even more time on my hands.'

'That's a few years away, surely?'

'I don't know. I can't help but feel that Sue would be better off, and Martin put Michael down for his old school as soon as he was born. Financially it won't make any difference to me. He set up a special trust fund for their education.'

Jock pulled out his pipe and tobacco pouch and with a great deal of concentration began teasing the tobacco and packing it into the bowl of the pipe.

'Have you thought of marrying again?' he asked casually.

Stevie repressed a smile. 'I've thought about it,' she told him noncommittally.

'And what form did your thoughts take?'

He looked up keenly for a moment from the pipe he was lighting.

'Well, Susan seems to think it would be a good idea — if I chose the right man, of course!'

Jock raised an eyebrow. 'The right man?' It was a question, not a statement.

'She looks for potential husbands for me in one light only, whether or not they would be good stepfather material.'

'And how do I rate?'

'Pretty high.'

'And with you, as a husband?'

'We-e-ell . . . ' Stevie pretended to give the matter her full attention. But Jock was not joking. In fact it was a long time since he had been so serious.

'Dammit, woman!' As always when he became emotional, his Scottish accent thickened. 'I'm asking you to marry me; do I have to spell it out?'

'I thought you might be!' Stevie's smile was gentle. 'But I was sort of hoping you weren't.'

'Does that mean the answer is 'No'?'

Stevie shook her head. 'I'm not sure. Sometimes I think that there is nothing in all the world that I would like better than being married to you . . . '

'But?'

'Oh, Jock — I don't know that there is a

but, it's just that . . . ' She shrugged, unable to put her feelings into words.

'Maybe I'm too old for you?'

Stevie shook her head. 'No, it's not that. There is no more difference between us than there was between Martin and me.'

'And that was a success — wasn't it?'

She nodded, but for a moment her face looked sad, almost old, recalling the price she had paid to ensure that success. Now it seemed Jock was asking her to do almost the same thing.

'Forget him, Stevie!' Jock had been watching her face and had seen the shadow that crossed it. 'He won't come back now.'

Stevie was startled. Were her thoughts so easy to read? She gave herself a mental shake; unconsciously squaring her shoulders. Her smile was rather shaky, but it was a smile.

'Do you know — I think you are right, Dr Campbell. I shall endeavour to take your advice.'

'You still haven't answered my question. Will you marry me?'

Stevie sighed; her tactic of using the doctor-patient relationship to deflect him hadn't worked. But she knew she was not ready to give him an answer yet, she needed time to forget Tom and get him right out of her mind.

'I'm taking the children to Portmadoc to stay with Nanny for a couple of weeks. I'll give you my answer when I come back, will that do?'

Jock smiled and reached for her hand. 'It will have to, my dear!' At least she hadn't turned him down flat; though he felt that if she really wanted to marry him she wouldn't need the best part of a month to make up her mind. He got to his feet, pulling her with him. 'Let's see what the youngsters are doing.'

12

Stevie was so busy over the next week getting ready for the first real holiday she had taken since the war began, that she had little time to think about Jock and his proposal. Her days were filled with washing, ironing, packing and generally preparing to be away from home for two weeks and by the time she got to bed at night it was all she could do to keep awake to read a few pages of her current library book.

Finally she and the two children were in the car. Looking at the cases and bags also packed in with them, Stevie thanked the powers that be that petrol was no longer a problem; it would have been an impossible journey by train. The excited children had ensured that she made an early start and even before they hit the Welsh border Michael was jiggling up and down asking when they would see the sea.

The cottage that Nanny and her sister had bought together was actually a couple of miles out of Porthmadog at a little place called Borth-y-Gest. There was no containing the excitement of the two children as they drove into the peaceful little village nestling round a natural bay where a small fleet of diminutive pleasure and fishing craft bobbed on the tide. Opposite this little harbour the swinging sign of a tearooms, aptly called 'The Bobbing Boats', creaked gently in the breeze.

The road took them on through the village and upwards to a row of grey terraced cottages overlooking the estuary. As she drew the car to a halt outside them and stepped out, thankfully stretching her limbs, Stevie took a deep breath. She could smell the sea, and far away across the estuary she could just see the fairytale outline of Portmeirion, the self-contained holiday village built Italian style. 'Look — ' She would have pointed it out to the children but they were racing up the garden path with shouts of joy towards Nanny. Dear, kind Nanny who had been her friend and helper for so many years and whose homely features were now split wide into the broadest smile ever seen as her two former charges ran into her outstretched arms.

Thanks to their early start, it was still only midday. They had a quick lunch then nothing would satisfy the children but the beach.

'Now don't forget,' Nanny waved an admonitory finger at Stevie as she set off with the children, 'this is an estuary and the tides can be tricky, so take care!'

'I promise, Nanny. I'll do no more than paddle.' Stevie felt young and light-hearted, little more than a child herself, as she set off with her children to find a place where they could dig and paddle.

It was not difficult; the golden sands in little private inlets between the dunes were sparsely populated. She spread a towel and lay, relaxed and at peace with the world, as the children dug and built and paddled and collected shells. Her thoughts slid to Jock. She knew she would have to make a decision soon. He was a good man, and a good friend. He would be a good father to the children. She thought she could be happy with him. They all could. Happiness and security — what more could she ask of life?

She sat up, wrapping her arms round her knees, and gazed at the scene before her. It was beautiful, a foreground of golden sand and rolling golden-green sand dunes; in the middle the sea shimmered in the afternoon sun, and behind, half hidden in the misty haze, lay the undulating shoreline across the estuary. To the right, the mouth of the estuary widened into the open sea, and sailing down towards her on the incoming tide was a small yacht, its bright sails billowing in the freshening breeze. It was all so beautiful and so tranquil. She wished she had her camera with her, or even better, palette, brushes and canvas and the skill to transfer the scene in front to a relatively permanent medium. In what seemed a whole lifetime away, before she had left school, she had dreamed of being an artist. Maybe she should take it up again, just for her own pleasure. She resolved to go into Porthmadog the next day and buy painting materials.

All too soon it was time to pack up and wend their way back to the cottage for tea.

'Don't worry,' she told the children. 'It won't go away; it will all be here tomorrow.'

But the next day dawned dank and cool, a heavy mist like a gauzy grey curtain hanging over the little bay and the estuary. Portmeirion and the whole far shore were hidden and in the little bay the waves were flecked with foam and the boats were indeed bobbing.

'No beach this morning I'm afraid,' Stevie told the children as she drew back the curtains. 'But never mind — ' she said in response to their wails of frustration and disappointment. 'We can go to Portmadoc and see what's there.'

She found it an interesting little town; what she called a 'real' seaside town. By which she meant that you couldn't imagine it dead and empty when the visitors left. Portmadoc had a life of its own apart from the summer visitors. She found several shops selling artists' materials, and in a wild splurge of self-indulgence she treated herself to all the basics she needed, including an easel and a small campstool.

'What d'you want those for?' Michael wrinkled his nose in disgust. This was almost as dull as shopping for clothes.

'To paint pictures with, silly!' Sue considered it her job, as the elder by four years, to instruct and inform her younger brother. Nanny called it being bossy. She turned to her mother now. 'I didn't know you knew how to paint,' she commented.

Stevie smiled. 'I don't know that I do, but it's something I've always wanted to do.' Art had been one of her favourite subjects at school and she had been considered good at it. 'And sometimes it seems a good idea to do something you just want to do.'

Susan nodded sagely. She couldn't agree more, but she hadn't expected her mother to show such good sense. It seemed to her that Mummy usually did things to please other people, and always expected her to do the same.

By lunchtime a watery sun was struggling for existence but it was still not really beach weather. Nanny looked at the tired shadows round Stevie's eyes and mouth and thought that what she needed more than anything was some time to herself away from those two high-spirited children, and, she admitted to herself, what she wanted more than anything was time with the children. Busy though she and Mary were with their new life and their boarders, she missed the company of the children more than she cared to admit.

'Which would you like best, a ride on a train or a bus?' she asked.

'A train!' they chorused.

'Right! Eat lunch as quick as you can and we'll go on the train to Barmouth.'

'Is Mummy coming too?' Michael asked.

Nanny looked across the children's heads and smiled at Stevie. 'No, Mummy is going painting,' she told him.

'Am I?' She smiled. Nanny had always been an excellent organiser; one of the many qualities that had made her so indispensable in Stevie's life. She found the prospect of a whole long afternoon entirely to herself to play with her new toys in peace very appealing.

By the time Stevie had set up her easel in a sheltered spot on the headland, a light breeze had blown away the last of the mist and cloud. She could see right across the estuary; it was a magnificent view and suddenly her fingers were itching to capture it on canvas.

She had been working for a couple of hours or more when she felt a strange uncomfortable sensation at the back of her neck and knew she was being watched. She turned sharply, her heart thudding.

Standing quietly a foot or two away from her, watching her picture take form, was a man of about her own age or a little younger. His hair curled crisply back from his forehead; it was a bit too long and untidy compared with the short back and sides of the day. He was thickset, but just tall enough not to be called stocky; his eyes, like his hair, were dark. The shadow on his strong chin showed that he hadn't shaved that day. He was wearing a bright flame-coloured shirt with the sleeves rolled up and the neck unbuttoned, she could see the dark hairs curling on his chest. There was the odd daub of paint on his shirt and rather more than the odd daub on the faded baggy cords it was tucked loosely into. He had sandals on his bare feet and the arm that he reached out to her was strong and tanned.

Without looking at her, or saying anything, he took the brush from her and with a deft touch transformed the bit of mountain. She had been struggling with it for the last half-hour but was having difficulty putting on

161

canvas what she had so clearly in her mind's eye.

She stared at it in amazement then turned back to him again. For the first time he looked at her, and not at her easel. As their eyes met something too subtle, too deep for words, seemed to pass between them. To say they fell in love at first sight would have been trivial and meaningless. The expression Stevie saw in his eyes, and she knew was mirrored in her own, was recognition. But only for a second, before convention took over.

'I'm so sorry,' he said, and his words vibrated with the music inherent in his race so that she knew him for a native. 'That was very rude of me,' But his smile belied his words and Stevie knew that he wasn't sorry and nor did he think he had been rude, and that given the chance he would do it again.

'Yes it was,' she agreed, 'but as you made such a good job of it I'll forgive you.' He still had her brush in his hand. 'May I?' She held out her own hand for him to return it.

Almost reluctantly he placed it in her outstretched palm. Stepping back slightly from her he looked critically at the canvas, his eyes crinkling at the corners and his head first on one side then the other.

Stevie found herself almost holding her breath as she waited for his verdict, and suddenly she wanted, oh, she wanted so much, for him to say something nice.

'Not bad, not bad at all — for a beginner!' and the teasing smile that she already felt she knew so well, flashed again.

'What do you mean, how do you know I'm a beginner?' She bridled.

'We-ell — ' he drawled;

'Is it that bad?' Perhaps she shouldn't have wasted so much money after all. She looked at the absorbing work of the last couple of hours and it suddenly seemed nothing more than an amateurish daub. She wasn't a painter after all — she never would be. She put up a hand intending to rip the paper from the easel. But before she could do so his hand, strong, firm and warm, was on hers.

'Don't do that!' Her hand tingled under his; she pulled it away and dropped it in her lap.

'I like it — it has promise.'

'Thank you.' So he liked it, did he? How kind of him — how very condescending. After snatching the brush out of her hand and 'improving' it himself, and calling her a beginner, he generously told her he liked it and tried to stop her tearing it up. The *condescension* of the man! She reached her hand up again for the paper; but this time it was his words that stopped her.

'Go on then, tear it up if you want to.' Her hand dropped back into her lap again almost of its own volition. 'I wasn't talking about your painting when I said you were a beginner . . . it's your stuff.' He waved an expressive hand at her easel, the all-embracing gesture taking in the paints, the brushes, the stool, even Stevie herself and the clothes she wore which, unlike his, were free of paint stains. 'Everything is new.'

'Oh!' Suddenly she felt very foolish. 'I see, I'm sorry.'

He ignored her apology. 'Why don't you use oils?'

'Oils?' What an extraordinary man. In the five minutes since she had become aware of his existence — she didn't know how long he had been watching her — he seemed to have succeeded in rousing just about every emotion in her, from irritation to anger, from attraction to . . . She stopped her thoughts at that point. 'What do you mean?'

'Watercolours are too wishy-washy. That's a nice little painting, if you bother to look at it. In oils it could be a good painting that you would *want* to look at.'

She looked at the picture on her easel with a different eye, and knew he was right. 'Water colours were cheaper and simpler and . . . '

'You hadn't enough confidence in yourself

to invest in oils,' he supplied for her.

'Yes,' she said simply, and looking up at him now she smiled into his face. 'How did you know? How do you know so much, are you a famous painter or something?'

He shook his head, but the smile was back. 'Not yet. I teach. In Wolverhampton.'

'Oh, I thought you lived here. You sound Welsh.'

'I am, this — ' with a grandiose sweeping gesture he indicated their surrounds — 'is my home, or at least,' he amended, 'my birthplace. I actually live in Wolverhampton.' Each time he said the name of the town where he lived and worked his dislike of the place was evident in his voice. 'I escape back here for a few weeks or so each summer and pretend that I really am a famous artist.'

'Oh.' The monosyllable was totally inadequate, but it seemed to satisfy him. He looked down at her, a small frown drawing his brows together.

'And you — what about you? You don't live in Wolverhampton too, do you?'

Stevie shook her head. 'No — Shropshire.'

He was still looking at her, and still frowning as if something, some knowledge, was just hidden from him, just out of his reach. 'I feel I know you. I must have met you somewhere. I thought maybe if you lived in

Wolverhampton I could have glimpsed you in a crowd?'

'No,' Stevie repeated, 'I never go there.' As she spoke to him and looked up at his face she shared his feeling. There was something familiar about him, and yet as far as she knew he was a complete stranger to her.

'Sensible woman!' His rather sombre features broke into a smile.

'What? Oh — yes.' Of course; he meant not going to Wolverhampton.

He sat down on the ground beside her; and picking up a handful of the dry sand between the coarse tussocks of grass, he let it run through his fingers. She turned round on her stool so that she was facing him.

'Why aren't you painting today, Mr — er — ' She didn't even know his name and yet she felt they were old friends.

'Jones,' he supplied with a wry smile. 'Davey Jones. But you may call me David.'

She smiled at him. 'Is that your real name?'

'It is,' he assured her, 'and considering every second person round here is called Jones it isn't surprising. I can't get away from that; but I do draw the line at being Davey Jones. So to my friends I'm David. Now you know all about me, how about telling me something about yourself? Your name, for a start?'

Stevie smiled. She hardly knew 'all about' him, though admittedly he had volunteered more information than she had, but that, she suspected was only because he was naturally the more garrulous of the two.

'My name is Stephanie Colville, known as Stevie. I live in the country in Shropshire and I'm just a housewife.'

'With a yen to paint,' he added for her.

'With a yen to paint,' she agreed with a smile.

For a long moment they looked into each other's faces. It seemed to Stevie that they were together in a charmed circle, a sort of fairy ring. In that brief instant all she was aware of was his face, his eyes looking into hers, the muted sound of the waves breaking on the rocks below them, the warmth of the sun and the haunting cry of the gulls that circled and swooped, soared and dived. It was a moment encapsulated in time that she knew, no matter what, would be with her always.

She broke the spell herself by dropping her eyes from his face and in doing so missed his quick glance to her left hand where she still wore the platinum band that Martin had put on her finger so many years before.

Involuntarily David sighed. He too had felt the strange magic of the moment. What was it about this woman? He must have met her somewhere, but surely he would have remembered it. Maybe he had caught a fleeting glimpse of her in a crowd. And yet — and yet — it was so much more than that. He felt he knew her, really knew her.

As they shared Stevie's flask of tea and her packet of tomato sandwiches and biscuits, he kept returning to the subject, mentioning places he had been to for holidays, places he had lived in; but though they shared many memories of places in common, they never seemed to have actually been in the same place at the same time. Finally he lay back with his hands clasped under his head.

'I give up — for the moment. But I know I've met you somewhere, and one day it will come back to me.'

Stevie smiled to herself. It seemed far more interesting and important that they had met now; not where they might, or might not, have met in the past. But she kept her thoughts to herself.

As she packed away the picnic things she shivered slightly. The sun was disappearing again behind thick dark clouds. She looked at her watch. Heavens, she had no idea it was so late. Nanny would be back soon with the children and she had promised to meet them at Portmadoc station. If she didn't hurry they would be waiting. She scrambled to her feet, gathering up her things as quickly as she could. She didn't mention Nanny or the children, just that she had to go.

David walked some of the way back with her and when they parted they made no plans to meet again. Yet it was understood between them that they would.

As Stevie swung back down the hill to the cottage she felt a springiness in her step, a lightness in her heart and a buoyancy that made her feel nearer fourteen than thirty-four.

★　★　★

'I suppose,' she said casually to Mary as she dried the dishes for her while Nanny put the children to bed, 'there would be quite a lot of artists living round here?'

'Oh, yes,' the older woman said, 'they come here in droves every summer, the artists and the would-be artists. And there are a few of course that live here all the year round. Those that either make a living at it or who have private means. There's not too many of those, though.'

'Are there many galleries around where you can see their work?'

'Well now, 'The Bobbing Boats' is a sort of

gallery. She hangs paintings round the walls of the tearooms and sells them if she can. Most of the locals put their paintings there. Then they have an exhibition of local art each year.'

Stevie made up her mind to go to 'The Bobbing Boats' at the first opportunity and look for David's work.

' 'The Bobbing Boats' is open in the evenings; she does evening coffees.'

'Oh, good! I'll take a walk down there when I've said goodnight to the children.'

Stevie found the two rooms of 'The Bobbing Boats' surprisingly well filled. It was an attractive place — small polished tables and ladder-backed chairs, with arts and crafts displayed cunningly on every available bit of shelf space, while the walls were hung with the works of local artists, including the proprietress herself. Stevie decided to have a coffee first and look at the paintings afterwards. She made her way to one of the few vacant tables, a small table for two against the wall. Hanging directly over the table was a bold seascape done in rich, sensuous colours. It appealed to her immediately and she looked for the artist's signature before she sat down. She saw the name 'David Jones' scrawled boldly in the bottom right had corner. She sat, waiting for her coffee, with her head tilted up so that she could see it as well as she could, though at this angle she certainly wasn't able to really do it justice. She liked it; it was what she would have expected of him. In fact, having met the man she thought she could probably recognise his pictures without looking for the signature.

By the time she had drunk her coffee the customers were beginning to thin out, for the tea rooms closed at nine, and she didn't feel quite so conspicuous walking round looking for more of David's paintings.

She found four more; but though she liked them all, none appealed to her nearly as much as the seascape. Looking at it closely she realised that it must have been painted from almost the same spot that she had chosen to set up her own easel. The difference was, she had chosen to paint in the sunshine while David had chosen to paint in a storm. And of course they had both chosen different materials to work in and each painted in a totally different style.

She went back and looked at the painting she was already beginning to think of as hers, and searched for the price. There was a small price tag on the bottom of the frame, fifteen pounds. She decided to buy it. Or, rather, she accepted the decision she knew she had made the moment she saw it.

'Looks like you had an expensive cup of coffee.' Mary smiled at her when she returned to the cottage with the painting safely tucked under her arm.

'I shall have to stay away from there,' Stevie laughed, 'it's a trap for the unwary.' She pulled off the brown paper wrapping and showed them the painting.

'Very nice.' was their verdict. But she could see they were also both thinking that she must have more money than sense to part with so much just for a picture; especially when she could paint one herself if she wanted to. After all, she had been out and bought all the materials.

As soon as she could Stevie went to her own room to gloat over her prize alone. She got her unfinished watercolour and stood it on the chest of drawers alongside the flamboyant oil. It looked a sad, drab thing. Her immediate reaction was to tear up her own painting and at worst give up the whole idea or at best go out again tomorrow and buy oil paints. But even as she reached for the paper to tear it up, something in her own work arrested her. She stepped back from it and tried to look at it critically and without bias; and quite suddenly as she did so, she knew that David was wrong. Oil paints just wouldn't be right for her; there was a charm, a delicacy, and a precision about her work that was almost Victorian. It wasn't the material she had used that was wrong, but the subject she had chosen. She should be using the qualities she had on something that would really benefit from them: flower paintings, or still lifes, or even landscapes if she chose the more intimate, cosy type of scene and not the grandiose and the flamboyant.

She left the two paintings side by side when she eventually climbed into bed.

13

She didn't see David for the next couple of days. The weather had turned warm again and she decided to make the most of it and spend time on the beach with the children. But at Nanny's suggestion they went a bit further afield. On one day they went to Black Rock Sands near Morfa Bychan, where the sand stretching for miles was so firm that it was possible to drive a car along the beach. Quite a contrast to Borth-y-Gest. The following day they went to Criccieth. The children found the pebble beach disappointing because they couldn't build castles, but Stevie helped them collect suitable round stones and shells to take home and make what Michael called 'funnies', comical shell and pebble animals and people. They were more than compensated for their disappointment in the lack of sand when they discovered a Punch and Judy show operating on the beach.

On the third day Nanny suggested that she take them out again, this time for the day. She would take them on the bus to Caernarvon, she told Stevie, and show them the castle.

Stevie decided to take a picnic lunch and her painting gear; but she would look for something other than a seascape to paint. With this end in view she took the track up the hillside away from the sea. She had barely rounded the first bend when she saw a familiar figure striding down towards her. They recognised each other in the same instant and both stopped in their tracks, then moved forward again at the same moment.

'Hello, you wouldn't be coming to see me, would you?'

Stevie shook her head with a smile. 'I'm just looking for a good subject to paint. Where do you live, anyway?'

'Up the hill, half-way up to Tan-y-mynyold.' He jerked his head indicating the way he had just come from.

'Oh.' It sounded totally inadequate, even to her own ears, but she could think of nothing else to say. They stood there on the narrow walking track, facing each other. He was effectively barring her way, as she was his. They would be there until someone made a move, and neither was ready to be the first.

It was David who finally broke the spell. 'Come with me I'll find you something to paint. And if I don't succeed then you can paint me, painting.'

'I just might do that,' Stevie responded in

the same bantering tone, and she turned round and began to retrace her steps.

'Look,' he said, 'I'm sorry, of course you don't have to if you don't want to; it's just that I've got this painting almost done and I want to finish it.'

'I shouldn't have turned round if I didn't want to.'

He set up his easel in a quiet spot overlooking the little harbour. It was like a scene from a picture book, and Stevie was tempted to paint it herself; but one look at the almost finished canvas he unrolled and fixed to his easel was enough. She could never compete with that. Anything she did would just be a pale shadow of a copy. Instead she set up her stool, drew out her sketchpad and pencil and proceeded to do just what he had laughingly suggested, a sketch of him, painting.

With very little demur he shared her sandwiches again at lunch. 'You always seem to be feeding me,' he said. Then, as if an idea had just struck him, 'How do you feel about a good walk this afternoon?'

'I'd love it!'

'Good! Then we'll go up to Tan-y-mynyold and have one of their special teas, how about that?'

'What is Tan-y-mynyold?'

'It's a tea room, right up in the hills, it's all there is up there. You walk up, you eat a good tea, and you walk down.' He treated her to one of his rare smiles, then, serious again, he added, 'Of course if you'd rather not . . . you may have something else to do?'

She shook her head. 'No, I'm quite free, and yes please, I'd love to walk up there with you.'

He looked at their combined gear. 'We don't want to take all this stuff with us. Do you want to take yours back to wherever you're staying, or you could drop it off at my place; we go past it on the way up?'

Stevie was suddenly loath to let him out of her sight even for the time it would take to get her things back to the cottage.

'I'll leave them at your place, if you don't mind.'

He held out his hand and pulled her to her feet and they retraced their steps back towards the path to the mountains and David's cottage.

They were well up the path before Stevie realised that her hand was still resting in his. Quite unselfconsciously, as if it was the most natural thing in the world, they were walking together, hand in hand. Almost as if he was picking up her thoughts, he turned and smiled into her eyes. He was only a couple of inches taller than she was, so that as they walked together their shoulders were almost level, and when he turned and looked directly at her their eyes met without either one or the other looking up or down.

He raised their entwined hands. 'Sorry, I forgot to put it down,' but he didn't offer to let her hand go, and neither did she try to withdraw it.

His cottage was a tiny two-up and two-down chiselled into the side of the hillside. Built of grey stone and roofed with the grey slate from the nearby quarry at Ffestiniog, it looked so much a part of the mountain itself that Stevie could scarcely imagine that it had actually been fashioned by Man. The small garden was an untidy wilderness. The rambler roses had been unfettered for so long that they had wandered far away from their original arch, and the whole was a riot of untrammelled perennials and self-set annuals growing happily cheek by jowl with the weeds. Yet, despite its untidiness, it did not look uncared for or neglected.

Stevie stopped on the path. 'Oh!' she said, 'but it's charming.' What an inadequate word she thought, and knew that this was just what she wanted to paint. 'Do you rent it?'

'No.' He shook his head; 'I own it. I was

brought up here, in fact.' The touch of defiance in his voice was not lost on Stevie. A sort of contrary pride in his humble origins.

'No wonder you don't like Wolverhampton.' Her smile was gentle as she spoke and she wondered why she was so acutely aware of this man whom she hardly knew; not just of his physical presence but of his very thoughts and feelings.

'Come on in,' he invited, letting go of her hand at last to unlatch the door.

The interior was in many ways similar to the garden, a mixture of exquisite antiques and modern everyday things jostled together. A beautiful old Welsh dresser dominated the room and with pure pleasure Stevie ran her hands appreciatively over the dark wood shining, beneath a thin layer of dust, with the loving polish of many generations of hands.

'That's a family heirloom too,' David told her. 'how about a drink, a glass of lemonade, before we set off any further? I'd offer you something stronger but I think we'd better save that 'till we get back down the hill, or we could find ourselves emulating Jack and Jill.'

'That would be nice. Lemonade I mean, not falling down the hill.'

★ ★ ★

Stevie enjoyed the walk up the hillside but was glad she didn't have all her painting things to carry with her. At one point David turned her round to look back, and as she let her eyes drink in the beauty before her another part of her consciousness was also registering that his hand was still resting on her shoulder.

'It's wonderful!' she breathed, and it wasn't only the view she was talking about.

'Tan-y-mynyold' was run on similar lines to 'The Bobbing Boats' — a cosy tearoom with crafts and paintings done by locals offered for sale. Stevie immediately began to look for David's work and was delighted when she recognised one and knew it was his before she read the signature at the bottom.

'Do you sell many?' she asked him, pouring tea for them both.

'Enough.' He shrugged.

'What does that mean?'

'It doesn't mean I sell enough to live on, by any means. But I do sell more or less as many as I can paint. I get as much as I can done while I'm here in the holidays — I don't get much, if anything, done the rest of the year.' His mouth had tightened as he spoke and his face wore a strange closed look, what she was beginning to think of as his 'Woverhampton look'.

'Milk — sugar?' she asked as she passed his cup over to him.

'Did you buy some oil paints?' David asked her.

Stevie shook her head. 'No. I don't think you're right.'

He quirked an eyebrow at her. 'You don't?'

'Oils are right for you; your whole style is so different; but I think watercolours are my medium,' she told him with a firm tilt to her chin and a stubborn line to her mouth that amused him, and in an odd way delighted him; as everything did about this woman.

'Then change your subjects — ' he began. But she held up a hand.

'Don't tell me. I've already decided to do that; and there is one thing I would just love to paint, if I may?'

'Anything, so long as it's not me!'

'Not you, but your cottage. May I?' Suddenly she felt hesitant. It would be awful if he thought she was chasing him, she would hate that. She needn't have worried — he seemed delighted.

The shadows were growing longer and a soft, but cool breeze blew in from the sea as they walked briskly down the hillside together. The tide was in and the sound of the sea grew louder as they got nearer. Following him to the cottage Stevie felt as if she were coming home and when he poured her a glass of red wine from the decanter on the dresser without even asking if she would like one, it seemed not casual, and certainly not rude, but the most natural thing in the world. He sat down, not by her, but opposite her at the table and raised the glass to her in a silent toast, she responded by lifting her own glass.

The sudden chiming of the grandfather clock broke the spell. Stevie looked at her watch. 'My God, is it half past six? Nanny will have a search party out for me!' She leapt to her feet and looked round for her things.

'Nanny?'

'Yes, I'm staying with her. She'll be worried, I must get back!'

He helped her gather up her belongings. 'But you'll come again; to paint the cottage?' he said as he handed her bag to her, he held on to the rest of the things. 'I'll carry these for you. I'll walk with you down to the village.'

They parted at the bottom of the hilly street that led to Mary's cottage and Stevie promised to be there as soon as she could, to paint his cottage.

★   ★   ★

David watched her climb the hill and turn in at the gate of a cottage half-way up; he saw

182

her disappear up the path and into the house before he too turned and made his way back home. He wondered about her; who she was, and who 'Nanny' was, what she was doing here, and all about her. Curiously, though they had been together for most of the day, the things they had talked about had not been biographical details but thoughts, ideas, and beliefs; the sort of conversation in fact that usually goes between two people who know one another very well and are good friends, not between comparative strangers. He marvelled at himself; he usually kept very much his own company on his visits back to his birthplace. Borth-y-Gest and his cottage on the hillside were his refuge and his retreat; he came there like a wounded animal to hole up and recover from the rest of the year and to draw enough strength to go back.

★ ★ ★

Stevie's thoughts were running along much the same lines. She wondered about him; and at herself. She had behaved quite out of character. It just wasn't like her to strike up a light-hearted friendship with a complete stranger. Yet somehow he didn't seem like a stranger at all and she knew, deep down, so deep that she couldn't even acknowledge it to herself, that whatever their relationship, it was not light-hearted.

* * *

It was several days before she saw him again. She didn't go to paint his cottage. In fact her painting gear lay untouched on the chest of drawers in her bedroom. She could, with a little manoeuvring, have easily found the opportunity, but the small nagging voice of caution, kept telling her to forget him, to stay away and not to get involved.

David for his part was restless and not getting nearly enough work done. He waited a little later each morning, hoping she would turn up, and left a note pinned to the door when he went; he got back a little earlier each day hoping to see her on her camp stool painting away with her schoolgirl watercolours and that look of concentrated determination on her face. She was never there, and the note was always still on his door.

He was striding along the headland three days later when he saw her. Down below him on the sands, with two children. In what seemed a couple of bounds he was through the dunes and beside her on the beach.

'Oh, hello.' Stevie, trying hard to sound

casual, was annoyed to feel warm colour flooding her cheeks as she looked up. Why did she have to blush like an adolescent?

The two children stopped digging and Michael straightened up, squinting in the sun. 'Hello,' he said, and with child-like directness, 'who are you?'

'This is Mr Jones,' Stevie introduced him to the children, 'he is a painter,' she added.

'What sort?' Sue wanted to know.

'What sort?' Stevie repeated the question blankly and her daughter looked at her pityingly and in tones of great patience and condescension explained, 'I mean houses or pictures,' she turned to David and demanded, 'Well, which?'

He didn't laugh as many grown-ups would have done but answered her quite seriously. 'Pictures,' he told her, adding, with a smile at Stevie, 'like your Mummy.'

'Oh, Mummy doesn't paint, not really,' Sue told him. 'She hasn't even finished one picture while we've been here.'

So they were her children. David wondered about their father; he didn't seem to be in evidence anywhere, but maybe he had just stayed home. There was a heavy feeling somewhere in the pit of his stomach at the thought of her involved in a family situation. Which was, he knew, totally illogical. For wasn't he involved too? He knew that he should stroll on and leave them to themselves, a happy family group. But he couldn't.

As if guessing his thoughts Stevie patted the sand at her side. 'Sit down,' she invited.

He hesitated for a moment, then squatted till he was on a level with Michael who, with just the same look of concentration that he had seen on Stevie's face, was filling a bucket with sand to make the turrets of the castle he was building. His face fell as it dropped apart when he turned it out.

'Can I help?' David asked, talking to the child as if to an equal.

Michael nodded. 'Can you make it stick together?'

'I think we need a bit more water; let's go and get some.'

'I'll go!' Sue snatched up her bucket and ran down to the water.

'Me too!' Within seconds Michael was running after her, and Stevie and David were alone.

'I thought you were going to paint my house?'

'I — I haven't had time.'

'Please find time,' he said softly, his dark eyes holding her blue ones.

She nodded. 'I'll try,' she promised, and

then the children were back with their buckets slopping seawater as they ran.

★ ★ ★

Stevie was almost as sad leaving the beach as the children were when, all too soon, it was time for lunch. She looked at David almost guiltily. 'I hope we haven't kept you from your painting?'

'You have, but it's been worth it.'

They parted without actually arranging to meet again; but she knew they would, and she fully intended to paint his cottage at the first opportunity.

The children prattled on happily about David as they walked home. Michael simply accepted his existence but Sue of course wanted to know all about him.

'Where did you meet him, Mummy? Do you like him? I do.' She fired a string of questions at Stevie, either not waiting for the answers or supplying them herself.

'Yes, I think he is very nice.' Stevie smiled inwardly at the understatement; she considered him utterly charming and knew that if she were honest she would have to admit that she was well and truly charmed.

Michael was bursting to tell Nanny all about his new friend who had helped him build the best castle in Wales. 'As good as Caernarvon!' he boasted.

Nanny looked over the child's head at Stevie, a world of enquiry in her eyes.

'He's talking about David Jones — an artist who comes here in the summer. I bought one of his pictures — remember?'

'I know who you mean,' Mary said, 'he has the cottage on the way up to Tan-y-mynyold. Spends quite a lot of time here in the summer. I believe he is quite successful, there are always a lot of his paintings in the annual exhibition and most of them sell.'

Stevie longed to ask more about him — was he married? For instance, but a thread of caution bound her tongue. Mary had probably told her all she knew, and Nanny, it seemed, knew even less.

★　★　★

It was another couple of days before she had a chance to take the path up the mountain and set up her easel outside David's cottage. She did not see him in between and there seemed no sign of him at home but, as he had promised, a note was on the door bidding her welcome and telling her he would be back soon. Stevie smiled to herself in some exasperation at the 'soon'. How long before he actually got back depended, on just when he had written the note.

As it turned out, David's 'soon' was well over two hours. But she did not really mind for this gave her the opportunity to make a rough sketch of the cottage and to begin painting in the background. She was standing back, brush in hand, looking critically at her work when she sensed, rather than heard, his presence. She turned round to see him standing a few feet away from her, his own painting gear in his hands. He smiled at her and moved closer.

'Not bad,' he approved, 'and you're even beginning to look like an artist.'

She felt an absurd little thrill run through her when he approved her work but her natural perversity and pride wouldn't let her admit it. 'What do you mean — I'm beginning to look like an artist?'

His face creased into one of his rare smiles as he lifted one hand and, so gently that his touch was like the whisper of a feather against her skin, ran a finger down her cheek. 'You've paint all over your face.'

'Oh!' Stevie was chagrined. She had really hoped that in some mysterious sort of way she looked different from her everyday self.

'How about a cup of tea?' he asked, 'or have you already had one?' He glanced down at the flask that Mary always insisted on filling for her whenever she went out.

'Well, I have, but I could use another,' she told him, following him inside.

Cupping her hands round the mug of tea and leaning her elbows on the table, Stevie looked up to meet his eyes. He was looking at her intently, a small frown of puzzlement making his face even more serious than usual.

'You know, I still can't help feeling I've met you before. There's something so familiar about you. Are you sure this is the first time you've been to Borth-y-Gest or Porthmadog?' She nodded. 'Then it must be Wolverhampton.'

'But I've never been there.'

David shrugged. 'Maybe it's not recognition but precognition.'

'Meaning?'

'Some part of me knows that I am destined to see a lot of you in the future.'

Stevie searched his face but could see that he was quite serious. It unnerved her. 'The fey, Celtic part, I suppose.'

Yet even as she tried to make light of it she had to admit that he felt so familiar that it was hard to remember how short a time they had known one another and how little they actually knew about each other.

David ignored her remark. 'And your

husband — what does he do?'

'My husband is dead. He died when Michael was a baby. He was a solicitor.'

'Oh, I see.' He didn't say he was sorry; he just went on looking at her. Stevie dropped her eyes, hoping he would see she didn't want to talk about her life away from here.

But he persisted, 'And you've been alone since then?'

She shrugged slightly. 'More or less.'

He wondered which — such an attractive woman would have plenty of men friends — but the noncommittal answer and the slight shrug had warned him not to encroach too far into her privacy. When she looked up again and raised her lids so that he could see her eyes, he saw the hurt there, and guessed intuitively that more than the death of her husband caused it.

'And you?' She almost whispered the tentative question, as unwilling as he was to pry, yet longing to know.

He nodded and the warm, sensual mouth tightened into a hard bitter line that she had never seen before.

'I'm married.' His tone was almost curt. Abruptly he got up from the table, pushing his chair back with a scraping noise.

He knew he was being totally unfair. He had asked her questions and was unwilling to answer them himself. He avoided meeting her eyes; knowing full well that if he did he would see his rebuff mirrored in them.

'I think I'd better be going. It must be getting late, and — '

'Nanny will be getting anxious,' he supplied, more than a hint of mockery in his voice.

'Yes she will.' Stevie tilted her chin, angry and hurt by his tone. 'Thank you for the tea, and for letting me paint your cottage.' She gathered up her belongings and turned to say goodbye. She tentatively moved a hand in his direction and, almost as if against his will he moved a hand towards her. But they didn't touch. It was as if strings were jerking their limbs and the puppet-master suddenly snatched them away.

'Goodbye.'

'Goodbye.'

They spoke in unison. Neither smiled. Stevie stood irresolute for a moment, aware of an almost magnetic pull towards him. He stood opposite her, holding her with his eyes but with his arms rigid at his sides. He dare not move them in case they opened to draw her close. It was a strange, tense moment when time seemed suspended, but which neither would forget. Stevie broke it by turning on her heel and almost running from the cottage.

David did not move for a second or two; then in one swift bound he was at the open door. He watched her retreating back flying down the hillside path as fast as she dare and he longed to call her back. But he knew he couldn't. It would not be fair to either of them. He watched until she had disappeared from sight, then with a sigh he turned and went back inside, closing the door behind him.

★　★　★

Stevie didn't go back to the cottage. She had done enough of the painting to finish it from memory the following afternoon. After a cool and misty morning a steady drizzle set in after lunch. Seeing not only the children but Stevie too getting more and more irritable and snappy, Nanny volunteered to take them in to Porthmadog on the bus to the cinema, which was showing a matinée of a children's film. Stevie watched them go, and then settled down in the empty parlour to finish off her painting.

She found it was not difficult. Every detail of the cottage was etched deep in her mind; forever, she suspected.

She had just finished when they all came

trouping back, damp, tired, excited and hungry, Sue and Michael vying with each other to tell her the story of the film.

'Mummy, you're not listening!' Sue accused in the middle of explaining the plot for the third time. 'You're just looking at your old painting,' She stepped closer to have a look at it herself. 'That's quite nice,' there was an unflattering note of surprise in her voice. 'I didn't know you could *really* paint.'

'Mmm, quite pretty.' Michael conceded pushing in closer to have a look. Stevie rumpled his hair and smiled at her daughter over his head.

'Yes, I'm quite pleased with it myself,' she admitted. 'Now run along and wash your hands. I think,' she lowered her voice to a conspiratorial whisper, 'Mary has made muffins and a chocolate cake.'

She turned back to her painting. She was glad she had stuck to watercolours. Her efforts pleased her own critical eye; when she got back home she might frame it.

She didn't see David again after that. Once she caught a glimpse of his retreating back striding through the village. Another time she thought she saw him setting up his easel on the headland, but she quickly turned in another direction. Better not meet, nothing permanent could come of it. She pushed down the sense of loss and resolutely cut short any stray reminders of his sexual attraction. Perversely she didn't use her paints again either. She told herself it was a good thing she had only bought watercolours and not expensive oils, if the 'spasm' was going to wear off so quickly.

★   ★   ★

The two weeks holiday had come to an end. Nanny was hugging the children with tears threatening to spill and Stevie was thanking Mary for the wonderful holiday they had all had; then they were piling into the car which seemed about twice as full as when they left home. There was a last-minute panic when Michael remembered he had left Teddy in his bedroom, but then they were on their way, down the hill, past the little harbour and the boats and finally inland, away from the sea, and heading for home.

14

'Home again, home again, jiggety jog.' Michael sang monotonously as he bounded up and down on the back seat, looking for familiar landmarks.

Yes, home. Stevie stepped out of the car, glad to stretch her legs after the drive and wishing she felt more enthusiastic about being back. She managed to return Mrs Evans' warm smile as she came out with a warm welcome for them all and a special hug for each of the children.

'Did you have a lovely holiday and bring me a bit of rock back?' she asked them.

'Of course we did.' Sue assured her, pulling away. Never as demonstrative as her younger brother; she was going through a 'touch-me-not' phase.

'Here, let me take those.' Mrs Evans turned to help with the piles of baggage Stevie was unloading from the car.

'Hey, you two, don't go in empty handed.' The children were already dashing into the house with no greater burdens than Michael's Teddy.

'Sue, carry some of these things for your

mother.' Michael and Teddy had already disappeared. With none too good a grace the older child turned back and snatched one of the cases from Stevie's hand and humped it into the house.

'Kettle's on,' Mrs Evans said. 'I reckon you need it.'

Stevie sat down at the kitchen table and leaned back in her chair as she set her cup down in the saucer. Mrs Evans was right; She looked round the large homely kitchen and across the table where the children were giving the housekeeper the rock they had brought back for her and showing her the shells and pebbles they had gathered on the beach, both talking at once as they tried to tell her about their holiday. She smiled to herself. Listening to the children prattling away it all seemed so far away, so long ago. She wondered if she had really felt the strange turbulent emotions that had threatened to engulf her when she was with David, wondered even if he existed or was just a figment of her imagination. The ringing phone snapped her out of her daydreaming.

It was Jock. Stevie hadn't given him a thought for the last two weeks beyond sending him a couple of obligatory postcards.

It was because she felt guilty that she didn't say 'No' immediately when he asked her for dinner. He sensed her lack of enthusiasm.

'Or perhaps if you're feeling tired I could come round and see you?'

'That would be nice. But you'll have to take pot-luck if you're coming to dinner; I don't know what Mrs Evans has planned.'

'I'm happy with that.'

Stevie walked slowly back into the kitchen, a frown on her face. She guessed Jock wanted an answer, but was she ready to give him one? Despite her promise, she hadn't even considered it; other things, like David, had pushed it to the back of her mind. Now she had to bring the idea out and look at it.

While Mrs Evans was feeding the children, Stevie ran herself a bath. She had half an hour of peaceful solitude aided by warm water and the relaxing perfume of lavender bath oil. Conscientiously, as she stretched her long legs, she thought of Jock, weighing up the pros and cons. It did not occur to her that such a clinical attitude to marriage might in itself be a con.

On the debit side was the difference in their ages: twenty-five years, one year less than between her and Martin and that had been a success in the end. She had nothing against older men; on the contrary, she liked the feeling of security, something she had not enjoyed in her relationship with Tom. The experience of being passionately in love was certainly wonderful, but would it have lasted? Whereas the affection she felt for Jock . . .

Remembering Tom inevitably made her wonder why she had never, ever, heard anything of him again. Reliving the pain of those silent months she told herself, for the umpteenth time, that he had obviously decided that his future lay with his wife. She splashed water over herself and lathered her body vigorously as if to wash away the memories that could still haunt her; of the way he had looked, how they had laughed at the same jokes, of his hands on her body. She must stop thinking along those lines; Jock was right, Tom was not coming back.

Her thoughts turned to David, who had touched her life so briefly. She reminded herself that their meeting had been so unimportant that they hadn't even exchanged addresses when they parted. But she knew that it had not been so insignificant, he had stirred her senses as no man had since Tom. She allowed herself the brief luxury of wondering 'what if' and knew that if he had not already been married she would not now be agonising over what to say to Jock.

The reasons why she should marry Jock were clearer, but why did they also seem less convincing? She ticked them off in her mind:

companionship; no need to make all the decisions about the children by herself; Sue and Michael needed a father — she stifled the thought that he would, in reality, be more like a grandfather to them. She herself was almost thirty-five, She had to be realistic and face the fact that at times like this, in the aftermath of a war, there were all too many widows with children. She was by no means unique; above everything else Jock represented security for all of them.

She stepped out of the bath and pulled a towel round her body telling herself that it was her duty to marry for her children's sake, that she was getting old and would probably never get another chance. She liked, loved Jock, had known him all her life; there would be no surprises there.

Afterwards she would look back and wonder at her naivety. It didn't occur to her that she was running true to form, doing as she had always done, opting for security.

She looked at herself critically in the full length mirror in her room, cool and elegant in a white blouse and one of the new, longer full skirts in navy, her pale blonde hair lightly permed and stylishly cut, healthy and tanned after her holiday. She looked younger than her years. David had found her attractive, she knew; what would Tom think of her now? It did not cross her mind that it was Jock's feelings that should concern her now if she had made up her mind to accept his offer of marriage.

She was halfway down the stairs when Mrs Evans opened the front door. She smiled as Jock looked up. He was comfortingly familiar — she would give him the answer he wanted.

Jock thought he had never seen her look so lovely. For a moment he felt anxious, but who could she meet staying with Nanny in Borth-y-Gest?

'My dear, you do look well. Your holiday has certainly done you good.'

Stevie laughed. 'Spoken like a true doctor.' she teased, but her eyes were warm as she looked into his face. 'Come and have a glass of sherry before dinner and tell me what you've been up to while I've been away.' She led the way into the drawing room and, indicating the two cut-glass decanters gleaming with amber liquid asked, 'Sweet or dry?'

'Dry — as usual.'

'Of course!' What on earth had she been thinking; a liking for dry sherry was one of the things she and Jock had in common. Her momentary lapse caused a slight tension between them but Susan, bursting into the room more like an ungainly colt than an eleven-year-old girl, dispelled it.

'Hello, Uncle Jock.'

'Hello yourself, young lady, and how is life treating you?' He smiled at her. 'You're growing up.'

Sue laughed. 'I've only been away two weeks; I can't have changed much in that time.'

Looking at her daughter, Stevie realised that Sue *had* grown, almost without her noticing. Her cotton dress was several inches too short, it strained across her chest and revealed two faint pubescent curves. With a faint shock Stevie realised that in just a few years Sue would no longer be a child. The realisation reminded her that time was passing for her too.

Sue settled herself on the sofa next to Jock, leaving Stevie to sit opposite them in one of the big armchairs. She leaned back in the chair, sipping her sherry, aware that, child or not, her daughter was flirting with the man her mother intended to marry. She felt angry and had to bite her tongue to stop herself from saying something As if aware of her thoughts, in the uncanny manner she so often displayed, Sue looked sharply across at her mother then back at Jock.

'I wanted to stay up and have dinner with you, but Mummy wouldn't let me. She said it would be too late and I needed an early night, so I've had my supper in the kitchen with Michael.'

Jock patted the bare brown knee pressed against his own thigh. 'Mummy is right; an early night is a good idea.' He smiled across the room at Stevie and she took her cue.

'I promised you could stay up and see Uncle Jock, and you have. Now you keep your part of the bargain and be off to bed, please.'

The child looked quickly from one to the other; sensing something between them. When Jock said firmly, 'Goodnight, Sue.' she didn't argue as she would have done with Stevie alone but dutifully kissed her mother goodnight and went to the door.

Two seconds later she poked her head into the room again. 'Mrs. Evans says to tell you dinner's all ready in the dining room.'

When she had gone Jock looked across at Stevie. 'She's growing up,' he remarked. 'Have you thought any more about boarding school?'

Stevie shook her head. 'Not really — have you any suggestions?' Maybe he was right. Sue needed a good deal more than the local school now and, unbidden, came the thought that life with Jock might prove a good deal easier without her.

Jock had promised himself not to rush

things, but he found himself asking, as he took his place opposite her at the dining table; 'And what about you, Stevie — have you given any more thought to the question I asked you before you went away?'

She carefully helped herself to salad and passed it over to him. 'You mean about marrying you?'

'I think that was the question!' He smiled over the lettuce and tomato. 'Well, have you?' He had meant to be quite cool about the whole thing and here he was pressing her for an answer like some lovesick schoolboy.

She helped herself to mayonnaise with a meticulous concentration that he found maddening. Then at last she raised her eyes to his and smiled across the table.

'Yes,' she said.

'Yes you've thought about it, or yes, as in yes you will?'

'Both,' she was enjoying teasing him, even if this was not the most romantic of proposals. 'But,' she warned, 'there are going to be a great many problems and an awful lot of things to sort out.'

'Such as?'

'Our children, for one thing.'

'Matthew is hardly a child,' he pointed out.

'Which is precisely why he may not like the idea of a stepmother young enough to be his sister; not to mention actually having a stepbrother and sister.'

'I see no problem there, what about your children?'

'You know they both love you Jock, they'll welcome you as a stepfather.'

'Even when I pack them off to boarding school?' he asked with a thin smile.

'Even then, Sue won't blame you, she'll think it's all my idea.'

*　*　*

There were, as Stevie had predicted, plenty of problems to iron out. Where they would live, for one. Jock simply assumed that she would sell Wingates and move in with him. Which was, as Stevie was the first to admit, the most obvious and logical thing to do.

'But what about the horses?' she asked. If she sold Wingates she would have no field to keep them in.

'You'll sell them, won't you?' As far as Jock was concerned the problem was easily solved. But Stevie shook her head.

'No. I could never sell Fairy, I've had her so long, she's become part of my life, and anyway, she's getting old now.'

'What about Bobbin?'

'I couldn't sell him either. The children

205

love him; they both learned to ride on him. Sue is too big for him now — in fact I was thinking about getting her another pony, but Michael rides him.'

Jock could see by the stubborn set of her lips that she had no intention of giving up on this one.

'Well,' he suggested, 'how about a compromise? Sell Wingates but keep that one big field nearest the village then you can still keep the horses. There's an old coach-house and stables at the back of my house; we can always get that cleaned out for you to use.'

In the end that was what they decided to do, though Jock dissuaded her from buying another pony for Sue.

'If she is going away to school in September, wouldn't it be better to wait till next summer and the long holidays?' he suggested.

It seemed that Sue was off to school. Jock had selected several possibles and Stevie had written to them, finally selecting one not too far away at Wellington in Shropshire.

The next couple of months were the most hectic Stevie had ever known. She had to organise the selling of her house, decide what she was keeping and arrange a furniture sale for the rest of her things, get Sue ready to go away to school, and in her 'spare' time get ready for her own marriage.

One thing she was very pleased about. As both she and Jock each employed a housekeeper it was obvious one of them would have to go. Not unnaturally Jock wanted to keep his on; equally naturally Stevie wanted Mrs Evans. Taking over as mistress of an established household was, as she knew from past experience, difficult, doubly so if the former housekeeper still had a firm hand on the reins. This problem was solved however when the son-in-law of Jock's housekeeper was killed in an accident and she gave in her notice to go and help her daughter who had three young children and was expecting another. Mrs Evans was delighted when Stevie asked her to go with her to her new home after her marriage.

The wedding itself was finally fixed for the beginning of September. They would go away for a brief few days honeymoon, then come back home so that Stevie could get Sue organised and see her safely off to school, before taking a proper honeymoon in October.

15

Stevie woke early that first Saturday morning in September; her last at Wingates. The house had been sold, the furniture sale was scheduled for next week and the new owners would move in the week after that. She lay quite still for a while, gradually moving through that half awake, half asleep state to full wakefulness wondering why, instead of feeling elated she felt quite the reverse. As she emerged to full consciousness she knew. Today was her wedding day, and it was wet.

The curtains were drawn and it was barely light but she could hear the steady rhythmic patter on the windowpane and see it splashing against the leaves of the laburnum tree outside her window. She curled up into a foetal position, pulled the bedclothes over her head and tried to silence the words echoing in her head: 'Happy the bride the sun shines on.'

Stevie did not consider herself a superstitious person — any bride would prefer sunshine to rain — but as she listened to the depressing sounds of a wet morning she made a mental note to be sure that she had the traditional 'something old and something new, something borrowed and something blue'.

She married Jock Campbell in a simple ceremony at eleven o'clock in the village church, in the company only of their immediate family and their closest friends. Afterwards they returned to Wingates for the wedding breakfast.

The rain eased to a drizzle when they left for the church but when they came out the sky was lowering and the heavens seemed to have opened. Stevie and Jock had to run for their car beneath the shelter of a large umbrella.

They were able to slip away quietly after the reception, for Stevie was going away in her wedding outfit; a simple well-cut pastel blue linen dress with a matching jacket. For the ceremony she had worn a specially made hat that was a froth of flowers and veiling, her one concession to frivolity, and had carried a spray of deep red carnations.

As they drove away down the tree-lined drive with the rain on the windscreen and dripping from the trees, Stevie looked back at the house she had lived in for so many years. She had come to it as a bride and she was leaving it as a bride; the wheel had turned full circle.

They were spending a long weekend in London for this, their first honeymoon, at the Regent Palace Hotel. It had been Jock's idea but Stevie, who seldom went up to town, had acquiesced. It was only when she found herself alone with him in the well-appointed and luxurious room that she realised that this was about the first time she had ever been alone, *really* alone, with the man she had married that morning. She had known him all her life but how well did she know him? Since she agreed to marry him a few short months ago she had been so busy that she had barely had the chance to have a meal with him, and their intimate relations had been restricted to a few chaste kisses. A wave of panic swept over her as she watched him checking the amenities of the room and finally reaching in his pocket for the keys to unlock his suitcase. Suppressing a sigh Stevie snapped open her brand new handbag to find her own keys.

The next half hour was spent settling into the room, unpacking and hanging their clothes in the wardrobe. Stevie suppressed the sudden memory of her last meeting with Tom. The bedroom door had barely closed behind them before they were in each other's arms — to hell with the unpacking! But if she expected such passion from her new husband she was doomed to disappointment.

When they were settled in the room to Jock's satisfaction they barely had time to change before they went down to the dining room. Bother dinner! Stevie would much rather have wandered London, exploring the great city by night. Maybe afterwards?

She tentatively suggested it while they ate their meal, talking together more like polite strangers than lovers, or even the old friends they were.

'We'll give it a miss tonight. I feel a bit tired, don't you? It's been a busy day. We'll have a drink in the bar and then go on up.'

Jock ordered champagne with their meal and afterwards they went to the bar and sipped a liqueur each, then, dutifully she followed him to the lift and their room.

Stevie had chosen her trousseau with care. The nightdress she slipped into tonight was a diaphanous affair of sheer white chiffon, revealing and seductive yet giving her a look of almost ethereal virginity. She looked very young and very attractive. But Jock didn't say anything. Maybe, Stevie thought, it was a mistake marrying a doctor. They saw too much of the human body in its less attractive moments. She slid between the crisp clean sheets waiting for him.

He climbed in beside her and, reaching over, switched out the light. So much for glamorous nighties, she reflected wryly. He lay beside her quietly, without moving, then, slowly, tentatively, Stevie moved her hand until she felt it touch his arm. For a moment nothing happened, then abruptly he turned towards her, hoisted himself on his elbow and pinned her body beneath his own. He was already hard, she felt his knee pushing against her own and almost cried out; then he had entered her and before she knew it he had come and was lying limp on top of her for a second before he rolled over away from her. With a brief 'Goodnight' he was soon asleep, snoring none too softly.

Lying wakeful at his side, scarcely even aroused, let alone satisfied, Stevie tried to crush her rising irritation. She would have liked to take a pillow and smothered him, hit him on the head; anything to silence the irritating and rhythmic noise. She lay awake for a long time, inevitably comparing him with the other men who had loved her; Martin and Tom had both made love to her with passion and tenderness, making sure that she, as well as they, got pleasure and satisfaction from the act. Maybe, she told herself as she finally dropped off to sleep, Jock was tired and tomorrow would be better.

When they woke up the sun was shining and the city was alive. Jock showed no desire either to lie in bed or make love again as Tom, and even Martin, would have done, but was up and shaving almost before she was properly awake.

They spent the day being tourists. Jock enjoyed himself showing Stevie all the sights of the city he knew so much better than she did. He took her to see Buckingham Palace and Westminster Abbey and St Paul's Cathedral. They climbed the stairs to the Whispering Gallery in the great dome and, he on one side, she on the other, they whispered to each other like children. Afterwards he took her to afternoon tea and they ate the sort of cakes she hadn't seen since before the war, and then they went back to the Hotel to change for dinner, tired but happy. It had been a full day but they had enjoyed each other's company. After dinner they went to the bar again and then to bed. Stevie was tired and didn't want to go out again tonight. They lay and talked companionably for some time, then, saying 'Good night,' Jock leaned towards her and gave her a chaste peck on the cheek. Stevie accepted this, she had no intention of making any advances herself, she smiled grimly to herself in the darkness; at least she knew where she stood, and this was preferable to last night's performance.

The next day, at Stevie's request, they went to the National Gallery. She could have spent the whole day there, and more, but Jock soon seemed bored and suggested they have lunch, then go to Harrod's. Amazed when he learned that Stevie had never actually shopped there or indeed entered its famous doors, he was determined to take her. That evening they had an earlier dinner as they were going to the theatre and the following day they were due to go home. Honeymoon over, though as far as Stevie could see it had begun and ended that first night in bed, for Jock made no more sexual advances until they had been home for nearly ten days. And then it was as before.

★   ★   ★

With the business of settling into a new home and getting Sue safely off to boarding school, Stevie didn't have much opportunity to dwell on her personal problems. And after all, were they so bad? She and Jock got on well, out of bed, they were excellent friends and life was, in many ways, running more smoothly than she had dared to hope. Michael had taken the change of home in his stride, though things had not really been so very different for him;

214

he still had kindly Mrs Evans and Jock had been a part of his life, almost of his family, ever since he had been born.

As it turned out their second and 'proper' honeymoon didn't eventuate. There was an outbreak of 'flu in the village and Jock couldn't spare the time away from his practice. Stevie was only mildly disappointed. She was finding that now she had settled down, her new home life was little different from what it had always been. She took Michael to school, did the shopping, discussed the meals and the general running of the house with Mrs Evans, helped with the cooking and did her share of the household chores; she messed about in the garden, drove over to see her horses and sometimes she and Michael rode together. It was a quiet but busy life with all the security she had craved.

Stevie would have been quite happy to have another child but Jock was adamant that he was too old to start another family; she could readily understand his viewpoint, and was happy to go along with it. Their first serious disagreement came when he suggested Michael should be sent away to boarding school.

'But Jock, he's too young!' Stevie protested.

'He will be eight next birthday. I went away to school at that age. So did Matthew.'

'Because you went and you sent your son doesn't mean it's right for my son.' Deliberately she stressed that Michael was hers and not his.

'It's high time he left the village school. It's not good enough for him. He's my son now, remember.'

'He is Martin's son. What is worrying you most, his education or the fact that he is at the village school and you don't think that good enough for Dr Campbell's stepson?'

'That's unfair of you, Stevie,' Jock snapped back; but unlike her he had his anger and his temper well under control. Stevie found herself shaking with rage — Michael was her son, not Jock's, and she did not want him sent away to school.

'If he doesn't go to boarding school where else do you propose to send him?' Jock asked reasonably.

'I can't see why he can't stay where he is.'

Jock sighed patiently. 'I've told you it isn't good enough for him. Besides, I think a boy is better away from his mother; you have to cut the umbilicus some time, you know.'

'Why don't you say 'apron strings' like anyone else?' she asked childishly; 'Can't you ever stop being a doctor?'

He ignored the taunt. 'Why don't you ask Michael?' he suggested.

Stevie agreed, quite sure the child would say no, he did not want to go away to school, but when the question was put to him his face lit up. 'You mean go away to a real grown-up school like Greyfriars?' He had recently become an avid Billy Bunter fan.

Jock nodded. 'That's what I mean!'

'But Michael, you don't know, you don't realise . . . ' Stevie tried to make him see that real life and fiction could be very different. But he wasn't listening. The idea that Jock had put into his head was taking root and seeming more exciting by the minute.

Before she knew where she was Stevie was immersed in school prospectuses again, interviewing headmasters and going round schools. Finally they settled on a small private Preparatory school, which Michael liked, Jock pronounced as passable until he was old enough to go on to a Public School, and even Stevie thought might not be too bad. A youngish headmaster and his wife ran it and his own two boys were part and parcel of the school, taking their place among the other boys.

Nevertheless it was with a heavy heart that Stevie took Michael to buy his uniform and sat for what seemed interminable hours sewing on his nametapes and marking his possessions. By the end of July most things were ready for him to go in September. Sue had already been away for a year and would be home soon for the long summer holidays and in August they would all three go and stay with Nanny. At least that was the plan.

A couple of weeks before they were due to set off together for the Welsh coast, Jock brought up the subject of holidays at the breakfast table.

'I have to go to London for a few days in August,' he told Stevie over the top of the *Telegraph*. 'You could come with me.'

'That would be nice. What date?'

'Round about the fifteenth, I think.'

'I shall be at Borth-y-Gest then with the children.'

'I thought you could take them there then come back. We could have that second honeymoon.' He lowered the paper and smiled at her.

'Yes, that would be nice.' Stevie was making a conscious effort to sound enthusiastic.

'Unless of course you would rather go to the seaside with the children?'

'No, of course not, Jock, it's just that . . . ' but he had taken refuge behind the paper again. Better probably not to admit that with Sue away at school and Michael off in September, she had been looking forward to

218

two whole weeks of their company, with time to enjoy it.

Jock folded up the paper and looked at his watch. He smiled. 'That's fine, my dear. It all works in very well. You can take them down there, stay the night, you'll be able to do the same thing to fetch them back. We'll be able to go away without having any worries about them. Well, I must go now. It's nearly surgery.'

As he walked past her chair he gave her a chaste peck on the cheek. Stevie did not quite turn away, but she did not respond.

Just at that moment Matthew came into the room, and caught the mutinous look on Stevie's face.

'Good morning!' he drawled, raising one eyebrow almost a couple of inches above the other. It was a trick that always made the children laugh and even Stevie found it hard not to smile. 'Or isn't it quite so good?'

'The morning is fine, just fine, and so am I,' Stevie assured her stepson. 'how about you?'

'Actually, no,' he smiled ruefully. 'last night was — well — one of those nights. A strong coffee and an Alka-Seltzer will make an excellent breakfast before I go out on the rounds. Good thing Father takes surgery this morning.' he gave Stevie a conspiratorial smile. 'I thought I timed my entrance rather well, what do you think?'

'Very well!' Stevie agreed drily as she pushed her chair back from the table. Since his return from the war Matthew seemed quite determined to catch up on the fun he had missed; or so it seemed. Jock was always cautioning him that a doctor could not afford to play and drink as hard as he did or both he and his practice would suffer.

Stevie liked Matthew well enough and often found herself more sympathetic to his point of view than to his father's — they were more of an age — but she deplored his habit of making himself her ally, as if the two of them were in one corner and Jock in another.

'If you're not having anything to eat then I can clear the table.' She began collecting the breakfast dishes up as she spoke and stacking them on a tray.

As she did her household chores and dusted Sue's room ready for her to come home from school the following day, Stevie resolutely repressed her disappointment about the holiday and instead looked forward to a week in London with Jock. Maybe, she thought ruefully, it might even turn out to be the honeymoon they had never had.

When she arrived at Sue's school the next day she hardly recognised her own daughter among the excited girls gathered round their trunks in the schoolyard. One of the regulations was that school uniform be worn at all times when travelling to and from school, and it was a minute or two before Stevie realised that the incredibly gangly girl bounding towards her was Sue.

'Good gracious,' she exclaimed. 'You have grown!'

'I know.' Sue stood on tiptoe to prove her point; 'I'm almost taller than you, now, and — ' she pulled Stevie closer to whisper in her ear, 'and my periods have started, so I'm really grown up!'

Stevie smiled at her. 'You are,' she agreed. She looked at her daughter, long legs below her school tunic; firmly swelling young breasts that even the hideous uniform couldn't hide. She felt a strange surge of emotion. Her little girl had grown up, become a woman, and she hadn't been with her. She quickly repressed the feeling; this was neither the time nor the place to get mawkish.

'Is this all yours?' she asked indicating the cabin trunk and the pile of cases, boxes and assorted parcels piled on top of it.

Sue nodded. 'It looks a lot, doesn't it? Do you think we'll get it all in the car?'

'Yes, but it's a good thing I came alone. Come along, we'd better start stacking it in.'

Together they carried the trunk over and just managed to slide it into the boot. The rest of the stuff was loaded onto the back seat.

'Sue — Sue, where are you going!' Stevie called to the flying figure vanishing among the crowd of girls. But Sue was temporarily lost in a flurry of excited farewells, good wishes for the holidays and promises to meet again next year.

16

Sue was full of excited chatter as they drove away from the school. At first it was all about the school, her friends, and what she had been doing during the term, but as they neared home she began to talk about the long summer holiday ahead.

'Are we going away, Mummy?'

'Yes, didn't I tell you in my last letter? You're going to Borth-y-Gest for two weeks.'

'Like last year?'

'Well, not quite like last year. I won't be staying with you. Uncle Jock wants me to go to London for a week with him. So I'll be taking you there and then coming back home.'

'Oh, well, that's all right.' Sue threw her mother a quick sideways glance. Her voice sounded flat and Stevie wasn't sure whether or not she did really mind. They drove in silence for a while then Sue said, 'I'd love to go to London some time.'

'You will,' Stevie assured her; 'I'll take you one day, I promise.'

Sue was still young enough not to trust 'some day'. It rang in her ears like 'tomorrow', which never really came. 'When?' she persisted.

'Oh, I don't know, perhaps next holidays.'

Sue sighed. 'That means 'never'!'

'No it doesn't.' Stevie protested and because she felt both guilty and let down herself over the loss of her own seaside holiday she said, 'We'll go up for a day at the end of this holiday. How about that?'

But Sue didn't answer. Crying, 'Hello everyone, I'm home!' she leapt out of the car and bounded into the house.

'That you are, luv, and my, how you've grown!' Mrs Evans came out from the kitchen wiping her hands on her apron and gave her a warm hug.

Watching, a suitcase in each hand, Stevie felt a sharp pang. Why was it that Sue would never let *her* hug her like that? Why did she always find it so difficult to get really close to her young daughter? At least, she reminded herself with a wry smile, Sue had told her about her periods.

'Guess what?' Sue was saying now to Mrs Evans. 'My periods have started!' She dropped her voice to a hoarse stage whisper.

'They have now? Then you are grown up!'

Stevie sighed and started up the stairs with the bags she had in her hands. She had tried to bring up her children to be unashamed of their own bodies; maybe with Sue she had overdone it.

Mrs. Evans and Sue hauled her trunk into the hall and they unpacked it there rather than try and carry it up the stairs but before she did anything Sue had to get out of the hated school uniform.

'Oh, dear,' Stevie looked at the cotton dress she had put on, 'we shall have to get you some clothes; that looks almost indecent.'

The three of them were having a much-needed cup of tea in the kitchen when Jock appeared in the doorway.

'Hello, Sue, I came home to have tea with you.'

Stevie immediately felt discomfited, guilty almost, as she set her cup down in the saucer, but Mrs Evans was already laying a tea tray and Sue, quite unconcerned, was chattering happily to Jock. Stevie wondered if he had always had this strange ability to make her feel in the wrong over the simplest thing or whether it was something he had developed lately. Picking up her cup and saucer and the chocolate cake the housekeeper had baked specially for Sue's homecoming, she followed her husband into the drawing room. As she crossed the hall the front door burst open and Michael came in like a tornado; only her quick reflexes stopped cake and china crashing to the ground.

'Is Sue home? Where's Sue?' he demanded, a big smile splitting his face when she appeared. 'I'm going to school next term too!' he told her, unable to contain his big news.

Did he really want to go away that much, Stevie wondered, or was it just that he was always so anxious to keep up with his elder sister, to minimise the four year gap between them?

'Go and wash your hands before coming in to tea.' Jock's voice was sharp when he spoke to the boy. Michael headed for the kitchen but Jock's voice recalled him. 'Upstairs, in the bathroom, please!'

Stevie bit her tongue to cut off the defensive retort that sprang to her lips. Why make trouble, or even meet it halfway?

The only person who seemed to have plenty to say over tea was Sue. She prattled happily to Jock about school, apparently oblivious to the fact that most of his answers were monosyllabic. Michael was too busy eating chocolate cake and Stevie, for some unfathomable reason, felt a miasma of vague unease settling round her. She was not sorry when they each went their separate ways, the children upstairs to their playroom, Jock to get ready for his surgery and she to the kitchen with the tea things.

The first week of the school holidays flew by. There was so much to do. She had to take Sue shopping for some holiday clothes and get ready for her own holiday. Jock had told her that they had to attend a dinner and Stevie would need a suitable dress. Sue had certainly grown up — she not only showed some interest in her own clothes now but even in what Stevie wore, and asked if she could go with her to choose her evening dress.

'But Mummy, that's so *dreary*!' Sue protested as Stevie took a soft grey crepe de chine with long sleeves off the rack. 'What about this one?' Her choice was a stark contrast, brilliant electric blue with a deep décolleté neckline. 'Try this one, please.'

'I couldn't wear that!' Stevie protested as she took the hanger from her daughter.

'Just try it. Please, Mummy?'

More to please her than anything else Stevie made her way to the fitting room with the two dresses and a plain, serviceable little black dress, that would do for anything.

She tried on the black first; it was a perfect fit and her tall slim figure and delicate colouring showed it off to perfection. It was a dress that Stevie knew she could wear for any number of occasions, and it was a perfect foil for jewellery. Over the last year she had grown her hair; which was still a delicate honey blonde, and now wore it in a neat chignon at the base of her neck. Jock liked it. He considered it both sophisticated and dignified.

She reached for the grey dress but Sue was dragging the peacock blue one off its hanger.

'No, try this one next, please, Mummy!'

Stevie took it, and slipped it over her head to please the child. She stepped back and looked at herself in the long mirror as Sue zipped up her back, she caught her breath.

'Oh, Mummy, it's super! Will you buy it?'

Stevie shook her head. 'I don't think so.' But she made no move to take it off. It was in fact a startlingly simple dress, relying entirely for its effect on colour and cut. The deep bodice was draped across the front in a way that did justice to her full breasts. This draping effect was carried over into the skirt, much longer than fashion had decreed for some time. The brilliant colour enhanced her eyes, which looked back at her now from the mirror with a bright glitter.

'Isn't it a wee bit long?' Stevie said to the saleswoman who had just drawn back the curtain to the fitting cubicle and was looking at her with undisguised admiration.

'Oh, no, Madam! That is the new length. Just thirteen inches from the floor.' She whipped her tape measure from round her neck and was down in a second with it. 'Exactly!' she exclaimed. 'I thought it looked it and, if I may say so, Madam, it suits you perfectly.'

'I *knew* it would!' Sue's voice rang with triumph. 'You must have it, Mummy.'

'I don't know,' Stevie demurred, turning and twisting so that she could see herself at all angles. The longer she wore it the more she loved it. But would Jock approve?

Finally she slipped it off and regretfully, almost tenderly, put it back on its hanger before reaching for the grey dress. This had a high neckline with a small stand-up mandarin collar embroidered with red sequins. It was a beautiful dress and had caught her eye immediately, as being suitable and yet becoming. She slipped it over her head and with nimble fingers buttoned up the row of little ball-like buttons, covered with the same material as the dress, up the front of the bodice. The long tight sleeves buttoned at the wrist and another row of little red sequins encircled the wristband. The tight-fitting bodice went down into a straight slim skirt, split to the knees to allow ample legroom. Though by no means as striking as the blue dress it was elegant and — yes — sexy on.

'That looks nice, too,' Sue admitted grudgingly; 'but you look *gorgeous* in the blue.'

Secretly Stevie wasn't at all sure that Jock would approve of this one either. His taste in clothes was conservative, his criteria being that they should be 'good' and 'ladylike'. The word 'sexy' didn't enter his vocabulary at all in any complimentary manner.

Stevie looked at first one dress then the other; at the blue dress on its hanger, at the grey one she was wearing and the good black dress she had not put back on its hanger because she intended to buy it. Memory, sharp and clear flooded back — she had worn a black dress, like this one, to Martin's funeral. When she took it off she had sworn never to wear black again. Impulsively she turned to the saleswoman.

'I'll take both these — but not the black.' She smiled at Sue.

'I wish you always wore clothes like that, Mummy. Not those tweed suits that make you look like a horsy old maid.'

Was this really her tomboy daughter talking? Obviously it was time Sue was allowed to choose her own clothes. With an effort of will Stevie managed to sit back and let her daughter select for herself; only offering an opinion when it was asked for.

As they carried their parcels into the house she felt well satisfied with the day's work. Not only had she refurbished both their wardrobes to their mutual satisfaction but something good had happened to their mother-daughter relationship.

17

'I wish I were staying, I don't really want to go back tomorrow.' Stevie sighed. She was standing at the familiar bedroom window looking out towards the sea in the little cottage.

'Maybe you can stay a day or two when you come to fetch them back?' Nanny sounded soothing and hopeful, just as Stevie had so often heard her when the children were disappointed over something. She turned and smiled at the woman she had grown to love over the years.

Nanny returned the smile. She felt a warm affection for Stevie; she had been with her since Sue was born and had seen her through the dark days of Martin's death and the not always easy years of the war. She had watched her unfold and bloom, like a flower, when that Mr Jefferies turned up again in the war. Mrs Evans had told her all about him and how he had helped with the horses and been sweet on the young mistress who he had known as a child. She had hoped it was going to be a second chance of happiness for her. But nothing had come of it. And then she had married the Doctor. A nice enough man, granted, but too old for her. Not that that would matter — after all Mr Colville himself had been older — no that wouldn't matter at all; not if she was happy, *really* happy, glowing, like she was when Mr Jefferies was around.

All that ran through Nanny's head as she watched Stevie standing pensively at the window. She watched her sigh and straighten up, a gesture that implied pulling herself together after coming to a decision.

'This won't do, No good crying over spilt milk. I must make the most of what I've got.' And with this mouthful of platitudes she turned back into the room, glancing at her watch as she did so. 'We've time to go down to the beach before tea, haven't we?'

'Plenty, Mary has only got a cold tea so it doesn't matter when you get back.' They always had a lavish High Tea round about six o'clock when they stayed at the cottage.

'Bless you!' Stevie bent swiftly and kissed the older woman on the cheek, her eyes bright with unshed tears.

The three of them half walked, half ran, down to the beach, breathing in heady draughts of the sea-scented air and rejoicing in the sound of the soft lap and swish of the waves breaking on the rocks. It was high tide so there was not a great deal of beach to walk on, but they soon had their shoes off and paddled among the rock pools looking for shells. And it was hard to know which of the three of them was the youngest at heart or enjoying themselves the most.

A shout made them all look up.

'It's Mr Jones!' Michael pointed to the figure waving on the cliff top. David began to run down towards them and simultaneously the children headed for the steep path between the dunes, running up to meet him. Stevie hesitated for the barest fraction of a second before she followed.

He met them nearly three-quarters of the way down, the steepness of the cliff lending wings to his feet. He caught Michael in his outstretched arms and over the heads of the children his eyes sought Stevie's.

'You're back,' was all he said.

Stevie nodded and dropped her eyes as she turned and started back down to the beach. 'I'm only here for a day.' she threw back over her shoulder.

'We're staying two weeks — she's coming back to fetch us,' Michael answered the unspoken question.

'How's the painting?' David called to Stevie.

'It's not!' Her words were almost lost in the

other sounds, the sea, the wind and the gulls.

'Oh?' The monosyllable was half comment, half question. He sensed there was something, not necessarily wrong, but different about her. It was almost as if she recoiled from his overtures of friendship, though the children were as open and warm as ever. He imagined a fence between them with a sign hanging on it: 'Trespassers will be prosecuted'.

When the children were out of earshot splashing their bare feet in the edge of the sea, he asked her to meet him later that evening in 'The Bobbing Boats' for coffee. She opened her mouth to refuse. Then changed her mind. Surely there was nothing wrong in having coffee with a friend?

'Thank you, I'd like to,' she said, and turned back to the children. 'We'd better get back.' They looked surprised and disappointed to be taken away from the beach so quickly, but their protests were wasted on her retreating back. David, too, wondered if she heard him say,

'I'll see you later, between seven thirty and eight?'

*　*　*

It was nearly eight when she closed the door of the cottage behind her after seeing Michael into bed and kissing him goodnight. She left Sue sitting with Nanny and her sister in the parlour looking through an old postcard album.

Stevie ran down the garden path feeling her heart lighten as the wicket gate clicked shut behind her.

At first she thought David wasn't among the evening crowd in 'The Bobbing Boats' then he saw her standing irresolute in the doorway, her eyes searching the tables, and waved to her from his corner seat.

The year since their last meeting dissolved as Stevie sat down opposite him, 'Hello,' she sounded breathless and suddenly self-conscious. 'I thought you weren't here.'

'I wondered if you would come,' his eyes held hers across the table, there was something different about her, but he couldn't quite put his finger on it.

He ordered a pot of coffee and homemade shortbread biscuits from the waitress.

'What happened to the painting?' he asked.

Stevie shrugged 'I don't know, it just got put on one side with — with all the other things,' she said bleakly, wondering herself why she had given it up so completely.

'Other things? Has it been such a hectic year?'

She looked down at her hands, absently

twisting the plain gold band that had replaced Martin's platinum one on her finger. For some reason she couldn't look at him, but the words had to be said.

'I got married,' she finally told him, looking up. Her voice was defiant — what was it to do with him anyway? — but she couldn't keep the apology from her eyes.

'Congratulations!' He forced himself to say, Stevie noted the distance, the lack of warmth rather than actual coolness, in his voice. 'I hope you will be — I hope you *are* — very happy.'

'Oh, yes, thank you, I am.' She smiled brightly as the waitress brought their coffee, but the tremor in her voice and the tightness in her throat belied her words. To cover the awkwardness of the moment she drew the coffee towards her and poured a cup for each of them. 'Black or white?'

'Black, please.' He reached across and drew his cup towards him, his eyes on her face. 'Are you, really?' he asked quietly, looking at her as if he cared; as if it mattered.

She nodded, not trusting her voice, her eyes on her own coffee cup as, with a hand that trembled slightly, she added milk. She could feel rather than see his gaze on her face, and slowly she raised her eyes to his; wordlessly she shook her head slowly from

237

side to side and admitted to him what, until that moment, she had not dared to admit to herself.

'No,' she told him, 'no, it was a terrible mistake.'

David longed to reach across the table and touch her hand; even more he wished he could take her in his arms and offer her what comfort he could. Instead he asked her, as gently as possible, 'Oh, Stevie, why?'

'I suppose I did it for the same reason I have done most of the things in my life. I want to be safe, I want my children to have security,' hearing the tremble in her own voice at this sudden flash of self-revelation which surprised even herself, Stevie picked up her cup and took a long sip of the hot, bitter liquid.

'Tell me about it — if you want to,' David invited, and suddenly she knew she must talk or burst.

'My husband is a doctor. In fact he used to be my doctor,' her lips twisted into a wry smile. 'he is a lot older than me; he was a friend of my first husband, he was older too. Jock — my present husband — was very good to me when Martin died. Sue was only a little girl, four, then and Michael just a baby. They grew up calling him 'Uncle'. I suppose he took the place of their father for them in

238

many ways. I think that was the main reason I married him, for the children's sake.' She gave a deprecating laugh. 'I know it sounds quite absurd and naïve, I suppose, but I don't think I really thought about him much as — as a husband. Only as a father to the children.' She stopped talking and drank her coffee in long, slow draughts, her eyes on the table in front of her, suddenly embarrassed by what she had told him.

'And as a husband he is disappointing?' David prompted gently.

She nodded, looking at him briefly over the rim of her coffee cup.

'And as a father, how does he shape up there?'

'Almost too well! No — that's not really fair of me; he is very good; it's just that he seems to think it is up to him to make all the decisions. Boarding school for instance. Even little Michael is going next year.'

'Does he want to?'

'Yes,' she admitted, 'but only because he has no idea what it will be like,' Absently she poured herself another cup of coffee. 'This holiday — he *knew* it was all planned and how much I was looking forward to it, then at the last minute he springs this trip to London; some Medical Convention he's going to, on me. He says the other doctors' wives will be there and he expects me to go.'

Looking across the table at her; the light falling on her smooth golden head; her lashes showing dark against her cheek as she absently crumbled a biscuit on her plate, David had a sudden rush of sympathy for the absent Jock. If she were his, he would want her with him too.

'Not altogether unreasonable,' his smile was sardonic. 'If I were him I would much rather have you with me than sitting around drinking coffee with some lay-about painter whose intentions are probably anything but honourable.'

'I suppose you're right. About Jock anyway; I don't know about you. I wouldn't have described you as a 'lay-about painter'.' She didn't comment on his remark about his intentions but at least she had managed a weak smile. 'I think you are a very good painter; that's why I bought one of your pictures when I was here last year.'

'You did?' He was pleased. 'I didn't know, did you get it here? And why didn't you tell me?'

'Yes, I bought it from here,' she looked up and glanced round the tearooms. 'I don't know why I didn't tell you,' she considered for a moment, 'maybe I thought you might misconstrue my motives, I had only just met you.'

'Implying that, had you known me better, you wouldn't have wasted your money,' he teased, determined to keep their conversation on a light note.

'On the contrary, now I know you better I would like more.'

'Thank you,' he inclined his head slightly in acceptance of the compliment.

'How is it going — your work I mean?' Suddenly she realised how little she really knew about him; and yet she had just opened her heart and admitted to him things she had not dared acknowledge even to herself. It was strange, as if she knew him and yet didn't know him; knew him as a person, without knowing anything about his life.

'By work do you mean my painting, or what I do for a living?' he asked her.

'Both!' Sensing that he was willing to talk to her about his life she added, 'What *do* you do for a living, anyway?'

'I teach Art at Wolverhampton Tech. You know what they say: 'those who can't — teach'. I guess that applies to painting as well as to anything else.'

'Oh, but you can — paint, I mean. You're good, David. *Really* good! So why . . . ' She tailed off, unwilling to pry into his personal affairs and remembering how he had closed

241

up abruptly when the conversation took the same direction before.

'But not good enough to support myself and my wife.'

Stevie nodded. The silence between them was heavy with unspoken words. She waited for him to continue.

'I am trapped in a more hopeless marriage than you are, Stevie,' he told her, his voice flat with resignation, 'but unlike you I didn't walk in with my eyes open. I got caught there.' He was lighting a cigarette and the lines on his face were drawn and bitter. As an afterthought he offered her one, forgetting she didn't smoke.

'Yes?' she prompted gently.

He inhaled deeply, and slowly blew out the smoke down his nostrils. 'My wife spends most of her days in a mental hospital.' His voice was flat and without emotion.

'Oh, David, I'm so sorry.' She reached across the table and touched his hand.

He didn't seem to notice, or hear her.

'We were married just at the beginning of the war; we had two, almost three, glorious years. She was so young, so pretty, so full of the zest for living. We were very much in love and very happy together. She got pregnant on my embarkation leave. When I knew, I begged her to leave Wolverhampton and get out to the country. She did, she found a cottage in a little place called Church Eaton, near Stafford. She was very excited about it, and about the baby. She arranged for her mother, who was living in Birmingham, to come and live with her. She was worried about her in Birmingham because of the bombs and frightened too of being all on her own and pregnant. I was pleased when she told me about her mother. The last letter I had from her she told me she had wangled some petrol coupons, God knows how, and as things turned out it was a tragedy she did. Anyway, she got the damn things and took our old car out of dry dock to go and fetch her mother.' He paused, reliving old memories and feeling again the sense of helpless rage and frustration he had felt when the news finally reached him, in a prisoner of war camp in Italy.

He sighed and picked up the threads of the story. 'They got caught in a day-time raid. Her mother was killed and Sheila lost the baby — and her mind.'

He looked across the table then at Stevie with eyes that were bleak with the hopelessness of his situation. Impulsively she squeezed the hand that still lay under hers. Her own eyes were pricking with tears and she found it very hard to offer sympathy through the lump in her throat.

'She has retreated into a sort of second childhood. Most of the time she doesn't even know me; just occasionally there seems to be a spark of recognition. I go and see her regularly; I even have her home when she's not too bad and I can cope, I'm all she has, I have to be around — in case — in case she ever comes out of it.' He gave a shrug expressing the hopelessness of his situation. He turned his hand over under hers and returned the pressure before drawing it away.

'So you must forgive me if I don't seem too sympathetic about your marriage.' The tone of his voice and the sudden warmth of his smile as he spoke took any sting or implied criticism from his words.

' 'I grumbled because I had no shoes and then I met a man with no feet',' she quoted, smiling back into his eyes.

Understanding, warmth, friendship, all these and more flowed between them.

'Yup! In other words, 'count your blessings' says Parson David Jones. Seriously, Stevie — on your own admission you married him to be a father to your children and for security for yourself. By all accounts he measures up.'

She nodded. 'Yes he does. Thank you,

David, for the mental and emotional shake-up — and for telling me about yourself,' she finished softly. She glanced at her watch, sat up and drew her handbag towards her. 'And now I think I must go.'

'Or Nanny will send out a search party?' It always amused him to think of her, a woman in her mid-thirties, under Nanny's jurisdiction.

'No, well she probably will — but I have to be off back home in the morning ready to go to London with Jock the next day. Will you still be here when I get back?'

'I'll be here,' he promised. 'Bring the painting of my cottage you did and show it to me. I would like to see it finished.'

'All right,' she promised. 'If it's a nice day — and if I can get away — I'll walk up to your cottage the evening I get back and show it to you.'

'And if it isn't — and you can't?'

'Then I'll try and make it the next morning.' She pushed back her chair and rose to her feet. 'Goodbye, David. Paint some wonderful pictures while I'm away.' And then she was gone. He watched her back weaving between the tables now thinning with customers. With a sigh he beckoned the waitress for his bill.

18

Driving back alone through the beautiful Welsh countryside, Stevie thought about her conversation with David. He was right, she should not complain about Jock. He had given her exactly what she wanted, security and a father for Sue and Michael. If, at times, security did not seem enough, then she had only herself to blame. She had known Jock long enough, and if in all those years he had shown no sign of being sexually attracted to her wasn't she being naïve to imagine that marriage would change him?

Their relationship was based on a long-standing friendship and he was no longer a young man; she could not expect romantic love from him, certainly not the passion that had made her relationship with Tom so exciting. She refused to listen to the small voice reminding her that Martin too had been as much her senior as Jock and in her marriage to him she had known both love and passion.

Tom she never thought of if she could help it. He was as dead to her as Martin was. Crying over spilt milk was a fruitless exercise.

She must learn to live fully in the present and make the very most of what she had.

With these sane and salutary thoughts, she turned the car into the driveway of The Firs, the home she shared with Jock and his son. A little of her determination ebbed and she felt a swift stab of disappointment and irritation, for the car already standing in the driveway was Matthew's, not Jock's. For the first time she resented sharing her home with her adult stepson.

She pulled her overnight bag from the car, slung the ubiquitous raincoat over her arm and stepped out. The house was quiet as she walked in and she made her way straight up to her room.

Tired and dispirited she flopped down on the bed, kicked her shoes off and relaxed. She woke to find Jock standing over her.

'Hello, my dear, I saw your car in the drive, but no one had seen you.'

'I came straight upstairs.' She smiled at him. 'I must have fallen asleep. I didn't know I was so tired.' She looked at her watch. 'Good gracious, tea time! I must have slept for over an hour.'

Jock sat down on the bed and took her hand lightly in his. 'You must have needed it. What on earth were you doing last night?' It was an innocent question and asked half jokingly but Stevie felt a sudden upsurge of guilt.

'It must just be the two days driving.' Afterwards she was to wonder why on earth she hadn't told Jock about David. After all there was nothing between them but friendship. Had she known that her silence would make two and two add up to five she might have spoken.

'It's nice to have you home.' He bent towards her and kissed her gently on the cheek.

'It's nice to be home,' she murmured, wondering at her own perfidy as she remembered how only last night she had said she didn't want to come back. She sat up and slid her feet off the bed, feeling around for her shoes. 'I'm dying for a cup of tea.'

The house seemed unnaturally quiet without either of the children. *It will be like this all the time when they are both away at boarding school,* Stevie reminded herself.

'It seems quiet,' she spoke her thoughts aloud as she poured the tea.

'Peaceful, don't you mean?' Matthew said as he took his cup from her. But he smiled to let her know he was teasing. 'Don't worry, stepmother dear, I miss them too. In fact,' he said, helping himself to sugar, 'I've enjoyed the last year so much and the company of my little brother and sister that I have come to the conclusion family life has much to offer after all and I am considering trying it.'

'You mean — ?' Stevie, pleased to find that he actually seemed to like her children, had got lost somewhere.

'I'm breaking the news to you that I plan to leave the family nest and build my own. In other words,' he ended as Stevie still looked blank, 'I'm getting married.'

'Oh, Matthew, that's wonderful! Is it anyone we know?'

'Her name is Pam, she was a student with me, and we've — er — kept in touch.'

'A student with you — she's a doctor?'

Matthew nodded. 'Yes, Dr. Baines, actually. She's going to join the practice here.'

'Where are you going to live? When are you getting married?' Stevie still had umpteen questions to ask. Instinctively she looked across at Jock. He was sitting back in his chair, his legs crossed, drinking his tea. From the expression on his face she guessed that none of this was news to him. They must have discussed it all last night while she was away. It made her feel an outsider. But she smiled brightly enough as she looked back to Matthew.

'The first week in September; and we've bought Willow Lodge — you know, poor old

Miss Davenport's house.'

Stevie nodded; she remembered the old lady well. She had lived alone for many years with a housekeeper and a dog and had died suddenly a few months ago, since when her executors had been busy winding up her estate.

'From one tree to another!' Stevie smiled at her own small joke, which seemed less funny when she had to explain it to Jock. 'He'll be moving from The Firs to Willow Lodge. So appropriate — for nests,' she murmured into her teacup.

When they were alone later that night she tried to draw Jock out about his son's marriage. He seemed pleased. With the practice growing they could do with another partner, he told her.

He was propped up in bed reading a book as she sorted clothes and packed ready for their trip to London.

'Is that new?' he asked, peering over his glasses as she took the electric blue dress out of the wardrobe.

'Uh-huh. Don't you like it?'

'It's rather — bright — isn't it?'

Stevie bit back a sharp retort, folded it carefully in tissue and laid it in the suitcase then turned and drew the grey dress out of the wardrobe.

'That looks better.'

Stevie didn't answer; but made a mental note to wear the blue one at the special dinner they had to go to. She shot him a defiant look and dropped the lid of the case down.

★　★　★

Jock came into their hotel bedroom from the adjoining bathroom just as Stevie was doing her hair. He stood and looked at her for a moment in the blue dress. He could not deny that it suited her and that she looked extraordinarily attractive in it — in a sexy way. Moulded under her breasts and with the low neckline showing just a glimpse of cleavage, it fitted to perfection and made the most of her good figure.

'Are you wearing that?'

'Jock, I bought this dress specially to wear tonight.' Stevie spoke patiently, as if explaining something to a child. She didn't turn round to look at him but focussed her eyes on his reflection in the mirror.

His face seemed to draw together as a small frown puckered his brows and he pursed his lips.

'It suits you,' he admitted grudgingly.

'Thank you!' Stevie was determined not to

notice his lack of enthusiasm.

'I suppose you'll be wearing a — a wrap or something?'

'Of course,' she smiled as she reached for her pearls. 'Would you mind doing up the clasp for me?'

He stepped forward and did as she asked; as he did so a wave of Chanel Numero Cinq, the perfume she always wore, assailed him. He met her eyes in the mirror and smiled, dropping his hands on her shoulders.

'You look very beautiful tonight, my dear.'

'Thank you,' she murmured again as she got up and turned to face him. She handed him her stole and he placed it gently round her shoulders. In that moment they seemed closer than at any time since their marriage.

Stevie had no regrets about her choice of dress. Many of the wives, in fact the majority, were extremely well dressed and what she privately termed the 'fuddy-duddy matrons' were in the minority. She enjoyed the evening far more than she expected to and found more than one male eye resting appreciatively on her cleavage; and not, she was sure, for medical reasons.

Jock noticed too, and she turned round once to find him watching her with an expression on his face she couldn't fathom.

'I enjoyed this evening!' she told him as she

dropped her bag and stole on the bed.

'So I observed,' his clipped voice matched the glacial glint in his eyes and was in direct contrast to her own pleasant, almost sensual, feelings. She looked at him sharply, anger dissipating her caution, helped along by the alcohol that had flowed fairly freely during the course of the evening.

'And what does that mean?' Her tone matched his in its cool civility.

He didn't answer immediately but continued to undress, folding his clothes and laying them neatly on the chair in his usual methodical way.

Stevie slipped out of the blue dress and hung it carefully on a hanger but threw the rest of her clothes casually down. She was slipping her nightdress over her head when he answered, so the expression on his face was momentarily hidden from her.

'I thought you behaved rather like a tart,' he told her in a flat voice as he drew back the sheet and climbed into bed.

Two bright spots burned on Stevie's cheeks and her eyes blazed as her face emerged from the folds of her nightdress. 'How dare you say that?' she hissed at him; in spite of her anger at his totally unjust accusation, she remembered they were in a hotel bedroom and it was not the place to raise her voice.

'I take that back; I should have phrased it differently and said I didn't think you behaved like a lady.'

'You can't take it back — you said it. It is what you really think,' her throat ached with the effort not to shout and she could feel tears of outraged indignation pricking behind her eyes, 'as for being a lady — well, I'm sorry, but I don't want to be one; I just want to be a woman!' Her voice broke on a sob as she scrambled into bed. She switched the light off and pulled the bedclothes up high over the shoulder that was turned to him. 'And,' she muttered only half out loud, 'I just want you to see me as a woman — just once in a while!'

'Oh, but I do!' he assured her. 'No other woman makes me feel like you do. I just don't like to think of other men feeling that way about you.'

He pulled her over towards him; and because she *was* a woman and needed so desperately the feel of a man's hands on her body, loving her — desiring her — she swallowed her pain and her hurt and turned willingly into his arms. He took her, as he usually did, with few preliminaries, and when it was over he turned over with a brief 'goodnight' and was soon snoring.

Stevie lay at his side, wakeful and

unfulfilled, wondering how a man who could so often be so considerate and thoughtful in daily life could be so lousy in bed.

★ ★ ★

Jock was fully occupied with his medical convention the following day but, assuring him that she was quite capable of entertaining and looking after herself in London, Stevie looked forward to a whole day to herself.

'What will you do?' Jock asked. 'Go window shopping?'

'I think I shall go to the National Gallery,' she told him, suddenly irritated that he should think her incapable of anything more intellectual than gazing in shop windows all day.

'That should keep you out of mischief for a little while; and then?'

'I don't know,' she snapped. Jock had no interest whatsoever in art and his paternal manner with its faintly patronising overtones annoyed her.

She spent the day enjoying a feast of visual delight. To see such great paintings as Constable's Flatford Mill in its original state was she realised, a totally different experience from looking at a print. Wandering through the tranquil halls of the gallery drinking in the works of so many 'greats' fired Stevie with renewed enthusiasm to take up her own brush again, and she promised herself that she would take her painting of David's cottage back to Wales as he had asked her to.

She spent her morning in the National Gallery and the afternoon in the Tate searching out in each place those artists who had made their name using her medium, watercolours.

Though Jock was occupied during the days, he had the evenings free and they went to one or two theatres. Stevie wore the grey dress for these outings. When she first put it on Jock raised an eyebrow at the slit skirt but made no comment and he could scarcely disapprove of the high mandarin collar even if the well-fitting bodice was, in its own way, almost as revealing as the decollate blue dress.

Stevie did the shopping she had to do but for the rest of her free time in London she haunted the galleries and had she been able to afford it would have gone home armed with several paintings. But Jock, she knew, would not take kindly to her spending 'his' money on originals when, if she really wanted pictures, she could get prints for a mere fraction of the cost.

By the end of their stay in London Stevie was eager to be back and on her way to Wales. She planned a day at home to unpack and re-pack the very different clothes she would need and then, she told herself, an early start in the morning. She couldn't wait to see David again and share with him the discoveries she had made for herself about the world of painters and painting as she wandered the galleries in her private tour of self-instruction.

* * *

Stevie was on the road at first light and in Borth-y-Gest for lunch. She found Mary by herself at the cottage. Her face broke into a warm smile of welcome as she opened the door, and as Stevie stepped into the neat little hallway the rich, yeasty smell of home baking wafted towards her. It reminded her that breakfast was a long while ago.

'My, you're here in good time!' Mary exclaimed. 'Have you had lunch?' Stevie shook her head. 'Best come along and get some then. I've just baked.'

Stevie smiled. 'I can smell that; it's making me feel absolutely hollow.'

'We'll soon fix that,' Mary assured her. And indeed she did. In no time at all Stevie found herself sitting at the well-scrubbed kitchen table with a still warm home-made loaf in front of her, cheese, tomatoes and lettuce.

Mary, who had already eaten, sat down at the table and brought her up to date with the children's activities.

'Violet's taken them to Black Rock Sands at Morfa Bychan this afternoon; well she took them this morning with a picnic lunch. They didn't expect you so early,' Mary told her. For a second Stevie couldn't think who Violet was, then she realised; of course that was Nanny's name.

They all arrived home in time for tea, brown, sandy and laughing.

Sue was full of questions. 'Did you have a good time in London, Mummy? What did you do; where did you go? Did you wear your super new dress, and did Uncle Jock like it?'

Stevie laughed and held up her hands in mock horror. 'Hey — wait — one at a time! Yes, thank you, I had a great trip, I spent most of my days in Art Galleries but Uncle Jock and I went to the theatre three times in the evenings; and yes, I did wear the blue dress you chose.'

'And did Uncle Jock like it?'

'Of course.'

Sue looked at her shrewdly. 'Well, *I* thought you looked super in it!' she assured her mother, and Stevie wondered why it was always so hard to pull the wool over her daughter's eyes.

'What are you doing this evening, Mummy?' that same young daughter asked as she reached for yet another slice of Mary's delicious bread and spread it liberally with homemade strawberry jam.

Meeting the clear gaze across the table Stevie did not attempt to dissemble. 'I'm going to see David Jones,' she told her. 'I'm taking the painting of his cottage I did last year to show him.'

'Can we come with you?' Michael clamoured.

Stevie shook her head. 'I'll be back after your bedtime,' she told him. Then looking up she met her daughter's clear gaze once more. Impulsively she added, 'But you can come if you like, Sue.'

As soon as she had spoken she wished the words unsaid; why had she asked the child to come with her? Maybe she felt the need of something, a shield perhaps, between her and David? Sue's presence would effectively prevent any more revealing revelations like those she had made to him last time they met.

Walking with her daughter up the mountain path to David's cottage, Stevie reflected that the Sue who had come home from boarding school this holidays was an entirely different person from the child she had seen disappear within its doors nearly a year before. Sometimes she seemed like a stranger, at others a young woman whom she knew slightly and was getting to know better; occasionally the child she had once known. She turned and looked at her now, realising that she had been so lost in her own thoughts that she hadn't been taking in what Sue was saying.

'I'm sorry, Sue, what did you say?'

'You weren't listening, were you, Mummy?'

Stevie began to protest, then laughed and admitted, 'No, I'm sorry, I wasn't really. I was thinking about you and how you are growing up.'

'Do you like it? Or would you rather I was your little girl still?'

Stevie considered. 'I think I like it very much,' she admitted with a smile. 'Now what were you saying?'

Sue sighed. 'I was talking about Uncle Jock. I wondered if he would like the dress. I thought he might not because . . . ' She stopped, looking at Stevie in some embarrassment.

'Because?' Stevie prompted.

'Oh, I don't know — it sounds so silly. But

I sometimes think he doesn't like me as much as he used to, now I'm growing up. And I don't think he likes you looking — well — *womanly*. Come to think of it, I don't think he really *likes* women all that much,' she ended in a rush.

'Oh no — you're wrong; you're imagining things!' Stevie protested, suppressing the disturbing thought that maybe she had a point.

Sue shook her head. 'I don't think he does,' she repeated, 'he used to make such a fuss of me when I was a little girl, and now I'm growing up he doesn't seem to like me at all. He likes Michael, but not me,' she stated categorically, without jealousy.

'Oh, no Sue. I'm sure you're wrong!' And yet Stevie found herself wondering; Jock had always been so good with Sue, she had always been so special to him, but lately . . .

'It was Uncle Jock who thought that Michael should go away to school,' she reminded her daughter.

'Ye-e-es.' Sue sounded doubtful. 'I know he did. All the same; he *does* like him much better than me.'

David saw them climbing the hill path towards his cottage. When they rounded the last bend the door was open and he was smiling a welcome.

'Come along in. It's good to see you — both of you!' There was no doubting the sincerity of his greeting and Stevie was pleased that it was extended with equal warmth to Sue. She knew how sensitive a young girl's feelings could be; and after what Sue had confided to her about Jock, if she also sensed that David didn't really want to see her she might begin to feel there was something about her that repelled men.

'How about a drink? It's a beautiful evening; we can sit out and get the last of the sun.'

He poured a glass of the red wine he always seemed to have on tap for Stevie. 'And what about you, young lady? What would you like? Wine, cider, lemonade?'

'Lemonade, please.' Sue smiled at him; he was a nice man; and she appreciated the compliment he had paid her by offering her wine.

'Did you bring the painting?' he asked Stevie.

She nodded and took it swiftly from her bag to hand to him. He unrolled it and looked at it critically, turning it so he got the full benefit of the evening light.

'But this is good! I like it. What do you think of it, Sue?'

'I haven't seen it,' she admitted, getting up

262

to look over his shoulder at the picture. She stared at it for a minute. 'Did you do this, Mum?' she asked, a rather unflattering note of disbelief in her voice. 'It's good!' She looked from the picture to the model and back again. 'It's really good; I really didn't think you *could* paint. Why don't you do more — you might become famous!'

Stevie laughed. 'Hold on, my head is growing so fast I shall never be able to wear any of my hats again!' But she felt absurdly happy at their praise.

Sue looked at her mother with a new respect. Since she had come home for the holidays she had found her mother much more interesting. She wondered which of them had changed.

'You have a talent,' David told her seriously. 'And you should use it, have you ever had any lessons?'

Stevie shook her head. 'Only the normal Art classes at school.'

'Why don't you go for evening classes or something?' He looked speculatively at her, almost as if he were seeing something about her that others couldn't or at least that he had not seen before. 'Or maybe not. As an art teacher I shouldn't be saying this; but I often think that more would-be artists are ruined than made by teaching. Those who make the grade do it in spite of, not because of, being taught.'

'That view sounds like professional suicide.'

David smiled ruefully. 'I suppose so.' He held her picture at arm's length, looking at it critically through narrowed lids. 'You have a freshness, a charm, almost a naivete, that is all your own. It would take a skilled teacher not to destroy it. Your eye for detail and your ability to copy is good; have you ever thought of working from photographs?' Stevie shook her head. 'Try it; it will extend your working hours because you won't be so dependent on weather or even light.

'Can you paint horses, Mummy?'

'I don't know, Sue. I've never really tried, why?'

'I thought it would be nice if you could do a painting of Fairy; she's getting old now and — and we won't always have her; a painting of her would be lovely; much nicer than a photo.'

'That's a lovely idea.' Stevie smiled warmly at her daughter. Sue loved the old mare almost as much as she herself did. 'When we get home I'll try. I'll do as you suggest, David, and take some photos of her and work from them.'

All too soon the evening came to an end

and it was time for Stevie and Sue to make tracks for Nanny's cottage. David walked with them down to the village, parting company at the harbour with plans to meet on the beach the following day.

'I like him; he is a nice man,' Sue said as they walked up the hill to the cottage.

'Yes, I like him too, he is a very nice man indeed,' Stevie agreed.

★　★　★

The next few days were like an idyll. Certainly, looking back on them afterwards Stevie could not remember anything, not one tiny detail, which marred their perfection. Even the weather was kind of them; they lazed on the beach, swam in the sea, basked on the sand; ate Mary's delicious picnics full of homemade goodies; set up their easels side by side and painted. They walked together, and talked together, and in the evening they drank coffee at 'The Bobbing Boats', or red wine at his cottage. Their last evening, he came for supper at Mary's invitation and charmed her with his appreciation of her cooking and Nanny with his rather brooding Celtic charm and his courtesy to them all, including the children. Nanny thought he and Stevie made a handsome pair, David with his dark curls and Stevie with her smooth blonde hair, but kept her thoughts strictly to herself.

All too soon the hour to leave for home arrived; Nanny was hugging and kissing them all and extracting promises to 'come again next year.'

'I wish we didn't have to go home,' Michael, waving frantically, echoed all their feelings as the car rounded the bend that cut the cottage off from sight. Stevie silently agreed, but Mary had other visitors booked into their rooms and anyway with Matthew's wedding coming up she was needed at home.

19

A few days after their return from holiday Stevie and the children loaded the saddles into the car and drove out the couple of miles to the field she had kept for Fairy and Bobbin when she sold Wingates. In deference to Jock, who thought it an unnecessary extravagance and asked, 'Who is going to ride it and look after it when she is at boarding school?' she had not bought another pony for Sue, Fairy was still capable of giving anyone a good ride and Sue could always use her in the holidays.

They saddled up the two ponies and Sue and Michael rode them about the field while Stevie took as many photos as she could. Fairy was still beautiful; the dark grey dapples that had been so prominent when Martin bought her all those years ago had now faded and her sleek summer coat was snow white. Her dark eyes full of equine wisdom, seemed even more striking now her coat was lighter. Stevie wondered it she would ever be able to capture one tenth of their expression.

Sue was right; she reflected sadly, Fairy would not last forever. Today, in the warm summer sun with the grass in her field lush and green, she looked good. But last winter she had become stiff and arthritic and Stevie had bought a weatherproof rug for her and gone each day, sometimes twice a day, to feed her and see her through the worst of the cold. Jock's promise of the stables had not materialised; Instead Matthew had filled them with his 'junk' — perhaps when he was married . . . Stevie stroked the sleek white neck, remembering the good times she and the old mare had shared together in the past.

David, she discovered was right. Working from photos was a good idea. After carefully laying all those she had taken of Fairy out on the table round her and doing a few trial and error sketches, she finally selected a head study and decided to copy that. David had known her abilities better than she had herself; she was a good copyist, and as the painting began to take shape under her brush, she felt quite pleased with it.

'Mummy, that's super!' Sue exclaimed when she saw it. 'It's just like her; you must get it framed when it's finished.'

Stevie stepped back and looked at it. She had to admit it pleased her. When it was finished she would, as Sue suggested, have it framed. She had enjoyed working on it, finding a deep pleasure in creativity that nothing else in her life, even the children, had ever given her.

For some reason she had not told Jock about her painting but had done it while he was out of the house, clearing everything away before he came back. She would present him with a fait accompli once the picture was in its frame.

When she had finished it and taken it into town she put her paints away for a while; with Matthew's wedding and the two children to get ready for school, her days were full. If she had a studio she could do a bit here and there but when she had to get everything out and put it all away again she needed more then odd snatched bits of time. She smiled to herself; a 'studio' — what a grand word to connect with her amateur daubing.

However, once formed the thought took root, and one afternoon she made her way up to the attics. Full of the junk of more than one generation's living, they were musty and cobwebby; but there was nothing that couldn't be swept up and tidied away. The light from the north window was good and the view from up here superb. Stevie enlisted Sue's help; her daughter took an almost proprietorial pride in her newly discovered talent and thought she should have a proper studio. She was already planning the casual way she would tell them at school that her mother was an artist.

Thinking of artists reminded Sue of something else.

'Does Uncle Jock know about David?'

'No — no, I don't think I've ever mentioned him. Why do you ask?'

Sue shrugged. 'I just wondered,' she said and her face took on the shuttered look that Stevie knew all too well meant something was going on behind it. She determined to find out why she had asked such a question.

'I just haven't told him because he never asks much about our holidays.' Stevie sounded defensive and didn't really know why; neither did she connect the closed look on her daughter's face with the soft ripple of apprehension that ran down her spine.

She brought her painting home the day she and Sue took Michael away to school. He had been quite cheerful about the prospect until they actually loaded his trunk in the car and put on his new uniform. That was when he really seemed to grasp that this was for real, he was going away from home. He was unusually quiet on the journey, sitting beside her in the front seat, which Sue had magnanimously given up to him this once. Stevie glanced sideways at him as she drove. A small, oddly pathetic figure in the new blazer that was a size too big, his school cap set squarely on his head.

She tried desperately hard not to cling when she said goodbye and watched him walk bravely away from her down the long corridor.

As they drove through their hometown on the way back she remembered that her picture should be ready. She looked at her watch. 'How about stopping in town, collecting my picture of Fairy, and then having afternoon tea?' Sue was more quiet than usual as they drove home, perhaps thinking of the few short days left before she too went back to school.

She brightened up visibly and smiled. 'Yes, let's!'

She squealed with delight when she saw the painting in its frame, 'It's lovely, Mummy even better than I remembered.'

The house was quiet when they got in. Matthew was away on his honeymoon and Jock out on his rounds; with two lots of patients to see, it was unlikely he would be in till evening surgery. Stevie laid the painting down on a coffee table ready to show him.

But when he came in he looked tired and drawn, and something warned her to wait till he had finished dinner. She planned to show it to him when they were having coffee together, quietly relaxed in the lounge. But Sue jumped the gun.

'What do you think of Mummy's painting, Uncle Jock?' she asked him as she helped herself to potatoes.

'Painting — what painting?'

'Oh, just a watercolour I did of Fairy,' Stevie said lightly. 'I've had it framed. I'll show you afterwards.'

'It's good — it really is! She did it mostly from photos like Da — ' Sue stopped abruptly and concentrated on her meal.

'Like what? Sue, what were you going to say?' Jock asked.

'Nothing!' she muttered, cutting up her meat with great concentration.

Jock looked at her sharply for a moment then across at Stevie. 'Perhaps you will show it to me after dinner?'

'Of course; I put it in the lounge ready.'

'I'll fetch it now!' Sue offered.

'After dinner will do, Sue.' Stevie smiled. Who would have thought her daughter would become such a staunch champion?

Sue, who had leapt ahead of them into the lounge, picked the painting up and turned it toward Jock.

'You have a gift, I think,' Jock said as he studied it, 'you shouldn't waste it.' He turned and smiled at her; and Stevie felt her heart leap. She wondered why on earth she had held back from showing him her painting, or even telling him about it.

'It's just like Fairy, isn't it? Don't you think so, Uncle Jock?'

'I do indeed, Sue. I like it very much!' He turned to Stevie. 'Is this the only one you have or are there any more I can see?'

'One or two,' she admitted.

'Then may I — please?'

Stevie turned to Sue. 'Would you fetch my painting folder, please?' She saw a quick frown cross her daughter's face and was ready for a refusal but then saw her look across at Jock and obediently leave the room.

'What cottage is this?' Jock asked as she showed him her painting of David's cottage.

'Oh — just a cottage on the side of the mountain near Borth-y-Gest,' Stevie cut in swiftly as she saw Sue's mouth opening.

Jock looked at the picture so long and hard that Stevie felt quite nervous and wondered what secrets she could possibly have given away with her brush.

'Yes, you have talent,' he repeated, 'but I prefer your painting of Fairy.' With that he dismissed the folder and turned again to the painting of the horse in its frame. 'We should hang this — where do you suggest?' He held it in his hand and looked round the room;

finally moving to the fireplace. Taking down a somewhat dreary print of an oil-painting that hung over the centre of the mantel, he put Stevie's picture there instead, stepping back to look at it.

'I think it goes well there,' he said with satisfaction.

Stevie smiled at him; the rush of affection she felt showing in her eyes.

★   ★   ★

Two days later Sue was back at school. A week later Matthew and Pam came back from their honeymoon. They came to dinner the evening they got home; tanned and glowing with the unmistakable aura of two people in love with each other.

Matthew was unflatteringly surprised when he saw Stevie's painting over the fireplace but when he made some comment about it being a 'nice little hobby' Pam retorted with some asperity, 'Hobby! Don't be absurd, Matthew; with a talent like that she can make it much more than a hobby,' she looked across the room at Stevie. 'Why don't you do it professionally? I know lots of people who would adore a painting of their favourite animal.'

'Oh — I don't know. I'm not good enough

for that,' Stevie hedged deprecatingly.

'Of course you are! Can you paint dogs as well as horses?'

'I don't know. I've never tried.'

'Well, try!' Pam dropped her hand on Matthew's Golden Labrador spread out on the hearth at her feet. 'Use old Honey as your model; if I like it I'll hang it in my sitting room and I'm sure it will get you some commissions.'

Stevie smiled; she liked Pam and thought she was just what Matthew needed.

'I'll try!' she promised. 'But you had better let me get some photos of her before you take her,' it was tacitly assumed that now Matthew was married his dog would leave them and make her home with the newly weds.

Stevie spent the next morning taking photos of the dog and when she had the prints she took them up to her attic making a mental note that if she was going to be a professional artist she had better learn to call it a studio.

With both children away at school and Matthew no longer living with them, Stevie found that time could drag and the quiet of the house be depressing. Only in her attic/studio did she relish the quiet and in what she was beginning to think of as her work, she found a satisfaction that dispelled the loneliness.

She did several sketches of Honey and finally ended up by doing a head study, similar to the one she had painted of Fairy.

Pam enthused over it when she finally showed it to her.

'You have really got 'something', Stevie. You've caught her expression, the essential Honey, to a tee. I don't know how you do it.'

True to her promise she hung it in her own sitting room in a prominent position. Now the dog was living with them their visitors could not only admire it but were able to compare the painting with the real-life model.

★　★　★

Stevie was walking through the hall after breakfast one morning on her way to the kitchen to see Mrs Evans when the phone shrilled. She turned back and picked up the receiver.

'Can you paint cats?' Pam asked without preamble.

'I don't know; I haven't tried,' Stevie answered, just as she had before when Pam had asked her if she could paint dogs.

'Well, I said you could, so you had better try.' There were no 'ifs' and 'buts' about Pam and the chuckle that reached Stevie along the line rippled with triumph. 'I've got a commission for you to paint someone's Siamese cat. They are going to phone you and arrange a time for you to go over for the photographic sitting. Oh and by the way, I told them your fee was a hundred pounds.'

'Pam! A *hundred pounds* — I can't — ' But with a click the line went dead in her hand. Stevie looked at the receiver for a moment before replacing it in its cradle; then she began to laugh; softly at first but with rising hysteria as panic gripped her. It was one thing to paint pretty little pictures to amuse herself, quite another to do it for a stranger and to charge a fee — and such an exorbitant one. She couldn't do it.

Yet when the phone went a short while later she found herself meekly arranging to go round the very next afternoon armed with camera and sketch pad to do the ground-work, only making the proviso that there would be no fee unless the client was completely satisfied with the end result.

She was more than satisfied; and it turned out that her Siamese cat was no mere house pet but a famous champion and his owner, who was a breeder, well known in the cat world. When other breeders saw the painting they too wanted their cats painted and, to her utter amazement, Stevie found that she was soon in demand as an animal portrait painter, at a hundred pounds a picture.

Though she had never actually been short of money in her life, this was the first time she had money that she had earned herself; it was a new experience, and, she found, quite a heady one. It gave her a feeling of independence she had never known before, even in the years between her two marriages. The independence extended beyond financial matters too, for now she met people to whom she, as a person, was important. She became Stevie Campbell, or Stephanie Campbell as she signed her paintings, not 'Dr Campbell's wife'.

The overall effect was good for Stevie, but detrimental to her marriage. She remarked on this one day to Pam, who had become a close friend.

Pam, who was about her own age but many years her senior in worldly wisdom, looked slightly exasperated; she often did when dealing with her young step-mother-in-law, in spite of, or because of, the warm bond of affection between them.

'That's to be expected.' Pam was seldom soothing. 'You have always been the child to Jock's parent. Now you're 'growing up'.

You're rocking the boat — can't you see that?'

'Hmm — you mean I'm threatening his security?'

'Of course you are! You married him for the security of having a father, he married you for the same reason, but his security lies in being one. If you suddenly grow up and don't need him so much in that way he is going to feel insecure.'

It all sounded very simplistic to Stevie; too simplistic to explain Jock's tense, edgy behaviour lately. But, unwilling to probe too deeply into her marriage, even with Pam, she changed the subject.

'How are things working out in the practice?'

'We're very busy at the moment and everything's a bit chaotic with this National Health coming in and changing things, but personally, pretty well. I work as a sort of permanent locum, taking surgeries or making house calls when neither Matthew or Jock are available.'

Stevie had been so busy in her own world lately that she hadn't bothered much with either world affairs or even national ones. It was probably the introduction of the National Health Service with all its attendant ramifications that was bothering Jock and making him so tetchy. She resolved to try harder to be the sort of wife that he wanted — whatever that was. She did not know how soon she was to be put to the test.

He seemed unusually cool and distant — almost locked in his own world — over dinner. By the time they reached the second course Stevie had given up all attempts at pleasant chatter and relapsed into her own silence. She had just settled into a comfortable chair with a good library book when he broached the subject of their holidays.

'What do you plan to do with the children this summer?'

'Do?' she repeated stupidly. 'I hadn't really given it much thought. I expect I'll take them for the usual fortnight in Wales.'

She watched his lips tighten and his brows draw together, he began to drum the fingers of one hand on the arm of his chair. It was a habit he seemed to have got into lately. It irritated Stevie almost beyond endurance while making her feel anxious and apprehensive, perhaps because it was so often the prelude to some disparaging comments.

'You can send them if you like; they can go by train. But I don't want you going.'

'Oh — and why not?' Stevie could feel her gorge rising. He was speaking to her as if she were a delinquent child. She couldn't remember whether he had always spoken in that way to her, but it certainly rubbed her up the wrong way now.

'I think you know perfectly well why I don't wish you to go.' He spoke icily with the same inflection in his voice; then he picked up the evening paper and disappeared behind it as if, as far as he was concerned, that was that. He had commanded and she, naturally, would obey.

Stevie felt a sort of buzzing inside her; almost like steam rising in a kettle; and like a kettle she was coming to the boil. There was an odd prickling in her scalp as if she were, quite literally, going to 'flip her lid'.

'No, I don't know. I haven't the faintest idea, so you can come out from behind that bloody paper and tell me!' She could hear her voice rising, and she got to her feet as if she would snatch the paper off him. She couldn't remember ever having sworn at Jock in her life.

Neither could he; and in spite of himself he was shaken; but he remained behind the paper, using it like a shield.

'I do not wish you to do anything to jeopardise your good name, or mine.'

'Ah — now we are coming to the point — your good name!' Stevie's voice was rising almost to a shriek. 'What the hell are you talking about, Jock Campbell? When have I ever, in any way, jeopardised your precious name, for God's sake?' Now she lunged forward and snatched the paper away, crumpling it and throwing it to a far corner of the room.

Even Stevie, blinded with rage as she was, blanched before the cold steel in Jock's eyes and his implacable calm.

'Your affaire with that man — that painter.' He spat the last word at her. 'I do not wish you to see him again — ever! Is that clear? As far as I can gather you have not been in communication with him since last summer; but I do not wish you to continue the affaire this year.' He wrinkled his nose slightly as he repeated the word, as if it emitted a bad smell.

Stevie strove with all her self-control to keep her voice level, she knew that losing her temper was no good. It only made her appear to be in the wrong.

'I have never have had an 'affaire', as you put it, with 'that painter' whose name happens to be David Jones.' She enunciated the words slowly and carefully. 'And whoever has let you think so has misled you.' Curiosity got the better of her; and she asked, 'Who *did* tell you anyway? Nanny?' It was unthinkable; she couldn't imagine Nanny doing such a thing — but whom else?

He shook his head.

'Who then? Not that there was anything to tell. David and I are just good friends.' She watched his lips curl into a sardonic sneer at her words.

'Isn't that what everyone says; the accepted euphemism for an illicit sexual relationship?'

'In this case it happens to be true!' she snapped back. 'But having made such a *disgusting* accusation I think the least you can do is substantiate it and tell me who told you such a blatant lie.'

He ignored the question. 'I am asking you not to see him again, Stevie. You are jeopardising my good name, which in my position as a doctor is very important. Now, would you mind returning the paper?'

Automatically she moved across the room and picked up the scattered sheets of the newspaper. She was so used to doing what he asked that it was second nature. But she didn't hand them over immediately.

'You sound insufferably pompous!' she told him. 'And anyway, even if I was having an affaire with David, which I'm not, who is likely to know about it here if we confine it to Wales?' Suddenly she didn't even care what he thought any more, if all he was concerned about was his good name. The fire of her rage was subsiding, leaving in its place a dull anger, every bit as cool and hard as his own. 'If I want to go to Wales, I shall go. And while I'm there I shall see whom I like and do what I like. I'll worry about my reputation and you can worry about yours — since it has suddenly become so important to you. I think you are getting upset quite unnecessarily.' She handed him the paper and turned to leave the room; but his next words stopped her.

'Your children chattered to me — they might chatter to someone else.'

Stevie felt as if a bucket of cold water had been thrown over her but when she spun round on her heels the expression on her face was unfathomable.

'My children would never tell you such a wicked lie about me, Jock. You have been asking them questions and putting two and two together and making five.' She spoke quietly now, with all the dignity she could muster.

Jock didn't speak for a moment; he was too busy sorting the paper out and retreating behind it once more. 'Michael chattered,' he reiterated. 'I must admit Sue denied you knew the man; even almost that he existed, which of course confirmed my suspicions.'

In spite of herself Stevie smiled. Yes, such defence would be more damning than any number of lies.

'You asked what I intend to do with the children this summer. Well, I intend to take them to Wales and stay there with them a fortnight at least. As for your good name — well, you can look after that yourself!' She wheeled away and left the room, turning a deaf ear to his voice behind her calling her name.

There was a chill between them in the days that followed. But he had been so cool, so distant, lately, that Stevie didn't really notice it as much as she might have done. She still fumed inwardly at his accusation and what she considered his underhand behaviour in questioning her children about her behind her back. Far from deterring her from going, Jock's accusation had prompted her to contact Nanny and arrange to go a week earlier, as soon as the children broke up, and to stay a week longer so that they would be away for at least a month.

She was looking forward to the holidays. Michael had been at school a year now, but she hadn't missed him as much as she had thought she would; her painting had kept her so busy. Jock's behaviour had also given

David an added lustre in her eyes, quite the reverse of his intention, so that as well as meeting him again as a friend and a fellow artist she found herself thinking of him as a man.

20

As it happened, Sue didn't come away with them. She had an invitation to stay with a school friend in London for the first week and would join them later. Knowing how her daughter longed to visit London, Stevie could not say 'No' to such an opportunity. She firmly repressed the small voice inside that suggested that maybe this would give her a chance to see more of David alone.

She was eager, that first day, for supper to be finished and Michael safely in Nanny's charge so that she was free to tramp up the hill to David's cottage. She almost dropped the plate she was drying for Mary when she saw his stocky figure with its shock of black curls striding up the garden path to the cottage door.

'Oh, I forgot to tell you — I met Mr Jones in the Post Office yesterday and he asked me when you were coming,' Mary told her rather belatedly.

They walked out on the headland that evening, after he had chatted to the two elderly sisters and heard all about boarding school from Michael.

'Mummy paints pictures now — and sells them!' the boy told him proudly.

David shot her a swift look, and to her annoyance Stevie felt embarrassed and knew the warm colour was flooding slowly up her neck and cheeks.

'Does she now; that sounds great!' David said to Michael, raising one eyebrow in query to her as he spoke. 'I must hear all about this.'

As they walked along the headland in the long twilight and found a wooden bench where they could sit looking out to sea, she told him how she had taken his advice and how well it had turned out.

'And you?' she asked. 'What about you?'

'Oh, it's been a pretty good year for me too,' he told her. 'In fact I'm having an exhibition all to myself just before Christmas.'

'Oh David — that's wonderful! I would like to come, where and when is it?'

'Where else but Wolverhampton?' he said dryly. 'I'd like it very much if you would come, Stevie.'

'I'll come. I promise!' She put her hand over his for a second. 'And . . . other things — how are they, David?'

He shrugged. 'They could be worse. They let my wife home now for holidays; Christmas and that sort of thing. And what about you, how are things going for you? Other than your painting, I mean.'

'Not too bad.' Stevie shrugged noncommittally. 'Matthew — my stepson — got married last September. Pam, his wife, is a doctor too. I like her very much and we get on very well together. It was Pam, in fact, who really got me started on these animal portraits.'

Over the next ten days they met every day; often they set up their painting gear and worked side by side. Sometimes they swam together; often they ate together; and always they talked. The only thing they didn't do was sleep together.

'Tell me more!' Stevie urged as David lay in the sand reminiscing about his childhood. Suddenly as she spoke she seemed to hear an echo in her head; a much younger Stevie saying just the same thing — to Tom — as he talked about Australia. The memory brought in its wake others, more painful, and a shadow crossed her face. David, who had just turned to look at her, saw the shadow, as if for a moment the sun had hidden behind a cloud.

'What is it?' he asked.

'Nothing. Just a memory of someone else, years ago who used to talk to me about his life in Australia and I used to say 'Go on — tell me more!' ' Quickly she snapped memory's door shut; the glimpse into the past was just too painful. 'I guess I'm just a very good listener!'

David propped himself on one elbow and smiled into her eyes. 'You certainly are.' He let his eyes rest on her for a moment, wanting in that instant quite desperately to make love to her. Had he cared for her a little less he might have done so, but some inner prompting, a sixth sense, warned him that to want more from her might only mean that he would lose what he had.

She had as good as told him that her marriage was a dismal failure, and he guessed from the look in her eyes a few minutes ago that somewhere in her life there had been a special relationship that was anything but a failure. She was not the sort of woman, he was sure, to sleep around lightly; she would not jeopardise her marriage, however disappointing it might be, for what she would consider a second-best relationship. Close though they had grown, and deep as their friendship seemed to be, he was not sure enough of himself to put her to the test.

Stevie did not miss the expression in his eyes; and for a second she allowed herself to wonder what it would be like to have David make love to her, how would she feel if he were to take her in his arms . . . ?

As they strolled up the hill towards Mary's

cottage they could see the village policeman pushing his bike ahead of them.

'Jones the Police,' David said. 'You see, here are so many of us Joneses they have to tag our jobs onto our names to know who is who.'

Stevie smiled. 'And are you Jones the Artist?' she was saying when her voice sharpened, 'He's turning in at Mary's gate,' her step quickened. 'I hope nothing is wrong!'

'Probably just reminding them about their dog licence.' David tried to be soothing, even though, like Stevie, he could feel apprehension prickling his spine.

'They haven't got a dog.' Stevie glanced at her watch. 'I should have got home earlier. Sue gets in on the London train this evening and I have to meet her. I shall be late if I get delayed.' Somehow she was sure that the policeman was there because of her, though for the life of her she couldn't think why.

Stevie could feel the atmosphere in the house the instant she walked in; there was a kind of waiting silence. Mary was in the kitchen; she held out her hand to Michael as they came in throwing a strange look, first at Stevie, then at David.

'Jones the Police is here to see you; he's in the parlour,' she said to Stevie; then turning to Michael she said, 'You stay here with me;

291

we'll make a pot of tea.' Then to David as he turned to go, 'Reckon you'd better stay and have one.' She nodded to him, as Stevie shot him a look that silently begged him to go with her into the parlour. He followed her out of the kitchen to the scrupulously tidy best room where Nanny and the policeman waited.

Jones the Police was sitting awkwardly on the sofa; his helmet in his hands, looking down at his boots, so shiny that he could almost see his own reflection. He looked up when they came in, nodded a brief greeting to his namesake then shot to his feet. In those few seconds he had wondered how Davey Jones the painter fitted into all this; even whether somehow he was at the bottom of the whole sorry business. He and this Mrs Campbell seemed pretty close.

He looked at her now and swallowed hard. He wished to God someone else had been given the job of telling her.

'Mrs Campbell?'

Stevie nodded, her eyes, wide and dark in a face suddenly pale in spite of its sunburn.

'I'm sorry, ma'am, but I've bad news for you.' He twisted his helmet round, cleared his throat and glanced appealingly at Nanny and then at David; but they were both looking at Stevie. He gulped again and stared down at his boots once more. 'Maybe you'd better sit down, ma'am.' She was looking so white that he thought she might faint even before he told her. Obediently Stevie sat, like an automaton, and Nanny and David followed her example.

'Please tell me, Officer. What is it?' Her voice was little more than a hoarse whisper. The train, something in her head was saying — it's the train — Sue has been killed — there has been a dreadful rail disaster . . .

'It's your husband, Mrs Campbell. There — there's been an accident. He's dead, I'm afraid. Your local police station got on to us and asked us to tell you.'

'Why should the police tell me? Why couldn't Matthew just send a telegram?' In the sudden rush of relief that washed over her that it wasn't Sue, she could think of nothing else to say.

'Well — er — it seems the police were called in.' They had suggested over the telephone that it was suicide but he didn't want to be the one to tell her that; he had done his bit. Awkwardly he shifted from one foot to the other, still twisting his helmet round.

'Well — er — I'm sorry to bring you such news — I'll — er — ' He shot a look of appeal in Nanny's direction; thankfully she

293

intercepted it and, getting to her feet, led him to the door. 'Good evening!' he mumbled as he followed her from the room.

Stevie looked completely dazed for a moment. She turned helplessly to David. 'I suppose I shall have to go home?' It was a question more than a statement.

'Yes,' he nodded. 'I suppose you will.'

'I thought it was Sue,' she told him, and he noticed with relief that some of the colour had come back into her cheeks. Suddenly she remembered. 'Sue — oh, my God, she's due at the station in about half an hour!'

'Don't worry about that; I'll meet her.' He was thankful to have something practical to do to help. 'You should start back as soon as possible, then you might make it before dark.'

'Perhaps I should take Sue?'

'No — leave her here.' Nanny had come back into the room. 'She's already had a long journey and she'll be tired. Besides, you — ' She had been going to say 'don't know what you'll find when you get there', but thought better of it and repeated, 'Better for her to stay here with me; I'll tell her and look after her. You get on your way. I'll pour you a cup of tea while you pack a case.'

'I think that's the best plan,' David told her. 'Don't worry about Sue; I'll take Nanny into the station at Porthmadog to get her. I'll go and get my car straight away.' He took her hand in his and held it for a second. 'I'm sorry, Stevie, really sorry. I hope things aren't too bad when you get home.'

'So do I!' she said, raising her eyes to his face. 'And thank you, David; thank you for everything!' She withdrew her hand swiftly from his and turned to get ready to leave.

* * *

Stevie drove back as fast as she dared. For once she could not enjoy the magnificent scenery through which she was travelling but could only curse the everlasting bends and curves that kept her speed down. Her thoughts were in turmoil. What had happened? Why hadn't she questioned that wretched young policeman more thoroughly? She hadn't even asked him what sort of accident. He had said 'the police were called in' which seemed to rule out a motoring accident. She felt a pang of guilt as she remembered how she hadn't even given Jock a thought, she had been so convinced that something had happened to Sue when she saw the look on Nanny's and that policeman's face as she walked into the parlour.

She was exhausted by when she finally turned in at her own drive, yet instinctively she knew that whatever she had already heard, there was worse still to come. She reached into the back of the car for the small case in which she had hastily flung a few essentials, closed the car door carefully, took a deep breath and forced herself to go inside.

She stepped into the hallway; everywhere seemed unnaturally quiet. Softly she closed the door behind her and made for the stairs. Then, changing her mind, she headed for the kitchen.

Mrs Evans, dear, kind Mrs Evans, staunch friend, along with Nanny, of so many years, was sitting quietly at the kitchen table; just sitting looking into space. Her busy hands for once were idle; she looked old and tired and her mouth drooped. She jumped to her feet when she saw Stevie in the doorway and her eyes, already red-rimmed, filled with tears.

'Oh — Mrs Campbell — Madam — you're back!' She dabbed at her face with a hanky. 'I didn't hear you come in. Oh — dear me — it's been so dreadful — him missing — then finding him like that — then the police here asking questions and everything. Oh, Madam!'

The housekeeper was so distraught that Stevie was loath to question her too closely and was relieved when she added, 'Young Dr. Campbell and Mrs Campbell are here, they're in the sitting room.'

'Yes, I saw their car when I drove up.' Stevie sighed. 'I'll go and see them.'

She turned and left the kitchen; wondering why she had come to see Mrs Evans first — she supposed for some sort of maternal comfort. At that moment she felt both very young and very old.

She found Pam sitting in one of the big armchairs by the hearth and Matthew standing with his back to the empty fireplace, a stance much loved by Jock, especially when he had something he considered important to say. They were talking together in low voices. Matthew looked so much like his father that for a moment Stevie paused in the doorway, her heart in her mouth, Jock wasn't dead after all, the whole thing was a macabre joke.

They stopped talking abruptly when they saw her, and Pam jumped to her feet and held out her arms in a warm impulsive gesture.

'Stevie, my dear!' In that moment she felt older than her step-mother-in-law and her heart contracted with pity, as she took in the drooping shoulders, the travel-rumpled clothes, the eyes unnaturally large and dark in the pale face. She looked all-in, as well she might; the news itself was bad enough and she had the journey home on top of that. Pam wished to God that were the whole of it.

She gave Stevie a wordless hug of comfort, and then led her gently forward to a chair.

'Give her a drink, a brandy,' she said over her shoulder to Matthew. 'Pour us all one.'

Stevie looked up at Pam and managed a wan smile of gratitude. Thank God for someone to lean on!

'Thank you.' She took the brandy glass from Matthew and sipped it gratefully; as the fiery liquid coursed down her throat she lay back in her chair, closed her eyes for a second and took a deep breath, then looked across at them, now seated side by side on the couch.

'What happened?' she asked tersely. Whatever it was, she had to know. 'The police just said 'an accident'.'

'He killed himself. While you were on holiday.' Grief and shock made Matthew's voice flat and toneless; but to Stevie the words were an accusation. They reminded her that Jock had asked her not to go. In that instant she forgot all the disappointments, the minor heartaches in her marriage and only remembered the good times; the kindness Jock had shown her and the friendship and companionship they had known over the years. Guilt consumed her, reflected in her swimming eyes, as she looked across at the other two.

'You mustn't blame yourself; whatever you do — you mustn't feel it was in any way your fault. It would have happened; whether or not you were here.' Pam's voice was authoritative and she glanced quickly at her husband before going on. 'I think you should know just what did happen,' she laid a restraining hand on her husband's arm, 'however painful it is — for all of us.'

'Please tell me.' Stevie begged. 'If you have any idea why — why he — did it, then tell me.'

Pam looked to her husband; but he was sitting with his face buried in his hands. It had been so terrible he couldn't bear to think about it, let alone talk about it to Stevie of all people, his father's wife.

Pam sighed. She didn't want to talk about it much herself; but Stevie had to know the facts and she, as the in-law, was, she supposed, the least touched emotionally.

'The police came here yesterday evening,' she began, speaking slowly and carefully, 'we happened to be here for dinner or we probably wouldn't have known they'd been.' She paused and took a deep breath. 'They were investigating some — complaints — they'd had — ' she seemed to be having difficulty finding the right words; Stevie cut in with,

'What sort of complaints?' Somehow she knew this was crucial.

'Rather nasty ones, actually.'

'A lot of damn lies!' Matthew looked up for a moment and, meeting his eyes, Stevie felt herself flinch from the naked accusation as he added, 'If you had *been* here.'

'Matthew!' Pam's voice was sharp. 'It wouldn't have made any difference if Stevie had been here.' With difficulty she controlled the impatience in her voice. Personally she was thankful, for Stevie's sake that she had been away; at least she had been spared some of the horror. The children too — they, especially Michael, would have been questioned.

'Please, *tell* me!' Dear God, what complaints could anybody possibly have made about Jock; he was the soul of rectitude, and a good doctor to boot.

'Some boys — small boys — around Michael's age — ' Pam struggled on — 'claimed they had been — molested — and — and — they named Jock.'

'Small boys — Jock?' Stevie's voice rose on a crescendo of horror as she took in the full import of Pam's words. 'But that is ridiculous — absolutely — ' her voice trailed away as, like insidious poison, doubt crept into her mind. She thought of Michael, sent so young to boarding school; out of temptation's way? She remembered Sue saying he didn't seem to like her so much now she was older and showing unmistakable signs of the woman she would become. She thought of her own personal relationship with Jock, the times when he seemed resentful, almost afraid of her sexuality. How he had insisted that she bring no hint of scandal to his good name. Oh, he had needed her all right — as a buffer, a shield, a smokescreen. Anger, bitter as gall, seared through her, and mingled with it a pity that tore at her very being. She lifted the brandy glass to her lips to drain it and found her hand shaking so much that she had to steady it with her other one.

Pam, watching her closely, saw all these emotions chase across her face and, for the first time, wondered if it were at all possible that there was, after all, some truth in the accusations.

Matthew looked up then, his face ravaged and his mouth working.

'Lies — wicked, filthy lies!' he repeated vehemently. 'Nothing can bring him back, but at least we can try and protect his good name now he's dead. I've been on to my solicitor and I've talked to the police; there may be no need for any of it to come out now — now he's gone.'

And that will save your good name, too, won't it? The cynical thought crossed Stevie's mind; but she managed to bite off the words before she gave them utterance. Hard on the heels of that thought came the grateful one that Michael might also be spared an interrogation.

'And then what happened?' she asked. The hurricane of feeling had swept through her leaving her feeling drained of all emotion, even grief.

'He laughed it off as an absurdity — an obvious case of mistaken identity — and refused to talk about it after the police had gone. He seemed quite his normal self when we left, but . . . '

'What did he do?' Stevie asked in the flat tone that Matthew had used a moment ago.

With a choking sound he dropped his face in his hands. It was Pam who took up the story.

'When Mrs Evans took him his early morning tea he wasn't in bed. She thought he was probably in the bathroom and left it on the bedside table and went downstairs to get his breakfast. She still wasn't too concerned when he didn't turn up for breakfast; just thought he must have been called out on a case and forgotten to leave a note as he usually did. When he didn't turn up for morning surgery and his receptionist rang the house and asked her if she knew anything — then she began to worry and that's when she phoned us. She had already been out to the garage and found his car missing. When she discovered we had heard nothing either she really panicked and wanted to call in the police there and then. We managed to dissuade her — we still hoped — but anyway it wouldn't have made any difference. A farm worker reported his dead body, in his car, up Shingles Lane. He had seen the car there when he went to work; when it was still there at lunch time he was curious, or suspicious, or both, and went and investigated. Jock had been dead for nearly twelve hours.'

As Pam talked Stevie could see it all in her mind, just as if she were there. She listened with mounting horror, getting to her feet suddenly as the recital ended. The floor beneath her heaved; the carpet seemed to come up to hit her. She put out a hand to steady herself, knocking the brandy glass to the floor.

'I feel quite sick!' she muttered piteously before her legs crumpled and she fell in a heap on the hearthrug.

21

Stevie held the thick envelope in her hand; she could feel there was a card inside and she guessed it was either a belated sympathy card or an early Christmas card. She didn't care, and left it on her bureau along with the rest of her mail, mostly bills that she didn't have time, or inclination, to deal with at the moment. There were far too many other things to do. Finding a new home for one thing.

Jock had left the house to Matthew. He and Pam were certainly not turning Stevie out — in fact quite the reverse; they had begged her to go on living there — but the house that had been her home for two years now felt like a prison. She had also turned down their suggestion that she simply change houses with them and move into Willow Lodge. She wanted a complete change. The only thing was, where?

The children being at boarding school was a mixed blessing. She missed them dreadfully and found it almost unbearably lonely; on the other hand it did leave her free to live entirely where she chose and not be tied by schools.

Financially their education was taken care of by Martin's will, but she had no income herself from his estate; that went when she remarried, and was invested in a fund for the children. Jock had left her a small annuity and most of the furniture, a few family heirlooms excepted. The rest of his estate went to Matthew. With that and the income from her painting she was, thank God, financially independent if not rich. She could not have borne the role of poor relation, totally dependent on her stepson's charity, for although their relationship was fine on the surface, Stevie still felt that Matthew blamed her in some way for his father's death.

The fat envelope lay forgotten on her desk under a mounting pile of bills and junk mail, till a week later when she answered the phone.

'Stevie? It's David here.'

'Hello, David. How are you?'

'Fine, fine — but what about you? Are you coming?'

'Coming where?'

'My show — I sent you a special invitation to the opening and private viewing.'

'Oh David! I'm so sorry; I don't think I opened it. Did you send it about a week ago? Just a minute,' she dropped the receiver and rummaged amongst the papers on her desk, 'yes, it's here, I'm so sorry!' she repeated.

'Well, I should think so; but never mind that — are you coming?'

'Of course I am! How could I *not* come? I promised, didn't I?' She quickly checked the date to be sure she was free that day.

'Good. I'll see you there, and Stevie — don't forget!'

★ ★ ★

As she walked up the steps of the gallery in Wolverhampton where the exhibition of David's work was being held Stevie felt more alive than she had for many weeks. Jock had been dead for over two months now and the pain, and the anger, the hurt and the grief, were beginning to subside. Occasionally, like now, they almost disappeared.

As she walked into the hall and looked round for David she saw one or two heads turn in her direction; then mutter to their companions who also seemed to look at her. Nervously she put up one hand to her hair, smoothing an imaginary stray strand back into place. She was wearing a plain grey flannel suit, the jacket with a nipped-in waist, and a full skirt. It suited her tall figure and her particular brand of simple elegance. For one panicky moment she wondered if some whispered word, some awful scandal, had followed her, but when David disengaged himself from a group of people and hurried over to her, apologising for not actually seeing her come in, she dismissed the thought and even the idea that people were looking at her.

'You've come,' he held her hand for a second, the expression in his eyes dark and unfathomable, 'you're looking well.' he told her and she smiled her appreciation of the compliment. 'Come and see the *pièce de résistance* of the whole show.'

He led her to a large canvas called, quite simply, 'The Beach'. It was a rich, colourful picture of sand, sea and sky and, in the middle of it a woman with her sandals in one hand, testing the temperature of the water rippling round her bare feet. The woman was clearly and unmistakably herself. There was a large clear sign stuck on the frame: 'Not for Sale'.

'Oh, David. It's wonderful — but I'm not nearly as beautiful as that!'

'On the contrary — it doesn't do you justice.'

He invited her out to lunch and when she demurred he assured her that even the artist was allowed time off to eat. He took her to 'The Vic', securing a secluded table in the thickly carpeted dining room of the prestigious old hostelry.

As they settled in their seats he asked how she was coping and sounded as if he really cared. To Stevie, who seemed to have been bombarded over the last couple of months with sympathy that to her over-sensitive ears often rang hollow, this mattered.

He was aghast when she told him that she was leaving 'The Firs' because it had been left to Matthew.

'Won't you contest the will?'

She shook her head. 'No. I don't want the house anyway. But I do have to find somewhere else. I can't make up my mind where I want to live, that's the problem.'

David looked at her for a moment. 'You could have my cottage in Wales for the winter if you like. That would at least give you a chance to look around and decide what to do or where to go.'

She gaped at him, amazement and gratitude lighting her face. 'Oh — no I couldn't. But it's very kind of you.'

'Why couldn't you? I'm not really being kind; you would be doing me a favour by care-taking,' he assured her. 'I shan't be able to get there till the summer holidays anyway.'

The more he talked and the more she listened, the more Stevie liked the idea. By the time they reached coffee she had agreed to wind up her affairs, put her furniture into store and get there as soon as possible.

'Thank you, David, for everything. For inviting me today, for the lunch and most of all for the cottage!' she said as they parted. Leaning forward she touched his cheek lightly with her lips. 'A friend in need is a friend indeed!' she quoted with a smile.

* * *

Now that she had an objective, things moved quickly. She arranged to store the furniture she wanted to keep and for the rest to go to an auction rooms. The only really sad note was poor Fairy, whose arthritis had got much worse this winter. With a heavy heart Stevie made the hard decision to have her put down, but Bobbin she sold to an excellent home as a child's pony.

She wrote to the children and told them they would be spending the Christmas holidays in Wales. Her letter to Michael crossed with one of his telling her all about a wonderful new friend he had made this term — an Australian boy. ' . . . and he's asked me to go to Australia one day and stay with him on his farm there,' he wrote, 'so please may I ask him to come and stay with us in the hols?

He won't be going home because it's too far but he is going to stay with some aunts or something for Christmas.'

Stevie wrote back and told him that he could have his friend for the New Year because Sue was going to spend a week with her friend in London then — and promptly forgot all about it in the hectic days of sorting, packing and eventually moving to the Welsh coast.

She invited Mrs Evans to come with her; but the old housekeeper tearfully told her that she was too old now to move amongst foreigners and thought the time had come for her to retire. Stevie smiled to herself at the description of David and her other Welsh friends as 'foreigners', but did not try and persuade her.

★ ★ ★

The sun glinting on the rime was like a promise on the frosty morning in late November when she loaded up her car and left for Wales.

She sang to herself as she drove; she had written to Nanny and told her she planned to spend the next six months in Wales at least and had received an ecstatic letter back. Of all the many children she had looked after in her working life as a professional nanny, none had been more 'her' children than Sue and Michael; maybe because they were her last two charges. She gloried in the prospect of having them living so close, and immediately began plans for a special Christmas.

Stevie was glad that she had a few weeks to settle in before the children broke up. She had two commissions and needed freedom to paint. She had advertised in some of the glossy periodicals such as *The Field* and *Country Life* portraits of animals from photographs. One or two good photos she felt would enable her to capture the essence of an animal on canvas. With these commissions had come the chance to prove she was right.

She had completely forgotten her promise to Michael to have his Australian friend on a visit, until one morning she received a thin letter with an Australian stamp. It was a short, formal note thanking her for her invitation.

'*Dear Mrs Campbell, my son has written to tell me that you have invited him to spend part of his holidays with you. I do appreciate your kindness and trust that it will not in any way inconvenience you —* ' etc. etc. Stevie flipped through it and glanced casually at the signature when her heart stopped, it seemed, completely. There was a ringing in her ears and then she could hear it beat again — bump — bump as she read the name. Tom Jefferies.

22

She turned the letter over in her hand looking at the address. Damn — it was written from a hotel in Melbourne and the postmark was Melbourne, Victoria. She looked again at the handwriting; cursing the Tom she had known in the past for being such a poor letter writer that she couldn't even be sure she recognised the handwriting. The signature looked familiar, but there could be dozens of Tom Jefferies; even in a sparsely populated place like Australia. She read through the letter again; what was his son's name? She thought back to the day when he had told her about his wife and child — Simon — yes that was it. But not once in the brief note did he mention him by name; just 'my son'. She tried to remember Michael using his friend's name when he asked her if he could stay; she couldn't remember, but thought he had just said 'my friend'. She had thrown the letter away after telling Michael he could ask him.

She read through the letter once more, searching avidly for some clue, however insignificant, that would tell her that this was 'her' Tom. But there was nothing. All she could do was await the New Year and her young visitor.

Stevie made the most of her few weeks alone before the children arrived for the holidays. She had plenty of work to do and was not lonely for she always had Nanny and her sister to visit and, thank heavens, David had a telephone in the cottage so she was not entirely cut off from the outside world.

The cottage itself was simply but comfortably equipped and the atmosphere seemed to Stevie absolutely right for painting, probably the impression she thought, David had made on his surroundings.

It was a healing time for her, of readjustment, of gathering her resources to go on with the rest of her life. She was grateful to David for offering her this temporary haven, but it could not be permanent.

Fortunately both children's schools broke up on the same day and she was able to collect them in one trip; though squeezing trunks and school stuff for two people in the car proved a teaser.

'Why are we living in Mr Jones' house, Mummy?' Michael asked as they drove into Borth-y-Gest.

'Because our old house belongs to Matthew now. Mr Jones has lent us the cottage while we look for a new home.'

'Where are we going to live when we do get a new house?' Sue asked.

'To be honest I haven't really given it much thought!' Stevie admitted, 'Where would you like to live?'

'In London.' Sue was definite.

'By the sea.' Michael cried.

'Yes,' Sue said after a few moments thought, 'I think I would enjoy living in London for a while, but we might find it very difficult to get anywhere we liked, housing is still difficult; so much of London was destroyed in the war.'

'Well, I wouldn't mind living by the sea either,' Sue compromised. 'But I'd rather be somewhere with just a bit more life than Borth-y-Gest.'

Stevie smiled at her daughter; she understood. Borth-y-Gest was a delightful haven to retire to, a wonderful retreat when life had given you a bit of a buffeting, but even she was young enough to feel that it would not have enough to offer long term.

'Somewhere like Rhyl?' she suggested.

'Oh, no, Mummy! That's too much of a seaside town, a holiday town. I think it would be awful in the winter. What about somewhere like Barmouth? I thought that was a lovely place when we went there with Nanny.'

'Yes — let's live in Barmouth!' Michael bounced up and down on the back seat excitedly.

'That's settled then as we all seem to like the idea. Michael, tell me about your friend, the one who is coming to stay? Simon, is it?'

'No, his name is Andrew.'

Stevie's hopes plummeted. She was sure Tom had told her his son's name was Simon.

But Michael went on, 'Simon's his older brother; *he* is too old for me, he's nearly four years older than Andrew. He's going to Public School next year.'

Her heart soared. Of course, how stupid, she hadn't done her arithmetic correctly. Tom's son Simon was less than a year younger than Sue.

With a little bit more judicious questioning she discovered that Andrew Jefferies did, indeed, live in Tasmania. That his mother had died a long time ago — Andrew barely remembered her — and that he and his brother were spending the holidays with some 'dreary old aunts' — *really* old, according to Andrew. Gratified by his mother's interest in his friend, Michael was more than willing to answer questions.

They spent Christmas Day with Nanny and her sister. The two old ladies had rustled up a huge tree from somewhere and the little parlour seemed full to overflowing when they all piled in to open their presents. The excited shouts and happy laughter rang joyously in Stevie's head and seemed to chase the unhappy memories of the last time she had sat in this room into the shadows.

The phone was ringing when they got back to David's cottage on Christmas night.

'Hello there!'

'David! How are you? Have you had a good Christmas?'

'Can't complain. And you?'

'Terrific!'

'How's the cottage going? Enjoying it? I thought I might get there for a few days in the holidays but I'm afraid I shan't be able to make it — maybe at Easter.'

'Good. That will be lovely. David — ' She wanted to tell him that she was looking for somewhere else without making him feel that she was in any way dissatisfied with his cottage. But a sudden crackle on the line drowned her words.

'Sorry — I didn't catch that. Bad line, isn't it?' The crackling got worse and he continued, 'I think I'd better hang up — I only wanted to wish you a Happy Christmas anyway. I'm glad you are in the house to look after it.'

Stevie was only able to yell 'Goodbye'

down the receiver, before the line went dead. She hung up slowly, she was truly grateful to David for his timely loan of the cottage, but didn't want to feel in any way beholden to him.

She put her search for a new home on hold for the moment. There was more than enough to occupy her, getting Sue ready to stay with her friend in London and preparing for the visit of Tom's son. She thought of him as that now, instead of 'Michael's Friend.'

By a lot of juggling and some good management she managed to arrange for Andrew to arrive by train at Barmouth station the same day that Sue left for London. She planned to have a look round the town in the gap between trains and see if they really would like to live there.

After Borth-y-Gest, the small seaside resort town of Barmouth on the Mawdach estuary seemed like a bustling city. They parked the car and walked through the town to the beach.

'It's nice here.' Sue spoke for all of them as she took a deep breath of the salt air blowing in from the sea.

'Yes, let's live here!' Michael chimed eagerly.

'I think we might.' Stevie said. She liked the town and it was on a direct route to

Shrewsbury, which made the to-ing and fro-ing to school easier. She looked at her watch. 'We had better have lunch, we don't want to miss these trains.'

On their way back to the town centre to find a meal they passed a Real Estate Agent's office; impulsively Stevie opened the door and went in. They had not much for sale, though quite a lot to rent for the winter. But as Stevie had David's cottage till the summer holidays there didn't seem much point in taking anything else that only offered the same period. Stevie took the addresses of the few places for sale and said she would look at the outside of them and call back if anything appealed enough to investigate further. Almost as an after-thought she gave her phone number and asked them to let her know if anything suitable appeared on their books.

After this detour they hurried to the station to meet Andrew, whom they were collecting before lunch; there was a convenient two hour gap between the arrival of his train and the departure of the one Sue had to catch.

Stevie anticipated meeting Tom's son with a strange mixture of curiosity and excitement, but when Michael shouted, 'There he is!' and ran to meet the small boy about his own age clambering down onto the platform she felt

319

nothing more than disappointment. If this was indeed the son of the Tom Jefferies she had known and loved, there was no likeness whatsoever that she could see.

But later that evening as she sat across the supper table from the two boys and listened to Andrew talking about his home in Tasmania, which he obviously missed very much, Stevie caught a wistful look of pride in the child's face and heard something in his voice that suddenly, unbidden, brought the memories flooding back and dispelled completely any lingering idea that it was all some huge coincidence. She knew this was Tom's son and, smiling at him across the table, she said, 'Tell us about Tasmania, Andrew.' just as she had so often said to his father long before he was born.

The two boys were the best of friends and the week's visit passed swiftly and happily. Even though the weather, at this time of the year, was far too cold to enjoy the seaside they found plenty of things to do and excursions to go on and Stevie was almost as sorry to see him go as Michael was when they waved him goodbye on the Shrewsbury-bound train to spend the rest of the holidays with his brother and his two great-aunts who were, as he confided in Stevie, 'dreadfully old, but quite nice.'

Stevie had not organised things quite so well this time and Sue did not get back for another few days. Michael seemed lost without his friend, and Stevie, who had a commission to do, wished she had arranged for Andrew to stay longer. Finally she put her paints away and decided to give up for the school holidays and just work extra when term began.

★   ★   ★

It was a day in February when two things happened. The Estate Agents rang to tell her about a house, and she had another letter from Australia.

23

The letter from Tom was a polite bread and butter 'thank you' note for having Andrew for a week in the school holidays; the sort of letter anyone would write to a complete stranger who had done one a kindness. It was obvious that he had no idea that he actually knew Stevie. This letter however was written from home and had his Tasmanian address.

Stevie was reading it for the third time when the phone rang. It was the Barmouth Real Estate people. They had a house available to let for a year, they told her. The rent was reasonable but it would not be available until after Easter and it was not actually in Barmouth but at Capel Arthog, only a few minutes out of the town on the other side of the estuary, and the views were superb.

While they talked Stevie glanced out of the window. The sun was shining, even though it was only February. Earlier this morning she had noticed snowdrops outside the cottage. She looked at her watch; it was still early, not yet ten o'clock.

'I'll come straight away and have a look at

it,' she told the agent.

Driving through Harlech with its castle and its historic associations, and on towards Barmouth, Stevie thought of Tom and this morning's letter. Through her joy in the spring-like weather, the beautiful scenery, and thoughts of the house she was on her way to see, even beyond her pleasure in hearing from him, she felt again the pain of the months when she had waited, longing for just such a note — anything — some sign that he was still alive. She made up her mind there and then not to disclose her identity when she answered his letter.

She was not disappointed in the Arthog house up above the town of Barmouth. It looked down on the magnificent Mawdich estuary, the rooms at the back facing the splendour of Cader Idris towering over them. Set in the side of the hill, the house seemed remarkably sheltered, and it was all she had ever dreamed of — and more.

'It's beautiful!' she breathed as the agent pulled up at the front door.

The only thing that worried her was that it looked small. She murmured as much, some part of her mind cautioning her that it was not good business to seem too enthusiastic.

'Wait till you get inside,' the agent said; 'It's

very deceptive. It's built into the hillside and goes back.'

It was, as he had said, deceptive Stevie found, and gloriously topsy-turvy when compared with conventional houses. Though technically a bungalow; being all on one level inside with no stairs, the three bedrooms at the back of the house were on ground level while the kitchen, in the centre, was somewhere in between. A path wound round the side to the back door which was up three steps, and the front of the house — the sitting room, hall-way and breakfast room — gave the impression of being upstairs when one was inside. A flight of six grey stone steps led up to the front door.

Stevie knew she was going to take it long before she stepped into the hallway. Standing in the garden and drinking in the breath-taking views she felt as if she had come home.

After she had been shown round the house they all sat in the lounge with its panoramic views of the estuary below them, drank coffee and discussed the whens and wherefores.

'We are leaving immediately after Easter,' the owner, Mrs Llewellyn, told her. 'So — any time after that, in fact as soon as possible would please us, we are not keen to leave it empty.' She glanced round the room as she spoke and Stevie felt a quick bond of

324

sympathy; she was sure she was going to feel just the same when the time came for her to leave this enchanting house.

'Where are you going?' Stevie asked, more for the sake of making polite conversation than anything else.

'Australia.' Mrs Llewellyn's smile was somewhat bleak. 'It seems a very long way; but it's only for a year. My husband has been sent to the Melbourne office of his firm for twelve months.'

Stevie started slightly. 'Australia,' she repeated in surprise; 'a long way indeed.'

If she had any doubts before about taking the house, the coincidence that they were going to Australia the very day that she had a letter from Tom would have made her take it. To Stevie it seemed almost like an omen — a good luck symbol. She smiled across at the owners, 'You'll miss the view,' she said. 'but don't worry about the house; I'll look after it for you, I love it already.'

Back home she sat down almost immediately to write and tell the children, adding that as they would have an extra room in the new house there would be plenty of room for their friends to visit.

Then she answered Tom's letter. She also told him about the house; making it clear that Andrew was more than welcome to stay with them again in the holidays. She found it hard keeping her letter to the mere acquaintances level, and was tempted to reveal her identity to him. Then she reminded herself that Tom had left without any attempt to communicate with her over the years, not even when his wife died.

That evening she phoned David and told him that she had found another house. 'I'll be leaving just after Easter,' she told him. 'I hope that is all right with you?'

'As a matter of fact that will fit in with me very well. I plan to come down for the last couple of days or so of the holidays; I'll be able to help you move.'

'That would be marvellous David, I can't thank you enough for letting me have your cottage. It has given me a chance to breathe — to think what I really want to do. By the end of another year in Wales I shall either be completely hooked and want to stay forever or I shall feel the need to spread my wings a bit more.' She laughed; at the moment she could not see any possibility of ever wanting to live anywhere else.

David arrived in Borth-y-Gest the day before they were due to move to Capel Arthog. Stevie and the children had spent the Easter holiday packing and tidying so when he arrived the car was filled to bursting point and the things they couldn't get in were standing in the kitchen in the hope that David would bring them in his car the next day.

When he walked into the cottage and saw the cases standing there and the cottage itself looking ready to receive him but almost as if Stevie and her children had never lived there, he felt a sharp stab of disappointment. He had hoped for a few days with her at least.

'David! How good to see you!' Impulsively she held out her arms to him and stepping forward he embraced her in a tight bear hug. Then he held her at arms' length and looked at her critically; his head slightly cocked to one side.

'You look a different woman! Wales agrees with you,' he nearly added 'and so does widowhood.' Gone the correct but repressed doctor's wife and in her place there was a vibrantly alive and attractive woman, daring to be herself.

'I feel different!' She smiled, about to add, 'and I'm so happy.' but enough of the old Stevie remained to caution her that widows of less than a year were not really supposed to be happy. 'We've done all the packing and clearing up.' She waved an arm vaguely round the house. 'We're all ready to go.'

'Yes, I see.' The bleakness of his voice was

lost on Stevie in her pleasure at the prospect of moving to her new home.

'Where are the children?' He looked round, half hoping that they were staying somewhere else.

'I sent them down to the village to stock up with some food,' she told him. 'I didn't like to leave it completely bare for you, like Mother Hubbard's cupboard,' Then, remembering that he had been travelling all morning, 'would you like a drink? A cup of tea or coffee?'

'I'd much rather have a glass of good red wine, if you haven't drunk it all.'

'Of course not, I haven't touched it,' she told him indignantly.

They took it outside and sat on two kitchen chairs in the warm April sun. David's cottage, like her new house, was sheltered from the inland weather by the mountains; today only a faint breeze stirred the trees and the sea, lying out beyond and below, was as calm as the proverbial millpond.

' 'A jug of wine, a loaf of bread — and thou — ' ' David quoted as he raised his glass to her.

Stevie laughed. 'Poor David, are you hungry? I'm afraid I haven't any bread till the children get back.'

Sensing an underlying seriousness in his

words she made light of it, but she knew Omar Khayyam as well as he did and, raising her glass to him, she quipped back, ' 'Better be jocund with the fruitful grape than sadden after none, or bitter, fruit.' '

David's face was still sombre over the rim of his glass. 'I shall let you have the final quote. If I continue we may get too maudlin, and today is too beautiful a day to think of anything but how good it is to be here — together — in the sun — with a glass of wine in our hands.'

'Well, here is your loaf of bread, anyway,' Stevie said lightly as the children appeared round the bend in the hill track with the shopping.

They were excited to see David and as she unpacked the basket and got a simple light lunch ready, Stevie did not know whether to be glad or sorry that the moment of intimacy — and promise — had been turned lightly away. She liked David so much; in fact he was quite one of her favourite people; she felt easy and comfortable with him, as if in some way he had always been a part of her existence. Added to that she found him immensely attractive as a man; and yet . . .

The clerk of the weather was thoroughly contrary the next day. Stevie woke in the upstairs room, David's bedroom, and drew back the curtains to see a wall of misty rain hanging over the sea. She went to the bathroom at the back of the house and saw the same grey pall shrouding the mountains. She pulled her dressing gown tighter round her and padded downstairs to put the kettle on for a cup of tea. The camp bed creaked as David rolled over, pulling the clothes closer round his shoulders. Then, as if suddenly aware that she was in the room, he rolled back and opened one sleepy eye and then the other.

'Hello! It's not a good morning; but would you like a cup of tea?' Stevie asked.

He stretched and yawned, 'What luxury to have early morning tea brought to me in bed, though the bed isn't exactly luxurious.' The camp bed creaked and groaned as he pulled himself up to watch her moving about the kitchen getting cups and making a pot of tea.

He sat up as she took it over to him. Patting the bed, he invited her to sit down.

Stevie pulled a face. 'It's not the best, is it?' she remarked as she sat on a hard lump that turned out to be one of the supports sticking through the canvas. 'I feel very guilty, sleeping in your comfortable bed while you had this thing. It should have been the other way round.'

David sipped his tea slowly, wishing he had

had the sense to suggest they shared the one comfortable bed. The idea had crossed his mind and if Stevie had given him any indication, however small, that she might have said yes, he would have chanced his luck.

He looked at her now, sitting on his bed. As she relaxed, the front of her wrap-around dressing gown unwrapped slightly and dropped forward, he caught a glimpse of the firm line of her breast disappearing into what looked like a very sparse nightdress.

Aware of his scrutiny she turned towards him as she sipped her own tea; annoyed to feel a warm flush creeping up her neck and cheeks.

'Stevie.' His voice croaked with feeling as, gently, he took her cup away from her and put it down on the floor beside his own. He shifted over on the creaking canvas and held the bedclothes back for her. 'It'll be a helluva squash, but never mind.'

She leaned against him and silently laid her leg beside him; her other leg was following and she was melting into his embrace, nothing else in her mind but the urgency of her need. His lips were just about to meet hers when noisy footsteps on the stairs and a shout of 'Mum!' brought her hastily to her feet and, she afterwards thought, her senses.

David could have cheerfully strangled Michael, or at least hurled his teacup at him, when the child burst into the kitchen a few seconds later full of excitement and moaning about the unkind weather. David looked gloomily out of the window and felt that the weather was just perfect for his present mood.

He continued to think so as he drove behind Stevie in thick sea mist-cum-drizzle along the coast road; his car loaded with the last of her belongings from his cottage and Michael, who had chosen to ride with him, still chattering with excitement about the new house.

Stevie looked round her in panic as she stopped the car outside the house and fumbled in her bag for the keys. The sky was a dull leaden grey and the rain was coming down very straight, and very wet. As she stood on the doorstep struggling with the unfamiliar lock, there was no view whatsoever; not a glimpse of the estuary and certainly not of Barmouth or the sea. She looked up; behind the house Cader Idris was hidden completely and in that moment seemed unlikely ever to reappear from its refuge in the clouds. Sue sat on her own in the car, watching her try to unlock the door. Michael and David waited stoically in the car behind. All three faces wore the same glum expression of sheer disbelief wondering what had possessed her to take this gloomy place for a whole year.

At last the door opened under her hand. She shook off as much rain as she could and went inside. The other three followed.

Stevie shooed them out again to help with the luggage; rain or no rain, the cars had to be unloaded. By the time it was all in everyone was wet and cranky, and Sue and Michael were quarrelling vigorously, each accusing the other of not doing their fair share.

It was David who organised everyone and everything. 'Come on — it's no good complaining about a bit of rain if you live in Wales. It's a lovely country but even I have to admit it can be wet; and needs roofing in. Now you two help your mother put some of this stuff away and I'll get a fire lit. Who knows; by this afternoon the sun may even be shining!'

The sun wasn't actually shining by when they had unpacked and eaten a makeshift lunch in front of the fire that blazed bravely in the hearth, but at least the rain had stopped.

'Come on,' David urged. 'We'll go down into Barmouth and blow the cobwebs away with a walk along the beach; then I'll take you to a café and buy you the biggest ice-creams we can get before I go back.'

Michael turned at the door. 'Which car are we going in?'

'Well, I don't think we've much choice; your mother can't get out of here till I move mine; unless she chooses to drive over the mountain.' David pointed out.

They all piled into his car and as they drove down towards Barmouth and the sea the mist rolled back and revealed the estuary below them and up above, through a break in the clouds, Cader Idris appeared as if the mountain wanted to welcome them to their new home.

They walked through the town and along the beach till they were all tired and hungry; but, as David had said, the cobwebs and the crankiness were blown away. True to his promise he took them to a café and bought ice creams and for Stevie and himself a pot of tea and a huge plate of hot buttered toast.

'I shall have to go; I have to get back tonight,' he told Stevie over the empty teacups.

'Must you?' she queried. 'Why not stay here for the night?'

He shook his head. 'No, I must get back. I can only stay a couple of days then I have to go back — home.'

Feeling in some way rebuffed, Stevie dropped her eyes to her plate and did not press the point, little knowing how small an amount of persuasion would have made him change his mind.

He had not felt such warmth toward anyone for a long time. He cursed the fates that gave him holidays only when her children were at home and wondered if it would be worth coming down for a weekend during term. His sixth sense detected some withdrawal in her, something he found hard to place — but it was there even in that moment when she had almost given herself to him. Maybe it was just too soon after her husband's death. He wished with all his heart he were free to ask her to marry him.

He dropped them at the garden gate of the new house, suddenly anxious to be on his way. Stevie could not know that it was because he knew that if she asked him again to stay the night he would weaken. She waved him off then turned to the house with the children. She felt curiously flat, instead of pleased to be settled in her new home. It was as if she had left something undone — some unfinished business.

She tried to phone David the next day, but could get no reply.

★ ★ ★

Stevie did not see David again that holiday. While Andrew was staying with them they went over to Borth-y-Gest to see Nanny and her sister, but David's cottage was closed and had that peculiar shut-in feeling of an empty house.

Once the children had all gone Stevie was able to really settle into her new home, and also to get down to some work. Advertisements in papers like *The Field, Country Life* and *The Lady* had brought her in enough commissions to keep her busy for some months and the money she earned more than paid the rent.

The weeks slid by pleasantly enough, and with the warmer weather she was able to enjoy not only her glorious scenic views, but the amenities of the pleasant little seaside town as well.

24

Stevie dipped her brush in the paint and with a deft stroke painted in a soft line that somehow altered completely the expression on the face of the Red Setter on her easel. She stepped back critically to look at her work, comparing it with the photographs in her hand, then, satisfied, she glanced at her watch. Ten o'clock — the postie should have come by now. She wondered if there would be a letter from Tom.

On her way to see if the post had come she stopped in the kitchen and put the electric kettle on, then went through the hallway. There was nothing lying on the mat beneath the mail flap. Disappointed, she was about to turn away when there was a rat-tat-tat on the old-fashioned cast iron knocker at the door.

Expecting to see Lloyd the Post, possibly with a parcel or some other package too big to go through the door flap, she turned back quickly.

'David! I thought it was the post.'

'It is,' he told her, handing over a small bundle of letters. 'I met him just at the gate.'

'Come on in.' She held the door wide and

stepped back. 'What are you doing here so early in the morning, other than delivering the post?' She smiled her thanks as she took the letters from him, her mind quickly registering that there was one with an Australian stamp.

'Spur of the moment decision. I woke up this morning thinking how nice it would be on the Welsh coast; jumped out of bed, shoved some things in a case, and here I am!'

He didn't add that he had originally planned to come the following weekend, which was Whitsun, but, guessing that would also be the half-term weekend and her children home, he decided to make it a week earlier and have her to himself for once.

'You mean you've been driving since — when? Come and have a cup of tea or coffee; the kettle is on,' remembering, she hurried into the kitchen, 'are you hungry? Have you had breakfast?' she called over her shoulder.

'Now you come to mention it, I don't believe I have,' he admitted with a rueful smile, 'but I did remember to shave.'

'I didn't have breakfast either,' she told him. 'I had a picture to finish and I was so anxious to get it done I just got up and started painting. How about we have some brunch?'

'Brunch?'

'A cross between breakfast and lunch. It's my favourite meal when I am on my own.'

Stevie scrambled eggs and made coffee while David made toast. They carried it through into the breakfast room where she had been painting, and sat at the table in the long low window, eating and catching up on each other's news. As always they fell into the easy camaraderie of good friends. The letters lay, temporarily forgotten, on the kitchen dresser.

When they had finished, David sat back in his chair and drew out his cigarettes; he lit one, and leaned back to watch her through lids narrowed slightly against the smoke. Her hair hung loose about her shoulders; eager to begin painting she hadn't bothered to roll it into the usual bun but had tied a ribbon quickly round it when it got in the way. When she had cooked their meal she had, for some reason, whipped this off again. She wore old slacks and a man's shirt flecked with paint that, even though it was several sizes too big for her, was curiously sensual. Her bare feet were thrust into sandals, and she looked far younger than her years. He knew that he both loved and desired her; and wished with all his heart that he were free to offer her more than love. Nevertheless, that was precisely why he was here. After he had left last time he couldn't get her out of his mind. He cursed the malignant fate that had tied him up in a totally unsatisfactory marriage, and he determined to tell her, at least, that he cared for her.

'Sorry?' He had been so lost in his thoughts that he hadn't heard her speak.

'I was just asking about your work; are you doing anything special just now?'

'Everything I do is special,' he told her. 'At the moment I'm working on a portrait of you.'

'Of me? But how can you — I'm not there.' Stevie protested, feeling confused and embarrassed.

'I'm working from memory. That is why I am here, I needed to refresh it.'

'Oh.' Stevie mumbled inadequately. She was flattered that he thought her a worthy subject to paint, embarrassed that he was looking at her as a model — with an artist's eye. 'And how is your memory shaping up?' she felt forced to ask into the lengthening silence.

'You look younger, and yet I feel you have matured over the last year,' he told her after some consideration. Stevie felt uncomfortable under his intense scrutiny. She had the feeling he had two pictures of her in his mind's eye and was weighing them up against each other.

'Flattery, Sir, will get you everywhere!' she said flippantly, in an attempt to diffuse some of the intensity between them. She got up to take the dishes out to the kitchen.

'I hope so.' David murmured to himself, as he followed her.

'Would you like another coffee? We could have it outside — it's beautiful now.'

He nodded, not trusting himself to speak in case he shattered what rapport there was between them. He was seized with an intense longing to sweep her up in his arms, carry her through to the bedroom and make love to her. God, how he wanted to do just that. But sensing this was not the moment he carried their second coffee out to the little cast iron table where he sat, somewhat morosely, opposite her in the sheltered garden.

'You've forgotten your letters. Shall I bring them out for you to read?' he offered in a conscious effort to please.

'Oh — yes, thank you.' Though she was longing to read them Stevie felt it would be impolite, so she was grateful for his offer.

There was one from each of the children and one from Tom, as she had guessed. A bumper day; but for David she would have eagerly devoured them the moment they arrived.

She smiled over Michael's letter; his spelling seemed to owe more to inspired imagination than anything else. He wanted to know if Andrew could spend the half-term holiday with them. She passed it over to David as she opened Sue's letter. She, in contrast, wanted to spend the long weekend with her friend in London.

'So it looks as if I'm going to lose one and gain another.' She smiled as she passed her letter over to David. There was nothing in either that was in any way private or personal.

'Who do you know in Australia?' he asked as he handed them back, nodding toward Tom's letter which still lay unopened on the table.

'Oh,' she said lightly, 'that's Andrew's father. I expect that will just be a polite little note thanking me for having him.' She dropped her hand over the letter as it lay on the table. It was a subconscious gesture not missed by David. All his instincts told him that her distant manner was in some way connected to the letter from Australia.

'Do you mean to tell me that he sends a little kid the same age as Michael, to the other side of the world to school?' he asked disbelievingly. 'It seems a bit tough to me.'

'Oh, I don't know.' Stevie bridled at the implied criticism of Tom; though privately she had thought exactly the same thing. 'It's not so bad. He has his elder brother at school, and relations, some aunts who live here, for the holidays.'

'And you.'

'And me,' she agreed. Her eyes dropped to the letter and, watching her, he wondered why, if it was only as she said, a polite courtesy note, she didn't open it and read it there and then. Suddenly it became terribly important to him that she did.

'Aren't you going to read it?' he urged, nodding at the letter still under her protective hand.

Stevie wanted to keep it till she was alone, to savour in secret. But David was watching her, and in some strange way she didn't quite understand it had suddenly become an issue between them; as if he had thrown down the gauntlet and was waiting for her to accept the challenge. She picked the letter up, turned it over once more in her hand, and slowly and carefully began to tear it open.

She glanced quickly through the letter; then began to read it through again, slowly, as if she needed the second reading to fully take in the contents. As she read a small smile hovered round the corners of her mouth and he watched a soft colour tinge her cheeks. When she finally looked up and her eyes met his he had the impression that she wasn't really seeing him at all.

He had no idea what was in the letter; but he knew, with a dreadful certainty, that he had lost her.

'Well?' Some masochistic demon inside him prodded him on.

'He's coming here — to England.' She seemed to be speaking as much to herself as answering his question. Her eyes, looking somewhere beyond him into the middle distance, shone as they never had for him; yet this man was supposed to be a stranger to her.

'But you don't know him — do you?'

With an effort she focused her eyes on him and nodded slowly. 'I do,' she told him. 'I've known him all my life — only he doesn't know that.'

'What do you mean?' David was torn, the rational, curious part of him needed an explanation; the emotional fey side already knew and didn't want to be told, had no need to hear about this person who had usurped Stevie's heart.

'I thought he was dead — that I'd never hear from him again!' There was awe and disbelief in her voice; he felt she was talking to herself, rather than to him, as if opening the letter had dismissed David altogether.

'Stevie, either don't tell me anything or tell me the whole story — from the beginning.' David wasn't sure he wanted to know, but she took a deep breath and began at the beginning when she and Tom were children; once she started nothing could stop her talking.

David sat quietly opposite her, not interrupting, only prompting now and then with a nod, though when she told him how she had never heard a word from Tom after he had left her on that last leave, he scowled and had to bite his tongue to stop himself saying what he thought. It seemed obvious to him that the scoundrel had had second thoughts and chosen his marriage rather than Stevie.

'So you see,' she wound up, 'he doesn't know that the Mrs Campbell he has been writing to for nearly a year, who Andrew has been staying with, is me.'

'Why didn't you tell him?'

'I don't really know.' She shook her head in genuine bewilderment. 'Maybe,' she admitted hesitantly, 'I was afraid.'

'What of?'

She looked up at him, and her eyes were suddenly deep pools of doubt. 'That he wouldn't go on writing if he knew,' she finally whispered.

'When you meet him — what then?'

'We shall see. I think I'm ready to take the risk now.' She tilted her chin and did, indeed, look ready for anything. 'You know,' she said, suddenly thoughtful again; 'I can see with the wisdom of hindsight, that I have really made my own life — we do, I think; it isn't as we like to believe, moulded for us by some mighty unseen hand. When I look back I can see that I have always plumped for security — I've never dared to chance it on my own. I've always had someone there to look after me — a father figure if you like. It has taken me a very long time to grow up; but I think I'm getting there at last.'

David's smile was rueful. He had never loved her, or understood her, as much as he did now, when he had lost her.

'Maybe you no longer need the pumpkin shell.'

'The pumpkin shell?'

' 'Peter, Peter, Pumpkin eater — had a wife and couldn't keep her — he put her in a pumpkin shell and there he kept her very well!' ' he quoted. 'You always looked for a husband who would put you in it and keep you there. You've outgrown that now — so if ever you make a commitment again it will be quite different; no one will have to keep you in the pumpkin shell to hold you.'

She reached across and laid her hand over his as it rested on the table between them. 'Dear David, I think you know me better than I know myself.'

'Maybe!' He turned his hand and caught hers in its grasp, imprisoning it. He was tempted to tell her just how he felt about her; but instead he just tightened his grip a little on her hand, with his eyes on her face. 'I hope you will always see me as 'Dear David' — your friend; and if — well — if things go wrong, if you ever need a friend, or just a shoulder to cry on, you'll let me oblige?'

'I promise,' she whispered, in a voice suddenly husky. 'Dear David!' she repeated.

'Well,' he said, as, suddenly brisk, he let her hand go and glanced at his watch. 'I had better be going. Thank you for brunch.' He smiled and moved towards his car. He stood for a moment; looking round him at the glorious views and then back at her, as if he wanted to remember the setting, and Stevie in it, for ever — or maybe just long enough to transfer to canvas. Then he held out his hand and shook hands with her, almost formally. 'Goodbye. And remember — I can't offer you a pumpkin shell, but everything else is yours for the taking.'

'Dear David!' she whispered yet again, and on a sudden impulse she leaned forward and kissed him on the cheek.

He stood still; he dared not trust himself to do anything else; then slid into the driving seat and switched on the ignition.

'Good luck! And keep in touch, whatever happens,' he said as the car throbbed to life and began to move forward.

'I will!' Stevie promised as she waved to him.

She watched him disappear down the hillside then turned back into the house to re-read the letter from Australia.

'I'm not too sure about the idea of the boys being at school in England after all,' Tom wrote. *'Simon doesn't seem at all happy. I'm not so worried about Andrew, even though he is younger; he is a more sanguine disposition altogether, and he has you. I can't tell you what it has meant to me to know that he has a happy home with young people to spend part of his holidays in. Simon is due to go on to Malvern, my old school, next year, so if I am going to make a change this seems a good time to do it. So I am coming to England before the school year ends to assess things. In fact when you read this I shall be on the high seas, due to arrive at Portsmouth on June 30th. Andrew tells me he is spending the half-term holiday with you and Michael. I appreciate your kindness to him and hope I*

shall have the opportunity to meet you and thank you personally.

Yours sincerely,
Tom Jefferies.

★ ★ ★

When the boys arrived the following weekend for the half-term holiday Andrew was wildly excited at the prospect of seeing his father again but, to Stevie's surprise, dubious about going back to Australia.

'I like staying with you,' he told her, much to her delight, 'and I shall miss Michael, he's my very best friend anywhere in the world!'

He chattered happily on to Stevie about his father's visit. He knew the name of the ship he was sailing on and Stevie already knew the date of his arrival, and the port. As she gathered and stored all this information a wild plan began to take shape in her mind. Why not meet Tom off the ship?

The more she thought about it the better the whole idea seemed. Cautiously she questioned Andrew about his relatives; were they likely to meet his father?

'Oh, no!' He told her seriously; 'they're old, Mrs Campbell, *really* old, not like you!' She smiled at the backhanded compliment. 'They never go *anywhere!*'

It seemed a wonderful idea until she actually stood on the quay watching the huge liner berth. As she stood with the crowd of relatives and friends all straining to recognise familiar faces amongst the passengers crowding the rails, it suddenly seemed quite mad. A terrifyingly ridiculous idea, which she wondered how she could possibly have entertained for a second, let alone brought to fruition. She would have turned and run then, even at this eleventh hour, if the crowd hadn't been so dense, hemming her in. Even so she might have fought her way through them if she hadn't suddenly seen a glimpse of Tom's face, up there above her, not directly on the railings, and looking down at the crowd below with a very half-hearted interest; not searching for a face, or faces, as the other passengers were.

As she watched she saw him suddenly push through to the railing and peer down at the crowd below. She knew he had seen her. Impulsively she raised an arm in greeting, her eyes never wavering from his face, far above her. Slowly, as if he were moving in a dream, Tom's arm rose in acknowledgement.

After what seemed an eternity of waiting, they were alone together. He had gone through customs and all the formalities of landing and had collected his luggage, now they faced each other and immediate practicalities.

'I have my car,' she said.

'I have a hotel room booked,' he told her, 'for one night.'

'I'll take you there.'

They walked to her car and stowed his luggage in the boot. The silence between them was heavy with all that was left unsaid, all that needed saying; all that they both wanted to say.

'How did you know I would be on that ship?' he asked her. He still felt as if he was in a dream and that any moment he might wake up and find it all gone. No Stevie — no car — and he would still be on board.

She smiled at him then. 'You told me.'

'I told you?' He looked totally bewildered.

'And Andrew, he told me too.'

Slowly light dawned. 'You're not — you can't be — Is your name Campbell now?'

She nodded as she let the clutch in and moved slowly away from the parking lot through the traffic.

He sighed. 'That explains a lot!' And then, as if remembering, 'But certainly not everything. I think we had better have lunch together and sort things out; if it isn't too late to get lunch.' It was well past one.

'I hope so — I'm hungry!' Stevie had been driving, it seemed, since the middle of the night and waiting on the quay for as long. The few sandwiches and the flask she had brought with her had long since ceased to sustain her.

Somewhat grudgingly the hotel agreed to serve them, because Tom had accommodation booked. They sat opposite each other in a fast-emptying dining room and began to fill in the missing pieces for each other.

'What happened; why didn't you write?' Stevie wanted to know above all else.

'I did,' he assured her. 'But you know what the mail is like in war-time, If you didn't get my letters they must have got lost, then I was injured and sent back home. The end of the war as far as I was concerned.'

'Injured? Were you hurt badly?'

'Well, yes, I suppose you could say so; it was all a bit of a fiasco really, a dreadful anticlimax to my heroic visions of 'saving the Mother Country'!' His lips twisted in a smile of self-mockery. 'I was injured in an accident with an army truck, and got a knock on the head.' He pushed back the hair dropping over his temple and showed her a white scar. 'Nothing to do with the bloody war; I also got a rather badly broken leg.'

Stevie nodded; she had noticed that he walked with a slight limp. She waited for him to continue - a broken leg and a bump on the head still didn't explain his failure to write.

'The leg mended reasonably quickly, I was left with a slight limp, so slight it wouldn't have been enough to keep me out of the war.' He paused as if searching for the right words to continue.

'Or to prevent you writing letters,' Stevie said with some asperity, recollection of those weeks, months and even years of waiting for news sharpening her voice.

He looked at her across the table, his eyes bleak. 'I lost my memory,' he told her. 'I know it sounds too corny, too neat an excuse to be true, but it is, you must believe me, Stevie.'

She nodded. It did sound weak and corny, and yet looking into his eyes she did believe him. 'Go on,' she said.

'I came round in hospital with total amnesia, I still can't remember anything about the accident itself. I was on the hospital ship heading for Australia when gradually the fog in my head cleared and snippets of memory returned. We were sailing into Sydney Harbour before everything had come back to me except the accident itself.'

'Why didn't you write then?' Stevie wanted to know.

'I had my memory back but I could only feel despair, there seemed no hope anywhere — everything, the war, and my small part in it, you, me, finished, as far as I could see.' He sounded bitter as he relived again the despair and the heartbreak followed by the acute depression of those weeks. 'Later, much, much later when the dark days were behind me, I wrote to you, several times, I never got a reply. My letters were probably on torpedoed ships but I didn't think of that, only that you, for reasons of your own, had not replied. Then one of my letters came back marked 'Not known at this address'. I didn't know whether you or the Post Office had returned it, either way it seemed hopeless and time to give up. What could I do anyway? I was married and on the other side of the world.'

Tom paused and looked at her expectantly, waiting for her to fill in the gaps.

'I was devastated when I heard nothing, I thought you had been killed, or taken prisoner or — or simply didn't want to bother with me any more. Eventually I did a really stupid thing, I gave up hope and married Jock Campbell.' She looked up and met his eyes across the table, begging him to understand; to forgive. 'I thought it would be for the best — I really did. I felt the children needed the security of a proper home, with two parents, and I knew him, and liked him . . . ' Stevie's voice sank to a whisper.

'And?' he prompted.

'And it was a miserable failure. He — he committed suicide nearly a year ago.' She could fill in the details later if necessary.

'So — ' The waiter had just put a plate of soup down in front of him, but he pushed it impatiently on one side and reached for her hand across the table. 'So we are both free — at last,' he said softly.

She nodded, closing her fingers over his. 'Yes — at last!'

As their hands touched a flood of mutual understanding flowed like a current between them. Smiling warmly at each other across the table they loosed their grip and began to drink their soup. They had all the time — all the time in the world now.

'I don't like the idea of you driving back to Wales by yourself,' he told her.

'I don't like the idea of going — by myself,' she agreed.

'Can you give me a lift tomorrow? It seems a shame to waste that hotel room.'

'I can give you a lift — if you can put me up for the night?' Her eyes danced as she looked at him.

'Done!' he said and blew her a kiss across the table to seal the bargain.

★ ★ ★

They were married quietly in the first week of the school holidays, with only their respective children, Nanny and her sister and Tom's two aged aunts as witnesses. A week later they all sailed for Australia.

'I always wanted you to marry Uncle Tom, so that we could go to Australia,' Sue said as the liner moved away from the quay, finally breaking the streamers that held them to England.

We do hope that you have enjoyed reading this large print book.

Did you know that all of our titles are available for purchase?

We publish a wide range of high quality large print books including:
Romances, Mysteries, Classics
General Fiction
Non Fiction and Westerns

Special interest titles available in large print are:
The Little Oxford Dictionary
Music Book
Song Book
Hymn Book
Service Book

Also available from us courtesy of Oxford University Press:
Young Readers' Dictionary
(large print edition)
Young Readers' Thesaurus
(large print edition)

For further information or a free brochure, please contact us at:
Ulverscroft Large Print Books Ltd.,
The Green, Bradgate Road, Anstey,
Leicester, LE7 7FU, England.
Tel: (00 44) 0116 236 4325
Fax: (00 44) 0116 234 0205

Other titles in the
Ulverscroft Large Print Series:

STRANGER IN THE PLACE

Anne Doughty

Elizabeth Stewart, a Belfast student and only daughter of hardline Protestant parents, sets out on a study visit to the remote west coast of Ireland. Delighted as she is by the beauty of her new surroundings and the small community which welcomes her, she soon discovers she has more to learn than the details of the old country way of life. She comes to reappraise so much that is slighted and dismissed by her family — not least in regard to herself. But it is her relationship with a much older, Catholic man, Patrick Delargy, which compels her to decide what kind of life she really wants.

PAINTED LADY

Delia Ellis

Miss Eleanor Needwood was about to be married to a most unsuitable suitor when Philip Markham came to her rescue. He arranged for Eleanor to be in London for the Season, a guest of his sister, who decided that everyone would benefit if Markham married Eleanor. And thus the rumour started. The surprised couple decided to play along with the mistaken impression until a scandal-free way to end the betrothal could be found. But when Eleanor agreed to pose for a daring artist, the result was far more scandalous than any broken engagement.

IF HE LIVED

Jon Stephen Fink

Lillian is a woman who feels too much. As a psychiatric nurse, she empathizes with her patients; as a mother, she mourns for her lost, runaway daughter. Now suddenly she has a new feeling, that her house, one of the oldest in the small Massachusetts town where she lives with her husband Freddy, has been invaded, violated by some past evil. And then Lillian sees the boy . . .